# Maid For You

## Lexi Blair

Leannan Press

First Published in Great Britain 2025 by Leannan Press

# A Little Disclaimer from the Author...

Hey there, lovely reader!

Before we leap headfirst into the romance, here's a quick heads-up...

This book is set in **Edinburgh, Scotland**, and while I've done my very best to make it accessible for readers everywhere (including my amazing friends across the pond), you *might* still stumble across the occasional *car park*, *biscuit*, or *pair of trousers*.

Don't panic—no one's getting undressed in public unnecessarily (unless they *really* want to). It's just that here in the UK, our pants go *under* our trousers, our mums don't spell it with an *o*, and if we're popping to the shop, we're probably not driving to a mall the size of a small city.

Language is a funny thing, and regional quirks are part of the charm—hopefully you'll enjoy them as part of the setting, just like the cobbled streets and questionable weather.

Thanks for embracing the Britishisms and sticking with me. Now go forth, enjoy the drama, and fall head over heels in love (ideally with someone tall, dark, and slightly broody).

With love and cheeky winks,
**Lexi Blair**

# 1

# Rose

These shoes looked great in the shop—better still, when I unwrapped the tissue paper and took them out of the box in the bedroom, back at Freddie's townhouse. And even on my feet, they look amazing. They're classic Manolos after all, silver satin slingbacks with a jeweled buckle, but jeez, they're a nightmare to walk in on this shiny marble floor. One misstep and I'll be on my back; it's like a skating rink.

Where's Freddie got to? He should be here so I can hold on to his arm, at least. The chandeliers in this place are so huge and sparkly, they're more like glitter balls. Their light reflects off the shimmering fabric of my dress, making me feel like I'm wrapped in stardust. And sometimes I think it must be magic of some kind that brought me here.

Laughter and the tinkle of fine crystal fill the air in the high-ceilinged event room at the Gladstone Hotel in Edinburgh as I ease my way through the crowd—a crowd I don't belong in. So many unfamiliar faces, though a few of them glance my way with a flicker of recognition. If they've seen me before, it's only because of Freddie. He's connected to everyone here. This is his world, not mine.

"Rose! Darling, you look absolutely ravishing!" says a woman draped in pearls and silk.

I stop and smile, hoping I don't look too 'rabbit in the headlights', but I honestly have no idea who she is, even though I'm sure I should.

"Hi." I give her a little wave with my free hand while clinging to my clutch bag with the other. My nails dig into it. Where the hell is Freddie? I twirl a lock of my blonde hair around my finger and hover near the woman, not sure if she wants a full-on conversation or if she is just making chitchat.

"Where's Freddie tonight?" she asks. "You're not here on your own, are you?"

"No, Freddie's here... somewhere. Not sure where he's got to." I bite my lip and look around. My eyes land on a man not far off. He's tall, with dark hair that skims the edge of his collar—neat but effortlessly stylish—and a jawline that could cut glass. The bright lighting catches his sharp cheekbones and straight nose. And his eyes—my God. They're a striking sea blue I can see clearly even from here. He's dressed smartly in a tailored jacket and crisp shirt, the picture of quiet confidence. All around him, people are nodding and smiling as he talks. Whoever he is, they're drinking him in. And I get it. He's handsome, undeniably so, though I shouldn't be looking or noticing.

"Perhaps he went out onto the terrace for some air," pearls-and-silk woman says, drawing my attention back to her. She tilts her head, her perfectly arched brow lifting slightly.

"Yes, he might have done that." I brush off a slight pang of anxiety with a laugh. "That sounds like him."

Keeping up this charade is so hard. I don't belong here, not really. You know that old phrase 'fake it until you make it'? Well, that's pretty much me every day of my life right now. Especially at events like this. I'm lucky to have found Freddie, or lucky that he noticed me. Otherwise, I'd be nobody. I'm more suited for serving drinks here than being one of the invited guests. Stepping into Edinburgh elite society wasn't something I ever expected. I used to work as a chambermaid in a country club where Freddie came to play golf and use the gym. One day we got talking, and that was that. It was a bit of a whirlwind, but now I'm here, the girlfriend of a promising young MSP, and working in his parents' high-end gallery. It's better than a dream come true.

My gaze drifts back to the handsome man. I can hear his voice—or at least the tone of it—low and smooth with a rough, gravelly edge. The kind of voice that could whisper sweet nothings and make my knees weak. As if sensing my thoughts, his attention shifts from the group around him and lands squarely on me. The jolt of it scorches through me, sharp and sudden. I can't tear my eyes away, even though I know I should. I need to find Freddie—and I definitely shouldn't be checking out other men. No matter how dangerously good-looking they are.

I wrench my gaze from him, though I have an odd feeling he's still looking at me. Heat climbs up my neck. I need air.

Focus on finding Freddie.

Maybe I should message him, but is it bad form to be texting at an event like this? I've never learned the rules. Not from my family, anyway. My mum died when I was a kid, and my dad's been lost in a bottle ever since. He wouldn't care who I'm dating, unless it gives him someone new to blame. My siblings barely speak to me these days—think I'm a sellout for being with someone like Freddie. A politician, no less. They hate everything he stands for. But I don't care.

Maybe that makes me shallow, but I like having nice things—for once. A warm house, decent clothes, dinner somewhere that doesn't smell of chip fat. Is that so wrong?

"Excuse me," I say, stepping away from the woman.

I should avoid the handsome man, yet something magnetic pulls me in his direction and I start to follow. I've barely taken two steps when a hand catches my arm.

"Hello. You're Freddie's girl, aren't you?" an older gentleman with a very shiny head asks.

"That's me." I smile. Who the hell is he?

"Indeed," he chuckles. His eyes move downward, falling onto my chest. Is he ogling my breasts? I mean, they are quite shapely, and this dress is low cut enough to show them off, but he's being so blatant. "Shall we get a drink?"

"I, um… need to find Freddie." And get away from this guy.

"I'm sure he won't mind." The man takes my arm, and I try to shake him off without making a scene, but his grip is firm.

"Please, I need to—"

"Unhand the lady, George. And come and tell us about the takeover."

My gaze flies to the source of the deep, velvety voice. The handsome man has his hand on George's shoulder and, although his expression is friendly, there's a sharpness behind it. I hold my breath, but I can't stop looking at him. He's in a dark suit and a white shirt, open at the top to reveal a wedge of tanned skin.

"Oh…" George makes a face, but his hand drops from my arm.

The handsome man guides George away with a hand on his back, but just before he turns, our eyes lock. I try to thank him without speaking. His lip quirks slightly, and I take it as a sign that he understands.

Without hanging around, I hurry off as fast as these shoes will allow, weaving through the crowd where everyone seems to belong to someone. Except me. As I slip through the throng of elegantly dressed guests, I feel another tap on my shoulder. Who now? Turning, I come face-to-face with a couple who frequent Freddie's parents' gallery.

"Nice to see you here. How is the new exhibition coming along?" The woman's voice is as smooth as the satin of her gown. Her husband nods in agreement,

"Great." My smile is fixed in place like a mannequin's. "The response has been really good."

"Freddie must be thrilled." The man glances around. "Where is he?"

"I wish I knew."

"Last I saw him, he was in the Renton Suite. I think he was talking to the owner of this place."

"Such a charming young man," the woman coos. She's right. He is charming, but doubts gather like storm clouds in my brain. Recently, things have been strange. Freddie's always been moody. He says I 'cured his depression' when we first met, but sometimes he has low moods. In fact, there are times when he loses it completely and goes into a right old rage. But hey, don't we all?

I push the thoughts away.

"Excuse me." I spot an opportunity as a waiter glides by with fresh champagne. "I should really try to find him."

I grab a glass of champagne and slip back into the crowd, letting it swallow me. Above the passing doors, I check for the Renton Suite.

Eventually I come to one with that name on a gold plaque. It's slightly open already, so I push it and go in. Compared to the glittering lights of the chandeliers, it's dimly lit in here and it takes a moment for my eyes to become accustomed to it. It's also a lot quieter, with only a few people involved in low conversations.

I spot Freddie standing near a bookshelf with his back to me. But he's not alone.

Instinctively, I draw back into the shadow of a large potted plant. He's leaning in close to a woman. Her tanned skin glows in the amber light of a nearby lamp, long black hair cascading down her back. She looks like a model who's just stepped off a yacht in the Mediterranean.

My attempts at looking glamorous suddenly feel childish and pathetic. I'm only twenty-five, and she's got to be at least five years older, maybe more, and she looks so effortless. My confidence, so carefully stitched together for the night, unravels at an unstoppable rate. I'm not sure what a politician's wife should look like, but I can imagine her taking on the role.

Me? Not so much.

And maybe that's not what Freddie wants. A wave of something cold sweeps over me. What if I'm just a bit of fun? A passing fling to liven up his life before he finds someone who truly *fits* into his world. Someone polished, poised—bred for this kind of life. Not a girl from a run-down estate with a drunk for a father and a second-hand education in how to act in rooms like this.

He makes no secret of how much he likes sex, and he has an appetite, alright. In fact, he's so desperate most of the time it's all done and dusted for him before I'm even in the mood. I've yet to achieve one of those fabulous orgasms I've read about—unless it's under my own steam. But it's a learning curve, right? We'll get there, won't we? Or is it possible he's using me while he keeps an eye out for someone more... *appropriate*?

God, I hate being so insecure, but I can't help it, especially when I'm faced with this.Freddie's hand brushes the woman's—a touch too intimate, too lingering for my liking.

A knot forms in my throat, and it's as though I'm seeing him for the first time. Is this how he acts with other women? I'm not sure he ever looks at *me* like that.

But I'm his girlfriend, and I'm not about to stand back and let someone else muscle in.

I glide across the room, my heels clicking on the polished floor, keeping each step careful and precise—just in case I slip.

"Freddie?"

He whirls around, and his jaw tenses. "Rose."

The woman's gaze flickers to me, her eyes narrowing ever so slightly.

"I've been looking all over for you." I keep my tone level but want him to know I'm not impressed.

Still focusing on the woman, he offers her an apologetic smile. "We'll talk more later." His gaze shifts to me, and his gray irises are cold, almost calculating. He leads me away. It's good to have him to balance on with these heels, but his grip on my arm is just shy of painful. Why is he holding me so tightly? And where the hell are we going?

He pushes open a door and almost thrusts me through it.

"Freddie? What the—"

The door snaps shut, and I register that we're in a carpeted corridor with a staircase in it. I assume it leads up to the bedrooms, though we're not staying here. Freddie's townhouse is close enough not to have to.

"Seriously, Rose." His eyes are hard, like chips of flint. "You know how important tonight is. You shouldn't have interrupted me; she's got connections that could make or break careers."

"Connections? It looked like you were auditioning for a spot in her bed." The words tumble out before I can catch them.

"I beg your pardon?" he hisses.

"Well, it's true. You were all over her. Have you been with her all evening?"

His lips curl. "This is exactly how you show the world your lack of class. Honestly, you haven't got a clue."

"A clue about what?"

His words cut like a blade, but I'm not letting him get away with this. He might be five years older and a hell of a lot richer, but that doesn't give him the right to walk all over me.

"About how to behave in public," he says. "It doesn't matter how many designer dresses I buy you or how much expensive makeup you slap on. In the end, you're still just a pathetic little nobody playing dress-up."

I gape at him. What the hell? I've heard him rant like this before, but this is so personal—and cruel. "I don't appreciate you talking to me like that. You need to calm down."

"Don't tell me what to do. You little—"

His hand moves too quickly to track, a blur that ends with a sharp pain exploding across my face. My head snaps back, and I taste something metallic. I bring a hand to my nose, and when I pull it away, there's a red streak—a stark contrast against my pale skin.

"Freddie... you..." I'm gasping, disbelief mixing with pain, my dress no longer a shimmering silver but a canvas for a spattering of blood.

I'm seeing red, and not just from the blood dripping between my fingers. The fury churning inside me is enough to set the room ablaze.

"Are you insane?" I spit the words out, my voice hoarse, my fingers still trying to stop the blood, and my brain trying to process what the fuck has just happened.

"Insane?" Freddie scoffs, towering over me. "You're the one making a scene. You know what's at stake here, Rose. Get in line, or you'll lose everything."

"What, like you?" My voice cracks, the words shaking, no matter how tightly I cling to my defiance.

"Yes. And if you lose me, you lose this." He tugs at my dress. "And your home, your job, your credibility. Everything. So, shut the fuck up, get cleaned up, start behaving, and get back in there."

"I'm not a child. Don't you speak to me like that. I-I don't need you." The words feel hollow, but I spit them out anyway, hoping they'll land with more strength than I feel.

"Oh, but you do." His gaze slices right through me, and I flinch before I can stop myself. Then he spins on his heel and strides away, leaving me trembling and alone in the corridor.

The clamor of the party feels distant now, as if I've been cast adrift. Blood is still pouring from my nose, and my pulse is throbbing in my ears, banging in my head like a bass drum. What the fuck just happened? And what do I do now? I hate to give credence to Freddie's words, but he's right. Everything I have has been sucked into a life with him. Without him, I have nothing. Even the clothes on my back aren't technically mine—he bought them.

The stairs creak with approaching footsteps, and panic skitters through me. I turn my face to the wall, hoping whoever it is will pass by without a second glance. I can't deal with a conversation—not now, not covered in blood with my heart hammering in my chest.

Please, just go past.

I need to find a way to get cleaned up and work out where I'm going to go. How can I go back to Freddie after this? Do I just suck it up and pretend it never happened? Or do I walk away with nothing?

I don't look around, but I sense the person is now at the bottom of the stairs and will have seen me. I focus on my breathing, willing them to walk on by.

The footsteps stop and out of the corner of my eye, I see a tall man in a black suit. Oh God. It's him. The handsome man I saw earlier. He pauses at the door to the main room, his hand on the handle. He turns, catching sight of me, and the shock that registers across his face is almost as sharp as the pain throbbing in my nose.

"Are you okay?" he moves back from the door, closer to me. His gaze is gentle, but his expression is grim, his thick eyebrows drawn together in a sharp V.

"Fine," I manage to choke out, but even to my own ears, it sounds like a lie. Tears mingle with the blood, and I can feel them, hot and relentless, streaming down my cheeks. When did I start crying? Freddie doesn't deserve my tears.

The man's piercing eyes scan my face; they're so ridiculously blue, they're almost dazzling. I can't look away, but the intensity is so strong I might implode.

"Who did this to you?" he asks.

I shake my head, pressing my sleeve against my nose in a feeble attempt to stem the blood flow.

"If it's someone in that room," the man continues, "tell me, and I'll have him dealt with."

My heart hammers at the thought, and part of me wants revenge so badly, but not like this. I don't know this man, who he is, or what he might do. I shake my head again, biting my lip to keep it from trembling. "No, it's... it's nothing."

"Can I help in some other way? Do you want me to call you a taxi or something?"

It's a kind offer, but I'm too scared to grab the lifeline he's holding out.

"Is there someone you can call? A friend? A brother or sister?"

"Um, yes." I do have a brother and a sister, but they both live miles away. So does my dad—not that I'd call him. He wouldn't leave the love of his life, whisky, to come for me anyway. Sienna, my best friend, would be the safest bet. But inside, my thoughts are a tangled mess. I don't want anyone to see me like this. Not even her.

The man doesn't move away but stands watching me. There's something about his presence that's strengthening. Part of me almost wants Freddie to come back and say something else. This man would take him down with one well-placed fist, I'm sure.

"Really, I'll be okay," I say, more firmly this time, hoping he'll believe it because I'm not sure I do.

"Do you have a room here?"

"No." I shake my head.

"I can arrange for one. You're in a bad way. I wouldn't like you to collapse. Come with me and I'll—"

The shrill sound of the fire alarm cuts him off, and a collective cry ripples from the main room. It's loud enough to make my ears ring, setting my already frayed nerves on edge. My breath catches in my throat, and for a moment, I freeze. Something tightens in my chest. It's just a drill, not real. But my heart is pounding. Don't let it be real. Don't let it take anyone the way it did to me.

"Oh, for fuck's sake," the man says. "The fire door's that way. If you wait on the street, I'll get someone to wait with you."

I start to walk. What else can I do? But my head is killing me. Where am I going to go? What will I do?

"Here." The man follows me. "Take this. It's cold out there." He puts his jacket around my shoulders. It's far too big, but it retains his heat and feels weirdly like a protective shield. "Now, excuse me."

Clutching his jacket around me, I head toward the fire door at the end of the corridor. I glance back and see him striding back toward the commotion. Why doesn't he get out too? But there's no time to ponder; I push through the fire door and tumble into the biting Edinburgh night.

The cold air slaps me hard across the face, and I gasp, pulling his jacket even tighter. My nose throbs in protest. Alone in the dimly lit back alley, I shiver. What the hell should I do? Should I actually wait for him?

"Must be a false alarm," someone says behind me as more people spill out into the alley. Panic blooms anew—I can't risk bumping into Freddie or anyone else who might recognize me. What if he comes out and sees me?

With a glance along the street, I catch sight of smoke curling into the sky, gray and misty against the dark backdrop. It's not a false alarm.

Oh God. What if Freddie is trapped in there? Maybe it serves him right, but even with the flames of revenge licking my insides, I can't bring myself to think like that. Not after what happened to my mum.

One thing's certain; I can't stay here. If the handsome man is pissed at me stealing his jacket, then I'm sorry, but I'm not risking a run in with Freddie.

I turn on my heel and start walking briskly away. Each step takes me further from the chaos, from Freddie, from the new life I thought would be mine forever.

# 2
## John

The shrill cry of the fire alarm is a piercing reminder that this is my hotel and there's trouble brewing, though I hope to God it's just someone who's had a bit too much to drink and decided to punch the alarm as a joke—albeit not a very funny one. Not for me anyway.

"Everyone, please, we need to move!" My voice cuts through the clamor of confused voices as I return to the room. I probably shouldn't have left that poor girl alone in the corridor, but I couldn't very well bring her in here in that state, and in case it's a real fire, we need people to get out. Why are they all just standing about as though this is a prank? "Come on, folks. Until we know this is a false alarm, we all need to get out. Keep moving."

It's like herding cats trying to get them to leave the champagne, and who can blame them? Fire alarms are more often false than true. Still, you never ignore them, not in my line of work. My hotel chain is built on prestige, so faulty electrics are unlikely, but it could be some dickhead smoking in the toilets. Wouldn't be the first time.

"What's going on?" someone shouts over the din.

"Fire alarm's going off, isn't it?" I bark back, sharper than I mean to be. "We have to assume it's the real deal. So, can everyone get to an exit!"

Some people have taken the hint and are moving toward the fire doors. I scan around, hoping to see someone I know, someone I can ask to go and wait with the girl in the corridor. I don't know her or what happened to her, but it looked to me like someone had hit her. A man I'd wager. Better not be George. I stopped him from creeping on her earlier, though lashing out doesn't seem his style. Then again, who knows? One thing I'm sure of is that if I find out who did it and I get my hands on him, I'll knock him out. Bastard. If there's one thing I detest, it's abusive men—like my thankfully deceased father.

And where's my wife? I've barely seen her tonight. That's why I went upstairs. I thought maybe she'd gone up to our room. I almost dreaded what I'd find. But she wasn't there.

Any time I did see her tonight, she was hanging around with a younger guy—stiff lipped, preppy, politician type. God knows what she was doing with him. It better be above board. But that thought needs to get out of my head; there's no time for personal dramas when safety's at stake.

"Is it serious?" a voice calls out.

"Can't say for sure, but do you really want to stick around to find out?" There's a gruffness in my tone that I'm not sorry about. People need to move, though I know from experience they rarely do without someone telling them to. The fire alarm's wail pierces the air, an ungodly shriek that has me clenching my jaw. "Listen up!" I bark over the alarm. "Everyone needs to leave the building now!"

A few heads turn toward me, startled out of their apathy. Murmurs ripple through the crowd, and then, like a sluggish river, they begin to move. They grumble about the noise, about the ruined evening, but at least they're heading toward the exits.

"Come on, let's go." I urge them on, propelling the reluctant stragglers.

As the room starts to empty, I scan the faces, still not seeing my wife. She's not among those I'm herding toward safety.

"Do you know what happened?" I ask the hotel manager, catching sight of her near the fire door.

"It's in the kitchen."

"What?" I stare at her. "It's real?"

"Sure is. I wish people would hurry up."

"Has anyone called the fire brigade?"

"Done," she says.

"Jesus Christ." I grind my teeth. "Everyone move!"

"We need help!" A panicky voice shouts over the alarm.

I barrel through the event room toward the shouter. "What is it?"

"The kitchen." The staff member looks frantic.

"Yeah. I know. The fire engines are on their way. You need to get out."

"There's someone stuck."

"What?"

"We couldn't get them out."

"You go." I send the member of staff to the door. Christ. Where are the fire engines? I know I shouldn't do this. I should get out with everyone else, but if someone's stuck. Can I get them out? Somehow?

My steps echo in the empty service corridor, the smoky haze growing thicker with each stride. My throat burns with the heat and the urgency.

I open the door and wrench a chef's apron from a hook and press it to my mouth. Through squinted eyes, I peer into the inferno that was once a place of culinary excellence. Flames dance along the countertops, mocking my efforts, the heat oppressive against my skin.

"Hello?" I call out. "Is anyone in here?"

"Help!" The cry is faint, but there—a figure huddled in the corner, coughing violently.

"Fuck!" Ducking low, I spot a path. I could reach her... but can she move?

At last, sirens wail on the street... They're here. Beside me, a flame leaps up, and I yell in pain, jumping forward. My face is in agony, but I'm closer to the woman. It's now or never. I lunge for her, grab her hand, and haul her to her feet. Without a second thought, I throw her over my shoulder and run.

# 3
## Rose

"Rose Darwin," Alexis calls out, and my heart jackhammers against my ribs. I wipe my palms on my black cleaning tunic, trying to look cool as I approach her office. She's the owner of the Maid for You Cleaning agency, where I'm lucky enough to have got a job. I've got a bad feeling about this as she waves me in with a smile that doesn't quite reach her eyes. I step inside, every muscle tensed.

"Take a seat, Rose." Alexis gestures to the chair opposite her desk. I take it and perch on the edge. What's this all about?

Since the night of the fire at the Gladstone, my life is hanging on the flimsiest of threads. My friend Sienna helped then, and I was lucky to get this job—and I need to keep it. Sienna also got me a room in the shared apartment where she lives, which isn't much, but it's better than being on the streets. I came so close that night—too close. All Freddie's fault. I'll never forgive him.

"Is everything okay?" My question comes out more as a squeak than my normal voice.

"Of course," Alexis reassures me, but I'm not convinced. She has a way of folding her hands together that looks like she's about to deliver bad news.

"I've got an assignment for you," she begins, and I brace myself. "It's a bit out of town, at the Lodge at Ardencairn Country Club."

The name sends prickles down my spine. It's the place where Freddie and I first crossed paths—the beginning of a chapter I'd rather forget.

"Are you familiar with it?" Alexis's eyes search mine.

"Um, yeah. I used to work there." I fiddle with a button on my uniform. "As a chambermaid."

"Good," she says. "That's helpful. And this would be a step up from that. The Knightons are looking for someone for their private residences on the estate. They're a prestigious family, and they need someone discreet and professional."

"Right." I nod. I haven't met the Knightons, but Freddie used to go on about them like they were royalty, and maybe in Edinburgh society they are. They certainly have a lot of money. Money Freddie would love to get his hands on. I know very little about politics, but I can imagine Freddie being involved in cash for favors. The ache for retribution against the bastard who left me bleeding in the gutter gnaws at me. Maybe this job is a chance to dig a little deeper into his shady dealings. How satisfying would it be to uncover something shady about him and these Knightons?

"So, what do you say? Would this be something you're up for?"

"Sure, I'll take it." I smile. "Sounds ideal." My mind is already dreaming of the moment I unearth something that will splatter egg across Freddie's smug face.

"Great." Alexis leans back in her chair. "The Lodge is where you'll spend most of your time and there are a couple of other properties too"—she checks her computer screen—"four days out of your five will be there."

"Got it."

Alexis clasps her hands together on the desk. "It's a trial period initially. If they're happy with your work, it could become a long-term position."

"Understood."

"Mrs Knighton would like to meet you on Monday morning. She'll go over what needs to be done, and then you'll start immediately. They've been without a cleaner for a week or two now, so they're desperate."

"Okay."

"This is a prestigious family. I'm trusting you with this because you've got the right approach—polite, attentive to detail... And you always remember to wear your uniform and keep it spick-and-span, which, believe me, has been an issue with some of the others."

"Thank you." I smooth down the black trousers. A far cry from the designer dresses I was in up to just a few weeks ago. This is me back to the lowest of the low. My fingers tremble slightly. This job isn't just about scrubbing floors, dusting shelves, and doing laundry—it's a lifeline, a way to claw back some control over my life after Freddie took so much of it away.

"Right, that's all then," she says. "And Rose?"

"Yes?"

"Good luck."

"Thanks." I need all the luck I can get.

As I leave Alexis's office, my phone buzzes in my pocket. It's a message from Sienna, a simple, 'How did it go?'

Later, I'll tell her where I'm going. She won't believe it. It feels like returning to the scene of a crime. Only this time I'm playing detective. Revenge is a dish best served cold, and I intend to make sure Freddie's is frozen solid.

That afternoon, I shuffle through the door of my shared apartment. This place is worse than student accommodation. It's in a hideous, run-down area where most of the places have boarded-up windows, and not a night goes by but there's an 'incident' of some sort or another. But it's cheap, and right now that's what I need.

Sienna's the only one of my flatmates who's home. And that's good because she's my BFF. We only met when I was in my final year at uni, and she was in her first. She's younger than me and still studying, though sometimes she seems older and wiser than me. The other two flatmates keep themselves to themselves and are either out or hiding in their rooms, gaming. Sienna is curled up on the shabby couch with a sketchbook in her lap, her mass of ginger curls piled atop her head.

"Hey," I greet her, dropping my bag by the door.

"Hi." She glances up and smiles. "How did it go? What did Alexis want to see you about?"

"A new placement." I collapse beside her. "And it's about to get interesting."

Sienna puts her pencil aside, her big glasses slipping slightly down her nose as she turns to me. "What do you mean?"

"I'm to clean the Lodge at Ardencairn."

"Oh?" Her sweet face is full of curiosity, but it takes a moment for the penny to drop. "Ardencairn? The place you met Freddie? Where you used to work?"

"Yes. Only it's not the hotel. It's the lodge." I bite my lip. "The owners are people Freddie was obsessed with. Wouldn't it be amazing if I could uncover something shady about them... and him?"

"Rose..." Sienna's voice is soft. "Are you sure that's a good idea?"

"Why shouldn't I?" I can't let it go. "I know it's a mad idea." I lean back into the cushions, feeling the springs press against my spine. "But he ruined my life. I'd love to get back at him."

"Revenge," Sienna murmurs. Her eyes are wide behind those large glasses; they always seem to see right through me.

"Yep. Sweet revenge." I can't help the grin that spreads across my face, even though I know it doesn't reach my eyes.

"Just be careful." She reached out to touch my arm. "It might not end well if you go digging."

"I know that." But the thought has sprung to life in my mind, giving me more energy and motivation than I've had for weeks. Maybe it's wrong to thrive on the negatives like this, but finding something positive is so hard right now. My mind is a dark place.

She gives me a small smile, one that doesn't quite hide her concern. "Just promise me you won't do anything too rash."

"Cross my heart," I say, tracing an *X* over my heart. But inside, I'm ready to fight back.

On Monday morning, I haul my bag of cleaning supplies onto the crowded bus and wedge myself into the last available seat next to a tall, gangly young guy who vaguely looks up as I sit down. He shuffles closer to the window when he sees the size of my bag. The air is thick with the scent of damp people and stale aftershave, but this journey is so familiar it's almost comforting. Ardencairn was my first job after leaving home—my first real escape. The live-in accommodation had sealed the deal. I needed somewhere to go. Somewhere that wasn't Thurso, with its gray skies, boarded-up shops, and a house that reeked of whisky and the kind of grief that never really lifts. And never will.

Getting out had felt like survival.

I'd only been at Ardencairn a few months when I met Freddie. What a Cinderella story it had seemed—rich boyfriend, champagne dates, and the promise of a bright future. Until he shattered it. Now I'm worse off than I was before. At least back then I hadn't known what it was like to believe you were safe.

My grip tightens on the strap of my bag as the bus rolls through the outskirts of Edinburgh, heading for the Ardencairn estate. Its high stone wall stretches along the road like it's guarding something important—or hiding it.

I hit the stop button and weave my way down the narrow aisle as the bus lurches to a halt. Hopping off, I walk a few metres along the pavement until the giant front gates and sweeping entrance to the country club come into view.

The directions point me to the lodge, but from here, it looks like a long walk. Maybe there's a quicker route through a back entrance—something to investigate later. The path curves through manicured lawns and past the imposing facade of the main hotel. It's a stunning building. Memories jump into my mind. We had some good times there—some naughty ones too. Freddie liked to 'christen the rooms'. I'd sneak him in. The forbidden nature of it was fun, but Freddie was shit in bed. That's one thing I don't miss. His brand of sex was so one-sided... His side. Sure, he liked to play, as long as it was me delivering the blow jobs, or rubbing him off between my boobs, smiling up at him while he came all over me. Why did I do it? The fucking loser gave me nothing in return. I was little more than his whore.

I scan the car park as I pass, half-hoping to spot his gleaming Audi. The sight of it would tempt me to drag a key along its flawless paint-work or sink something sharp into the tires. But it's not there, and I'm not sure if the feeling that follows is relief or disappointment.

The lodge eventually comes into view—larger than I expected, and grand in an outdated, brutal kind of way. All harsh angles, concrete cladding, and oversized windows that scream retro money rather than timeless elegance. It's a place that's meant to impress by sheer size, not beauty. These people must be seriously minted. No wonder Freddie was such a suck-up.

I head up to the main door. Should I knock? Or is there a back entrance? I raise my hand, but the door opens before I can do anything.

"Ah, you must be the new cleaner." An older lady with silver hair scans me over. She's beautifully dressed in a green skirt suit.

"Yes, I'm Rose from Maid for You."

"Mrs Knighton," she introduces herself, stretching out a wrinkled hand that's covered in rings. "Welcome to the Lodge."

"Thank you."

"Come in, and I'll show you around." She gestures inside. "Your agency speaks very highly of you." She closes the door behind me. "They say you're one of their best."

"Really?" How can I not be surprised? Since Freddie, I've felt so down about myself—like somehow I'm faulty.

"Indeed." Mrs Knighton's smile doesn't falter. "We value discretion and dedication here at the Lodge. I trust you'll fit in perfectly."

"I hope so."

"Excellent." Mrs Knighton ushers me through a set of double doors into the kitchen. My eyes widen. It's the biggest kitchen I've ever seen—more like something from an old boarding school than a home. The country style is dated to the point of being offensive, with heavy wooden cabinets, avocado-green tiling, and an industrial-sized Aga that looks like it's been there for at least fifty years. It might've once been impressive, but now it just feels tired and overdone. "This is where we need you to start today," she informs me. "Though I'll show you around the whole house first."

"I hope I don't get lost."

She chuckles. "Don't worry if you do. It's confusing at first, but you'll get used to it."

"Do you mind if I take notes on my phone, so I don't forget?"

"Of course not. Take as many as you like."

She leads me back into the corridor, the soles of my shoes squeaking faintly on the scuffed parquet flooring. The walls are lined with faded wallpaper—cream with a pattern that might once have been fashionable but now just looks dreary—and the light from ugly wall sconces casts a yellowish glow that makes everything feel a bit institutional. I tap out notes about what she wants done in each area, all the while trying to sketch a mental map of the layout.

At the end of the downstairs corridor, she pauses at a closed door. "This is John's study. It's off-limits unless the door is open. John is very particular about his privacy and doesn't mind if the room isn't cleaned every time."

"Okay." My eyes flick to the solid wood barrier, its varnish dulled and pockmarked with age. I assume John is her husband. Is he the man Freddie was so desperate to get to know? What secrets might be behind that door? I almost laugh, getting carried away with my own nonsense.

After the house tour, I get to work—and now I see why this job's going to take days. I'm here for three, cleaning and doing laundry, then I'm to spend another at a second property on the estate, which she'll show me tomorrow.

At first glance, the kitchen surfaces seem fairly clean, but a closer look reveals the telltale signs of neglect. I roll up my sleeves and get scrubbing until everything gleams. It's funny—I've got a reputation for being discreet, but truthfully, I'm a bit of a nosy parker. I can't help myself. I love seeing what's tucked away in the cupboards of the places I clean.

One of the best was when I cleaned for a very posh lady in a house in Leith. She had the best collection of vibrators I'd ever seen. Certainly beats the pitiful thing I've been reduced to using, though it gets me off better than any man ever has. In my shared apartment, though, it's not the kind of thing I want to be doing. The walls are so thin everyone in the building would know what I'm up to, and I'd rather not broadcast the fact. I know it's nothing to be ashamed of, but still, it feels awkward.

I have a quick snoop in the cupboards. Crockery, packets of food, jars of homemade jam, and an array of teas greet me. It all looks so normal, so painfully domestic. No hint of scandal or deceit. Not that I was expecting to find anything too shocking in the kitchen.

Once I've finished the kitchen, I move on to the hallway. Mrs Knighton has gone out—I saw her tearing off in a flashy red car—but as far as I know, her husband's still here, holed up in his study. The thought makes my skin prickle. This place is so big and echoey, I don't know what's worse—being alone or knowing there's a man I've never met lurking behind one of these heavy, shut doors.

The vaulted ceilings and dark wood panelling in the hallway are so thick with varnish they practically glow orange. I polish the over-lac-quered sideboard, edging open a drawer as I pass. Inside are some keys, a pack of cards, a few carved wooden boxes, and the kind of clutter you only get in houses like this. Upper-class junk, the sort that probably has a story or a price tag. Or both.

"Absolutely unacceptable! I won't stand for it!" The voice booms from behind the closed door of the study, making me jump a mile. I slam the drawer shut, my heart thudding nineteen to the dozen. He's not talking to me—at least, I hope not—but he's still grumbling away in a low, furious growl.

Who's he arguing with? Is there someone else in there? Or is it just a phone call?

I inch a little closer, listening. His voice is low and gravelly, and a prickle skitters down my spine. There's something about it—something that tugs at the edge of my memory like a loose thread I can't quite pull free.

Probably sounds like someone from the TV, I reason, because I can't place it. Still, I can't shake the strange, unresolved sensation in my chest. I gather my bucket and cloths, moving toward the living room, trying to put distance between myself and the study. But as I go, I cast one last glance over my shoulder. The door remains shut, but something still niggles.

Who is Mr Knighton?

# 4

## John

"It's not about the cost—it's about the integrity of the design," I argue, my voice echoing slightly off the porcelain as I lounge in the claw-foot tub. Warm water laps against my skin, and the scented bubbles are heady. "No, we're not cutting corners. Remember why we started this whole venture?"

I came up here to escape business, but wherever I go, business finds me. As soon as this call is done, my phone will start buzzing again. It's partly my own fault, according to my mother and brother. They always say I bite off more than I can chew and never know when to stop. Since the accident, I've been holed up here, focusing on something I've always wanted to do instead of the hotels that keep the lights on. I started designing golf courses. Crazy, right? But I've already designed the one at Ardencairn, so why not stretch my skills?

It's something I can do away from the prying eyes of people who only want to look at the beast.

Because that's what I've become. A freak show.

"Every tree counts on the course. It's not just a tree; it's part of the entire experience." I run a hand through my thick hair, letting the water drip back into the bath with a soft patter. My hair needs a trim. Before the accident it was neat and short, but three months on and it's longer than it's ever been, falling around my ears, and almost long enough to hide the scars.

"Alright, alright, I'll talk to the contractors again. You win, as usual." There's a smile in my foreman's voice, one that I can't help but return—yes, I like to get my own way.

"Thanks. I appreciate your efforts." I end the call and turn off my phone, then I sink deeper into the warm, luxurious water.

Silence settles around me, and I close my eyes. Taking a bath mid-afternoon is not usually my style, but my head is so full of crazy shit that I need to do something mindless—something to stop me from thinking.

My hand rises instinctively to my face, tracing the ridges of scarred skin that map out the left side like a grotesque mural. Okay, so this not-thinking thing... It isn't working. In fact, with the peace and quiet in here, there's even more room for my dark thoughts to push in.

What the hell was I thinking? The night of the fire plays over and over in my mind, vivid behind my closed eyes. I tried to be the hero, dragging the kitchen worker out of the blaze. Everyone says there's a fine line between bravery and stupidity—and I can't decide which one I crossed.

I'm not sorry I saved her, but I hate that I threw myself into danger like that. Not for me—I don't care about myself. But for Isabel. My sweet, brave little girl. What if she'd lost me that night? A shiver runs down my spine, even with the hot water pouring over me.

She needs me—probably more than ever now. I can't let her down. Not when Lydia's trying to ship her off to some boarding school like a package that's become inconvenient.

Opening my eyes, I lift a block of handmade soap and scrub at my skin with the gentle clary sage lather. If I could as easily wash away the memories. Lydia's betrayal cuts deeper than any flame ever could. Discovering her affair was bad enough, and now the constant fight over our daughter's future. Over my dead body is she going to boarding school. Isabel is terrified at the prospect, and I'm not paying for a ten-year-old to be separated from her family, just so that Lydia is free to fuck her new lover whenever she wants. She made her own bed, and she can lie in it—literally.

Hot water seeps into my bones, but it does nothing for the cold fury settling in my heart. The perfect life I thought I'd made for myself and my family over the years has crashed and burned. My control has slipped, and I'm spiralling toward an unknown destination.

A clicking sound from my bedroom makes me sit up. It sounds like someone opened the door. The soft hum of a tune trickles through the wall. I furrow my brow, listening. Who the hell is in my room? It's a woman. I can tell from the singing, but no one I recognize. Not my mother. Definitely not Lydia—she wouldn't dare come back here. Who then? I don't exactly have a stream of women through my bedroom door. Though maybe I should. God knows that would be a way to forget. Maybe some mindless sex is exactly what I need. But that thought doesn't answer the question of who's in my room.

Not wanting to shout out in case it's an intruder, I carefully and quietly lift myself out of the bath, water cascading off my body. The faded black-and-white tiles and chunky suite do nothing to lighten the mood—this bathroom hasn't seen a proper update since the seventies when my asshole of a father had this place built.

I know it's unlikely that an intruder would be humming to them-selves while ransacking my house, but I'm struggling to find another explanation.

Snatching a towel from the rail, I wrap it around my waist, and tiptoe across the chilly tiles, treading carefully, trying not to make a sound.

Peeking through the slightly ajar door, I spot a young woman with her back to me, dressed in a black tunic, cropped black trousers, and white tennis shoes. The tension in my shoulders eases—she must be the new cleaner. The last one was signed off sick. My mother took care of the handover because I... well, I can't face people right now. Even the idea of having a cleaner feels overwhelming, though I know I need the help. I just don't know if I'm ready to share my space with anyone, not even someone paid to be here.

The laundry is stacked neatly on my bed, which is impressive. It's been amassing in the laundry room for a couple of weeks.

She adjusts the clip holding up a pile of blonde hair, then reaches for the book on my nightstand. Her fingers brush over the cover, and she hesitates. Then she opens the top drawer and pulls it open, still humming to herself.

What the fuck?

Still leaning on the doorframe, I clear my throat. She jumps like a startled deer caught in the headlights as she whirls around to face me. Whatever I was going to say evaporates. Words die on my lips. Recognition hits me with the force of a golf swing—she's the young woman from the Gladstone, the one with the blood trickling from her nose. The one who disappeared into the night wearing my jacket. And now she's here, rifling through my drawers. Questions flood my brain, and I'm not sure what to ask first.

"Who the hell are you?" I gape at her. "And what are you doing in my bedroom?"

# 5
## *Rose*

Frozen, my hand clutches the edge of the drawer. What the fuck am I doing? Why did I have to open it? But that's not the question pushing its way to the front of my mind. Did I say question? If only it was just one. Thoughts are assaulting my brain like a hurricane. The man who's staring at me with ridiculously blue eyes isn't a stranger—not completely. I've seen him before. He's the man from the Gladstone, the one who draped his jacket over my shoulders when my nose wouldn't stop bleeding... after Freddie. And holy hell! Where to look? Those eyes, or the broad chest with the thin line of hair trailing down his sculpted abs? Or his face...? What happened to him? Those scars map out a story I don't know. He definitely didn't have them before.

He's still watching me, leaning his shoulder on the doorframe, a dark eyebrow raised as if waiting. And fuck, he asked me a question... Who am I and what am I doing in his room?

"I, um, I'm Maid for You..." My voice is squeaky. What the hell?

"What?" His frown deepens, etching lines into his forehead.

Heat floods my cheeks. "I mean, I'm from the agency Maid for You. I'm the cleaner—Rose Darwin." My heart thumps against my ribcage.

He's going to have me sacked, isn't he? I just know it. And I deserve it. But fuck, I need this job.

His gaze drills into me, so intense I can almost feel it physically. "We've met before, haven't we?"

I nod. Goddammit, his voice. It's so low, raspy, and seductive. Maybe he's doubly pissed; he hasn't just caught me snooping around his house, but I didn't wait like he said that night, and I ran off with his jacket. "I still have your jacket if you want it. But it's, um... covered in blood. I didn't know who you were, so I couldn't return it."

A smile flickers at the corner of his mouth, and he straightens up, tightening the towel at his snug waist. "Did you wait for me that night? Like I asked? I'm sorry I never made it back out."

My lip trembles under the assault of my gnawing teeth. "No, sorry. I had to go."

He crosses the room to the window, raking a hand through his damp hair. The muscles on his back shift under his skin, and I hold my breath, trying to focus on anything other than the clenching between my thighs. My fight-or-flight reflexes should be kicking in round about now, but my brain hasn't got the right memo—it's thinking more flirt or fuck, which is crazy as hell. But this guy—whoever he is—has really got my blood pumping.

"Well, it doesn't matter now." He pivots back to face me, his expression dark and a little menacing. "I was... Well, I couldn't get back out, anyway. I hope you didn't suffer any lasting damage."

"No." I shake my head. It's kind of ironic he's asking me that when he's clearly had lasting damage from something. How did he get those scars? I don't dare ask.

"Is it just a coincidence that you're here?" His velvety voice is calm, but I detect an edge—curiosity or accusation, I'm not sure. "Seems highly unlikely to me. And… no offense, but why were you at the Gladstone that night if you're a cleaner? The ticket prices are… Well…" He eyes me over again like he's X-raying me or trying to extract the information telepathically. My defences are so low, I'd surrender it straight away. The way he's looking at me is enough to get me on my knees.

"I was with someone at the Gladstone." I give a little shrug. "We split up, and I was left with nothing. So, this job…" Fuck. I need this job, but will I have to beg? Right now, I'm kind of into the idea.

"And does the job description include rifling through my drawers?"

"No," I mutter, and my cheeks burn. "I'm too nosy for my own good. I know that. But honestly, it's a coincidence that I'm here. I didn't know who you were at the Gladstone, and I still don't."

He lets out a little huff. "I'm John Knighton. I own this house."

"You're Mr Knighton?"

"I am."

How can he be? Mrs Knighton is too old to be married to him, surely? I mean, he can't be much more than forty; she looked like she was in her sixties.

"So, you're not Mrs Knighton's husband? When she showed me around, I assumed—"

A short bark of a laugh escapes him, softening his chiseled features. "That's my mother. She doesn't live here at all. She just likes to help out. I'm the only person who lives here. Well, except for my daughter, who's here every second week."

"Oh." My throat has gone dry. He's the owner? So, not just caught red-handed, but caught by the person in charge. "I'm sorry. I shouldn't have snooped. I'll collect my things and go."

His look is steady, probing, like he's seeing straight through me. My knees will surely give way. Time stretches between us. What does he see when he looks at me? My insides are trembling at what I see—a man I'd like to do wicked things with. Where are these thoughts coming from? He's too old for me... too... just not right, okay!

Forgive me, Father, for I have sexualized an older man, but really, it isn't me; he's done it himself by looking at me like that.

"That won't be necessary. I forgive you."

"You do?"

"Yes." He nods, and God, he's beautiful. No amount of scarring can hide that level of handsome. "But I expect you to be a good girl from now on."

I swallow hard. The heat in his eyes mirrors the fire spreading through me and pooling in my core. I'll be a good girl for him any day of the week.

"Okay."

He eyes me over, then moves to the bed, running a large finger over a stack of crisply ironed shirts. "How can I sack anyone who's this good at ironing?"

"Thank you." I hold my breath.

With a final pointed look, he retreats to the bathroom, pausing at the doorway. "And in the future, you might want to knock before you come in..." The door clicks shut behind him.

I stand frozen to the spot. Fuck. Fuck. Fuck. My head is whizzing all over the place. The fact that he's here at all, and that I'm here with him. His body, his voice, his face... and what they all do to me.

This is not normal, and I don't get it.

My feet feel disconnected from my body as I head down the wide staircase. Piles of clothes wait for me in the laundry room. Now, every pair of boxer briefs I iron will give me all levels of unholy thoughts. The shirts I did this morning are his. They've touched his chest.

"Get a grip," I mutter under my breath, willing my pulse to slow down. It doesn't listen.

Of all the houses in Edinburgh I end up in, it had to be his. I've heard it said that real-life is stranger than fiction, and this is wild. Sienna will have an explanation. She loves anything that's even remotely spooky, and she'll no doubt tell me this is fate. But if it is, then why? Seems fate has me destined to be stuck in a laundry room ironing shirts, while Mr Knighton lounges in the bath upstairs.

Thoughts of his naked body fill my mind as I pile up the clothes to iron. What would it be like if he'd pulled off the towel? I half close my eyes as I imagine his cock—large, thick, and hard. I used to resent giving Freddie blow jobs, but for John Knighton, I'd be on my knees begging. Nothing would give me more pleasure right now than to take his length in my mouth, have his fingers rake through my hair, hear his low, breathy voice say my name... "Good girl, Rose."

My insides are on fire. Tonight, when I get home, I don't even care if everyone in the apartment is listening; I need time with my vibrator or I'm going to explode. How much nicer it would be if John Knighton was the one to scratch that itch? But I know it's not going to happen. I might be thirsty, but I'm not delusional. I know my place. Look what happened the last time I tried stepping above my station. Lesson learned. No way am I going there again. From now on, I'm sticking to normal guys from plain and simple backgrounds.

John Knighton is everything I don't need, so he can get himself out of my head… Only problem is I have to work in this house. How can I escape seeing him? I really need to get a handle on myself and be sensible.

Lifting the iron, I run it over a pair of black boxer-briefs. Okay, so it isn't going to be easy, but I can do this. I'm here to clean, and that's what I'll do. No more snooping, no more nonsense. If I keep repeating it enough, maybe I'll start to believe it.

# 6

## *John*

I lean against the cool windowpane, my breath fogging up a tiny circle on the glass as I peer into the backyard from my daughter's bedroom. Rose tips a large bag into the trash can. She's singing, I think. It's too far to hear and too cold to open the window, but her lips move, and there's a rhythm to her steps. Wherever she is, she sings. It's cute. She might be a snoop, but at least she's a cheerful one.

Turning from the window, I survey the chaos of Isabel's room. Toys everywhere. Her endless collection of soft animals is strewn across the floor, on the bed, under the desk. I ask her to tidy up, but she never does. She probably doesn't even remember she has half of them—until I try to throw one out, of course.

Despite the clutter, she's got the best of everything—luxury bedding, expensive books, the works. But even with all that, her room still suffers from the same god-awful style as the rest of the house: fussy wallpaper, thick floral curtains, dark wood furniture that swallows the light. Decor frozen in the seventies, and not in a charming, vintage kind of way. I know I need to redecorate—Lydia was always on at me to do it—but the truth is I've been putting it off because what I really want is to knock the whole damn place down and start over. Strip it of the memories. Of him.

The problem? The council. They've rejected every planning application I've submitted. Apparently, the house is of "historical importance." Nothing about it feels worth preserving to me. I'd happily watch it burn—well, as long as no one was inside. I don't want to go through that again.

I exhale and rub the back of my neck. One day, I'll rebuild it all. Modern, open, light. Something new. Something safe.

I'll ask Rose to vacuum this room before she goes. She can just shove all the toys to the side, and I'll get Isabel to put them away when she gets here tomorrow.

Rose will be back from taking out the trash now, and I could go and find her, but something stirs in my chest. An odd feeling, a little like heartburn. Whatever it is, it's acting like a barrier. But a strange one—one that wants to see Rose... but not talk to her.

God, I've become such a fool. I'm just not used to being around women without the safety blanket of having a wife. Now my brain is shoving everyone at me as a potential partner when I don't even want one. I'm done with all that. Once I get used to my face, I might have the confidence to hookup with people now and then, but I'm not putting my heart through the pain of a relationship again.

Why am I thinking all this about Rose, anyway? It's not like she'd look twice at me. She's too young for me, and I'm too broken for someone as young and carefree as her. For all I know, she has a boyfriend. I just hope it's someone who treats her right—I swear to God if I find out who hurt her that night at the Gladstone, I'll murder him.

I shut the door of Isabel's room and head downstairs to my study. I've got work to do, numbers to crunch, emails to ignore.

"Morning, Mr Knighton." Rose's voice comes from behind as I reach the lower corridor. I turn around and nod. She's carrying a dustpan and broom toward the front door.

"Morning."

Her smile looks almost flirty—which is just my brain misinterpreting signals again. Maybe I'm not a safe person to be allowed out.

"How are you today?" she asks.

"Fine." I glance around, trying not to hold her gaze too long, but I can't stop myself. My focus won't settle anywhere else. She's all wild curls tumbling from a messy blonde updo, rosy cheeks, pink lips, and a trim figure beneath the smart black uniform. She's petite, and something about the idea of taking her in my arms sends hot bolts through me. "Um... Are you settling in alright?"

"Yeah, thank you." She smiles but nips her bottom lip. "I've not done anymore snooping." She raises the dustpan and broom as she holds up her hands in surrender, then makes an 'eek' face.

"I'm very glad to hear it. Otherwise... Well..."

"I swear I'm being good." Her eyes travel over me, and there's something almost suggestive in her tone. Isn't there? Or is that just me once more?

"You keep on being a good girl and we'll get along just fine."

She bites down on her lip again, and this time, there's no mistaking the flash in her eyes. "Okay. I'll be very good." She gives me a cheeky grin that's almost a wink. "I need to sweep the porch before I get back to the laundry. You really go through a lot of clothes. I've never seen so much ironing. I feel like I've spent the week spinning straw into gold."

"Meaning I'm some evil jailer who's locked you in a dark room until you complete the task?"

"Exactly."

I shake my head with a rueful smile. Isabel loves fairy tales, but Rumpelstiltskin is not her favorite. Still, I get Rose's meaning. "There won't usually be that much ironing. With the previous cleaner being signed off, there's been a big backlog."

"Good to know. I thought you might be trying to set a new world record or something."

"Well, you'll have all Isabel's stuff to do next week as well. She'll be here tomorrow until next Friday."

"No worries. I was kidding. It's part of the job, and I actually quite enjoy it."

"I wonder, would you mind giving Isabel's room a vacuum? Just shove all her toys to the side. She's terrible at picking them up."

"Of course, no worries." Another smile—each one lands deeper, like she's wearing down my defences one grin at a time. Such a far cry from the broken little creature she was at the Gladstone. This is shiny Rose, and I can even forgive her snooping. Natural curiosity seems part and parcel of who she is. I'm still watching her, and she's looking back. "What age is Isabel?" she asks.

"She's ten." I glance away with a smile. "And quite a character. Sometimes she's headstrong and lets her mouth run away with her."

"Does she get that from you?"

"I think not." I raise an eyebrow.

She chuckles and shakes her head. "I was just joking. I hope I get to meet her next week."

"She'll likely be at school when you're here, but we'll see." The thought of Isabel at school reminds me of Lydia's plans to send her to boarding school. No chance will that happen. I won't allow it. She needs stability, not a cold dormitory far from her family.

"I'll get on." Rose makes her way to the front door. "I don't want to add slacking to my list of faults."

"Definitely not."

Back in my study, I try to focus on the spreadsheets and emails demanding my attention. But the numbers blur, and the words become meaningless as Rose's singing drifts through the house, slipping under doors, into my very thoughts. I lean back in my leather chair, closing my eyes. It's like having Snow White here. It wouldn't surprise me if she's out there feeding a flock of birds from her hand—makes a change as I've been living with the wicked queen for the last twelve years.

I want to talk to someone about this. About how strange it feels to have her here—*her*—after that random meeting at the Gladstone. The odds of it are... well, they're slim. Too slim. But who would I even talk to?

Mum would scoff, probably say I was overthinking as usual and tell me to stop being so bloody intense. She'd never understand why this unsettles me, why it sits under my skin like a splinter I can't get out. And my brother, Jamie—God, Jamie would laugh his ass off. He'd think it was the best story ever. He lives for this kind of coincidence.

Darius, my best friend, might hear me out, but I haven't spoken to him properly in weeks. He's got a lot on his plate. And even if I did tell him, he might read between the lines, see something I don't want to admit. Something I'm afraid of. Would he think I'm interested? Obsessed? Is that what this is?

I don't know. I honestly don't. Is it unhealthy to be thinking about her this much? To replay our encounter at the Gladstone like it meant something? To read something into every smile she gives me. To wonder why she's here now, in this house, as if fate—or something darker—put her in my path? I keep trying to be rational, but it doesn't sit right. What if it *isn't* a coincidence? What if she's here for a reason?

Could she be running a scam? Targeting me on purpose? Maybe she's casing the place, getting the layout, working out where I keep the valuables. I wouldn't put it past someone—not anymore. Since Lydia, since I found out just how far someone can go with a smile and a lie, I see deceit in everything. I used to trust people. Used to think most were decent. Now? Now I question every motive.

But how do I stop? How do I break this loop in my head and just see her for what she is—a cleaner, a stranger, a woman who might just be as lost as I am? Or is that the most dangerous kind of lie yet?

Rose doesn't work here on Fridays. Today she's over at Jamie's place, cleaning the converted stable block he and his partner Owen call home. I wonder what he'll make of her. Jamie's sharp—he misses nothing—and he oversees the running of Ardencairn with that same attention to detail, while I manage the business on a broader scale. Together, we're carrying our father's legacy. Strange to call it that. The hotels are the only good thing the evil bastard left behind.

The Gladstone fire has buried me in paperwork. It's been a mess—PR, insurance, staff to reassure. And then there's the woman I pulled from the wreckage. Now she's under investigation. I hope to God she didn't do it deliberately. My gut says she didn't. But every possibility has to be examined. That's how this works. Still, she's clearly suffered. Mentally, if not physically.

Unlike me.

I tap my pen against the desk, each click a futile attempt to summon my focus. The insurance claim for the Gladstone is a mess. So many investigations have to take place, and all the while we're losing money. I spend the afternoon going through emails and paperwork until I hear the front door clicking.

"Daddy!" The shout snaps me out of my reverie, and suddenly there's a whirlwind of energy bursting into the room.

"Hey, monkey." I jump up from my seat as Isabel throws herself into my arms. I check out the window and see the school taxi driving away. "How was school?"

"Boring."

"It shouldn't be boring. That means you're not working hard enough. And speaking of that. You need to go upstairs and tidy your toys. They're in a right mess."

"Okay, fine." She runs upstairs, and her footsteps clump on each step. She's barely gone when I hear her calling. "Daddy! Daddy, come here!"

What the hell? I charge up the stairs. "What is it? Are you okay?"

"Look at this." She drags me into her room and points at her bed. "Did you do it?"

I peer inside to see every cuddly toy she owns arranged either around the bed or on shelves. Some of them are set up on the carpet like they're about to have a picnic.

"Wasn't me, sweetheart." I smile as I look around. "It must've been Rose."

"Who's Rose?" Isabel sinks to the floor beside the picnicking toys, picks up her favorite pink rabbit, and cuddles it.

"She's the new cleaner." I lean on the door, unable to stop smiling. She looks so happy.

"Is she like Mary Poppins?" She giggles. "I think she must be. This room was too messy to tidy without magic."

"Maybe she is." I shrug. "Though she doesn't look like her."

"Who does she look like?"

"Um... I don't know. Herself."

"Like Belle? Or Rapunzel?"

"Maybe a bit like Rapunzel."

Isabel nods. "I like her already."

"Me too, kiddo." I sit down beside her. Yeah, me too. My crazy mind has too much Rose on the brain.

# 7
## *Rose*

The saggy couch cushions swallow me up as I lean into them and pass the takeaway pizza box to Sienna. "You can have the last bit. I'm stuffed."

"Thanks." Sienna lifts it. "Though I'm not sure it's good for the hips."

"Like you need to worry. You're already too skinny."

"Because I can't afford food."

She's only half joking, and I know how she feels. After I met Freddie, I never thought there would be a day like this ever again. His money was the answer to my prayers. I guess there's more to life than money, but when you don't have any, that's a tough line to live by.

"How are the classes going?" I ask. She's younger than me by a few years and does art at Edinburgh University. She also works in a coffee shop to make money to pay for it all. I remember those days so well—when I was a chambermaid at Ardencairn. It's almost like nothing has changed.

"Yeah, they're good. What about you? How's the new job? I've been so busy this last week I've hardly seen you."

"It was okay." What else can I say? I'm a cleaner, but I have a degree in English. I'd love a better job, but who'll give me a reference now?

Freddie's parents? Why do I doubt that? And I don't even want to ask them. I never want to see them again. I can almost guarantee they'll have blacklisted my name. "Something weird happened though, and you'll love it."

"Oh, what?" Sienna peers at me from behind her large glasses. She's so pretty in a whimsical way. She reminds me of a fairy princess who should be dancing barefoot in a garden.

"Well, the guy who owns the house is someone I'd met before... He's the man who gave me his jacket that night at the Gladstone. This is so weird, but I always had a feeling I'd see him again. Is that stupid?"

"Oh, wow. It's fate. It must be. Did he remember you?"

"Yeah, he did." Heat rises in my cheeks. "And this is maybe super-weird, but like... Well, he's really handsome."

"Why is that weird?"

"Because his face is covered in scars, and it wasn't before. God knows how he got them, but the first time I met him..." No, I don't want to go back there. But I haven't forgotten him asking me who had hurt me and telling me he'd deal with them if he found out. If he was willing to do that for a stranger, what might he do for someone else? "Well, let's just say he doesn't seem violent, but how can you tell?"

I give you Exhibit A—Freddie. I didn't think he'd turn out to be violent.

"Then just do the cleaning and keep away from him."

"I would..." I nibble my lip for a moment. "But I can't. He draws me to him. It's like I can't help meeting him in the corridor..." Or walking in on him in the bath. "And he's kind of... You know..."

"You fancy him?"

I shrug and take a swig of wine. "There's something about him."

"And do you want to... have a relationship with him?"

"God no. He's got to be a millionaire. You should see his house. I mean, it's ugly as fuck, but clearly worth a lot."

"Wouldn't that be good then?"

"No, I've dated a rich guy in the past, and I'm not doing that again. I can make my own money, and I don't want some rich saviour. Anyway, this guy is older, and... well, not relationship material—for me. Though I would fuck him."

Sienna giggles. "Are you serious?"

"Hell yes. Freddie was useless in bed, but this guy... I just *know* he'd be good."

"How can you possibly know that?"

Good question and I'm not sure I have the answer. "I just do."

And I'll happily test my theory if the opportunity arises.

"Rose." John Knighton's commanding voice grabs my attention as I make my way toward the laundry room on Monday morning. Heat rises in my cheeks and neck as the chat I had with Sienna on Friday night dances into my head. If I meet his eyes, will he see right through me? Guess the filthy thoughts I've been having? Deduce that every night in bed, I lie awake seeing his face, and wonder about his scars, but more... So much more. I imagine his lips on mine, his hands touching me... Fuck, I've got this bad.

"Morning, Mr Knighton." I turn and smile at him, my breath catching as I take in his slim hips encased in black jeans, and his broad chest filling a crisp white shirt, open at the top, just enough to tease me. I know what's under there, and I wouldn't mind another look—or to run my fingers over it.

"I need to thank you," he says. A smile plays on his beautiful lips. They're so perfectly shaped, with a lush lower lip and a pronounced Cupid's bow on top. Even though a scar runs close, it doesn't take anything away from him.

"Thank me? What for?"

"For setting up Isabel's toys so thoughtfully. She loved them. It was above and beyond. We both appreciate it."

"Oh, that. It was nothing." I'd forgotten all about it, but as I've always had a soft spot for cuddly toys, I actually enjoyed doing it. We didn't have much money growing up, and I'm the middle child. It's funny how things often passed me by. "She's got a great collection. Lucky girl."

His eyes linger on mine, and there's something in them—gratitude, maybe, or more—whatever it is, it makes my heart flutter. "She is. And I admit I spoil her. She's precious."

I smile at his dreamy-eyed look.

"I better get cracking," I say, more to myself than him.

"Me too." He heads toward his study.

I open the laundry room door and start loading the machine. Once the first load is in, I nip to the kitchen to start cleaning. This is where a degree in English has landed me. Still, it has one plus point—I get to ogle John Knighton.

Where did he get those scars? He owns this house, so does that mean he also owns the country club? Or are the house and the club unrelated? I'll google it later and see if there's any information.

By the time I've cleaned the kitchen and the pantry, it's time to get the laundry out of the machine. I load it into the basket and put in another load. The box of powder is nearly empty, but there's another one on the top shelf next to what looks like a pile of old photo frames and faded biscuit tins.

I can't reach that shelf, and I don't want to go bothering Mr Knighton. There's an empty crate below the window, so I pull it over, and, balancing precariously, I stretch up. My fingers grab the edge of the box when it clips the stack of photo frames sending them toppling.

*Crash*!

The frames hit the worktop on their way to the floor. Fuck.

I put the box of laundry detergent on the worktop and stoop to lift the frames. Some of them have smashed. I thought they were empty, but they all have pictures in them. Family pictures, it seems.

My heart races. I'll have to confess that I broke them and somehow explain that I wasn't snooping. My eye catches the people in one of the pictures. There's John—pre-scars—smiling next to a woman with very long dark hair and a golden tan. On John's knee is an adorable little girl with sea-blue eyes just like him; her hair, thick and dark, is tied back in a half ponytail. That must be Isabel when she was younger. Then I freeze when I look closer at the woman.

"No way." I've seen that woman before. She's the one who was talking to Freddie at the Gladstone the night of the fire. Are they still together? Is that who Freddie left me for?

I shake my head. Something's gone wrong somewhere. This is all so twisted. I need to speak to John. Firstly, to confess about breaking the frames, but also to see what he knows about Freddie and his wife.

I knock on his study door, clutching the picture to my chest, but he doesn't answer. I put my ear to it. No sounds. He might be taking a break or gone for a walk. I head down the corridor, but as I approach the living room, I hear his low voice talking. The door's open and I look in to see him lounging back on the couch on his phone.

Oh hell. His arm is along the back of the couch, and with his posture so open, all I can think about it resting my head on that slab of a chest while he runs his fingers through my hair.

He glances up, sees me, raises his hand and flashes two fingers, mouthing "two seconds".

I hover near the door until he ends his call.

"Come in." He beckons me. "What is it you want?"

"Um, well..." I approach where he's sitting. "I wasn't snooping or anything—I promise." My words tumble out in a rush, and I hold out the broken frame. "Some frames fell from the top shelf when I was getting the washing powder, and they broke."

He glances at the picture. "Never mind." His voice is flat. "I won't be putting them up again anyway."

I bite my lip and don't move.

"Is there something else?" He raises an eyebrow.

"Is this woman your wife?"

He looks up now, his eyes meeting mine. "Soon to be ex-wife, yes. Why?"

"And did she... Well, did she leave you for someone else?"

"Why do you want to know that?"

"Because I saw her with my ex-boyfriend."

His eyes drill into me, and I really need to sit down... My legs are like jelly under his penetrating stare. "Is your ex Freddie Blackwood?"

I nod.

"Jesus Christ." John gets to his feet. "Yeah. That's who she's gone off with. A politician." He scoffs. "When did you see them together?" He scrapes his hand through his hair, not looking at me.

"At the Gladstone. The same night I first met you."

He turns to face me, and his eyes darken. "Is he the one who hurt you?"

I look away as a surge of emotion rises in my throat. I barely manage a nod.

"Fucking bastard," John growls. "He's just made himself a marked man."

"What do you mean?"

"First, for beating up a woman, and second, for stealing my wife."

I watch him pace from the window to the couch. Is this how he got his scars? Defending someone? I can't deny I like the idea of seeing him land a punch on Freddie's sanctimonious face, but at the same time I don't want him to get into any trouble.

"Mr Knighton." I fiddle with the photo frame. "This might be a conflict of interest now. If it's too weird, I can talk to my boss. You might want someone else instead."

He stops pacing. His gaze softens as it meets mine. "It's your call." The corner of his mouth twitches into an almost smile. "But as far as I see it, it isn't a problem. Unless of course you find any of her stuff and have a mad urge to burn it or slash it to pieces..." His eyes flash. "In which case, come and find me first, and I'll help you."

I let out an involuntary giggle. "Okay. That's good." I move closer, edging around the couch to where he's standing. "Because I'd rather stay here."

He nods. "I'd rather that too."

A bolt of energy crackles between us before John looks away. His expression darkens, his jaw tightening as he runs a hand through his hair again. "I don't want that bastard anywhere near my daughter."

His words hit me like a punch to the gut. "Oh God, of course. Can you warn your ex?"

He shakes his head. "I doubt it. She won't listen to me. She'll think I'm just being bitter, trying to sabotage her new relationship." His eyes meet mine, and I see the fear there, and helplessness. "But if he's capable of hurting you, then he's capable of doing it to others."

Without thinking, I bridge the distance between us and reach out, taking his hand in mine. His skin is warm, calloused, and I feel a jolt of electricity at the contact. "I'll help you. Any way I can."

He looks down at our joined hands, then back up at me. The intensity of his gaze makes my breath catch in my throat. We're standing so close now, I can smell his cologne—Jo Malone's *Wood Sage & Sea Salt*, which I've seen bottles of while cleaning his room. He's so tall, his chest so broad, shoulders so wide. I want to climb him like a utility pole, wrap my legs around him, and kiss him.

I'm acutely aware of every detail on his face—the faint scar above his left eyebrow, the flecks of green in his blue eyes making them almost turquoise. My gaze drops to his lips, and a powerful urge to push up on tiptoes and kiss him rips through me.

"Thank you," he says. "I'm not sure how you can, but if I think of a way, I'll let you know."

"Do you feel... Well, it's like we're bound together somehow?" I shrug. "I know it sounds silly, but—"

"It doesn't sound silly. I understand."

"Freddie makes me so mad." I grip John's hand even tighter. "I actually feel sorry for your ex."

"She doesn't deserve your pity. She's a cold-hearted manipulator."

I huff out a wry laugh. "I guess she's well-suited to Freddie then. Though I doubt she'll get any satisfaction from him."

"Not if what he did to you is anything to go by."

"He wasn't exactly a great lover before that. His own satisfaction was all that mattered." I let go of his hand. "Or maybe I'm just not attractive enough. Your ex is really beautiful."

He takes my hand again, and the heat from his hold radiates through me. "You shouldn't say things like that. This is on them, not on you. If you're not attractive to a vile man who hurts women, then it's no loss. Other men will be attracted to you... Other men *are*... I'm sure."

"Do you know what I want?"

His eyes bore into mine like he's reading my soul. "Tell me."

"Revenge."

He lifts an eyebrow. "And how do you plan to get it?"

"I don't know, but I want him to suffer."

"He will. Life with Lydia will be trials enough."

"No, that's not enough. I'll need to think of something. It makes me sick to think of him and your ex together... while we're..."

"We're what?"

"You're alone, and I'm... well, also alone." And cast into the gutter like an unwanted piece of trash.

"But we're not alone, are we? It's like you said—we have a bond."

I wrap both my hands around his and lift them to my lips. "Yes, we do. We've both been burned."

"That we have." His eyes lose focus for a moment.

"Can I seal our bond?" I raise my eyes to him, my lips still close to his hand. "With a kiss?"

He frowns and eyes me over. "You want to kiss my hand?"

"Well... I'd settle for your hand, or..." My eyes wander to his lips again.

"Then let *me* kiss *you*."

"Isn't it the same thing?"

"Not quite." His voice is barely above a whisper.

My heart hammers in my chest. "Then do it."

He slides his hand from my grip and snakes it around the curve of my waist. The sheer size of his palm sends heat to my core. He leans in slowly, giving me every chance to pull away. But I don't want to. I want this—want him—more than I've wanted anything in a long time.

His lips meet mine, soft and tentative at first. It's a gentle kiss, but somehow full of power. The way he's holding me is so strong, and I'm encased by him. And I get what he meant by *him* kissing *me*. He's in control, and I'm succumbing to him in a dreamy stupor.

His hand cups my face, his thumb caresses my cheek, and the kiss deepens. Our tongues meet, and electricity sparks inside me. My breasts strain against my bra, nipples peaked and desperate for contact. I want to rip off my cleaning tunic and have him touch me. His tongue finds mine again, and my insides clench. My pussy burns with need now, and my panties are soaked.

I moan against his lips, and he pulls me closer. My stomach rubs over his crotch, and his hard length presses into me. Fuck, he feels huge. A rippling ache in my vagina screams to be filled by him. He angles his head slightly, still kissing me with soft lips and deep sweeps of his tongue.

This is more erotic and stimulating than anything I ever got from Freddie. I'm so close to coming just from kissing.

How is that even possible?

Reaching up, I swing my arms around his neck, hungry for more. I nibble on his lower lip as a knot of sensations builds in my core.

"Oh, Christ," he groans, and pulls away, leaving me bereft. "I'm sorry." He turns away from me. "I got carried away... That was—"

"Was what? Why did you stop?" It was the best kiss I've ever had. Jeez, he knows how to kiss—like a real man, not a spoiled boy.

He looks back at me. "You're an employee—I took advantage."

"No, you didn't. I agreed to it. We're both adults. And you know what made it even better?"

"What?"

"That tasted like revenge. Right now, Freddie's probably drilling into your ex with his shitty moves. Let him do it. Let them have that... because our kiss was explosive. We're so much better than them."

"Maybe." He stares at me. "But we can't do anything else."

"I know that. It was just a kiss."

"Just a kiss... Yes... Now, I, um, have work to do."

"Okay."

"I'll... Well, I better get back to it." He leaves the room, and I swallow.

Shit. That wasn't what I was hoping for. The ache between my legs is so strong now, it's painful. But I guess it's not going to be relieved the way I wanted. Maybe I should just go sit on the washing machine and ride it out. "Ugh." I throw back my head. Now I not only look like a snoop, but a sex-obsessed maniac. He's probably counting the days until I leave, and he gets his old cleaner back. But I can't dismiss that kiss. And he can't deny he enjoyed it, because he couldn't hide it. Fuck. Fuck. Fuckety fuck. Why is my life such a frustrating place to be?

# 8

## John

My office door slams shut with more force than I intend, the echo chasing me into the silence of the room. My pulse hammers in my temples—a relentless pounding that matches the chaos inside my head.

Freddie fucking Blackwood is the man who hurt Rose! The man who's now screwing my ex-wife. A man I want nowhere near my daughter. *Ever.* I'm already pumped enough to do something more violent than I've ever done before. If anyone deserves a good thumping, it's him. How could he hurt Rose? How could he hurt any woman?

Is he hurting Lydia?

Surely, if he's hurt her, she's got the sense to leave. I know if I say anything, she won't listen. And I admit it sounds like sour grapes, but fuck, it's my daughter's safety I'm concerned about.

I grab the phone, dialling my solicitor and praying to God he answers.

Thank fuck he does.

"Michael, it's John." We get the pleasantries out of the way before I get straight to the point. "I need to talk about custody of Isabel. I want full custody." I already know what he'll say—he's already said so in a roundabout way. Getting full custody will mean lengthy court battles unless Lydia agrees to it. And she won't. Out of principle. Even if it would give her all the freedom she wants. But she doesn't want to lose face and be seen as anything but the perfect mother. "Yeah, I know it's not going to be easy, but..." I trail off, staring unseeingly at the antique golf clubs mounted on the wall of my study. I listen to what Michael has to say, and I tell him my reasons. He's as disgusted as I am about Freddie Blackwood, and wonders if the whole affair will blow over quickly. I certainly hope so, but I can't count on it.

Isabel hates the idea of boarding school—so do I, for that matter, but I'm almost swayed to the idea of letting Lydia have her way. It would take her out of Freddie Blackwood's path, anyway.

But how could I?

My daughter would lose all respect for me. I already promised I wouldn't let her go. So, I need to find another way to keep her safe.

"Alright, John. I'll prepare the brief and call you back when it's all set up," Michael assures me.

"Thanks." I end the call and slump back in my chair, my gaze fixed on the ceiling.

Lydia.

She's the root cause of all this. I never thought I was a vengeful man, but right now I can see her far enough.

When we were together, I excused her moods and tempers. I assumed it was hormones, periods, the stress of being a mum and running her own business. Christ, I spent a long time investigating anything and everything that could explain why she was so frosty. Sometimes she'd snap for no reason—none I could see anyway—and God, could she shout? She'd scream at me and smash things. Thankfully I never saw her behave like that to Isabel, but what about now?

Thoughts of my daughter alone with an unstable mother and Freddie Blackwood are enough to make me sick. Thank fuck Isabel's with me this week and I can keep her close.

I let out a long breath. The restless tension in my body is already close to breaking point, but I haven't even considered one of the main factors. One that's setting my nerves on edge and consuming me the same way the flames devoured the kitchen at the Gladstone. A flesh memory of that heat is branded into me, but it's also in my blood—right now. And it's all caused by Rose Darwin.

She's a forbidden temptation, weaving her way around my house and infiltrating my senses with her smiles and her fuck-me eyes.

That kiss! Why did I do it? Have I lost my mind?

In all truth, I must have. I can't blame Rose. But I get it—well, I get her. I know how she feels. We've both suffered the same pain, from different people, but people who are now together, leading the lives they should have been leading with us. It should make it easier that neither Lydia nor Freddie has shown themselves to be pleasant people. But it doesn't.

Rose wants Freddie brought to justice. So do I. And I want Lydia to be held accountable for her attempts to get her hands on my money, steal part of my business, and now for endangering our daughter. How to bring it about is another matter.

*Is* there some kind of bond between Rose and me? She seems to think so. I don't believe in any of that soul-connection stuff—but I do believe in shared trauma, in the pull that happens when two damaged people recognize something familiar in each other. And then there's the physical side—undeniable and raw. I've felt attraction before, sure, but not like this. This is sharp, immediate... consuming. Maybe it's just because it's been a while. Lydia lost interest in sex a long time before we split—again, I assumed hormones, and she brushed me off whenever I tried to talk about it.

Now I wonder how many others she was with. Why she needed them. Why I wasn't enough.

This sure as hell isn't doing much for my ego. I'm well aware I'm not in peak condition—face wrecked, confidence shot—and yet Rose looks at me like I'm still worth something. Like I'm a man, not a monster. And maybe that's why I can't stop thinking about her. Because her attention—it does something to me. She'll be in no doubt about my attraction. My cock responded faster than she could say revenge and was ready for action. But she's working here. I can't take advantage of her like that, though the desire for something uncomplicated, something purely physical, is like a siren song calling to me, urging me to yield to the temptation.

With another deep inhale, I get up from the desk and head to the kitchen. It's past midday, and I should probably eat or at least have a coffee. I flick the switch on the kettle, listening to the low hum as it bubbles away. My mind's still whirling with hundreds of wild thoughts when the door glides open.

"Hey." Rose steps inside with a smile. Her eyes fix on me, and the tension inside me rises again. I clench my fists to control it. Tension I can deal with, but if my cock rises too, we're in trouble. I can't let just the sight of her get me hard. That's ridiculous.

"About earlier..." she says. "I shouldn't have suggested that kiss. It was out of line."

"I was as much to blame as you." I lean against the counter. "In that moment, it felt right... and good." I hold eye contact, but she looks away with a little quirk of her lips. "But... Well, you work here. I'm technically your boss."

She nods, taking a step closer, her gaze searching mine. "I know that. And I wasn't looking for anything... serious or long-term or anything like that. I guess I just..." She lets out a sigh. "...wanted something mindless to numb the pain. And before you say anything, I know it's the kind of thing I could get on Tinder, but I felt something between us. Though it's probably just the fact we've both been hurt."

"Exactly. I was just thinking the same thing. We have a trauma bond. You understand me better than anyone right now."

The smile grows on her face, and she nods again, this time more enthusiastically. "Yes. That's what I felt like. You really 'saw' me because you understood what I'd been through."

"I do understand, and it hurts me. I feel your pain strongly."

Rose inches even closer and puts her hand on my arm. "And I feel yours. That was why I wanted to kiss you. To relieve my pain, but also yours."

"It worked... But only for a moment, because now it's left me filled with doubts."

She shakes her head and tightens her grip. "Let's not doubt our connection. I think fate brought us together... not forever—that would be crazy—but for this moment. We're here together to help each other."

I allow myself a smile. She's so cute and so open to believing this kind of thing. "I'm not sure I believe in fate, but I like your reasoning.

It's a better thought than any of the dark ones I've been plagued with today."

There's a mischievous glint in her eye as she runs her finger down the sleeve of my shirt and onto my hand. My pulse quickens as her skin brushes against mine. "Well, if you want to numb the pain, we're on a lunch break. Neither of us is technically working right now."

"You're very naughty," I say, a half-hearted attempt at chiding her, "and determined to get me into trouble."

"Trouble?" She raises an eyebrow, playful yet piercing. "You've already ruined me with one kiss. So what do I have to lose?"

I raise an eyebrow. "I've ruined you?"

"You have. And you could probably do a lot worse." She looks up at me and all I can think about is taking her right here in the kitchen. And God, I will ruin her. There are so many things I want to do with her... But do I dare?

She's still smiling at me.

"What exactly do you want to do?" I ask.

"I'd like you to kiss me again. We'll take it from there."

I watch her for a moment, undressing her with my eyes, and imagining everything we could do together. "Oh, fuck it. Why not?" The words are out before I can stop them. Maybe I didn't really try. Subconscious thoughts are becoming conscious—my mind and body are waking to possibilities.

Her smile doesn't fade as she raises her hand to my face, gliding her soft palm over my scars. There's very little sensation there, but when her fingertips reach my earlobe and continue down my neck, molten lava erupts in my veins.

I snake my arms around her, pull her close, and our lips crash together in a deep, all-consuming kiss. My body responds immediately, and my cock hardens. She rubs against me, and I run my palms down her back. I need to get her out of this uniform.

"Let me show you something I'm good at," she whispers against my mouth, "something that will help you forget everything."

She pulls back just enough to slip off her top, revealing a lacy black bra that cups her beautifully shaped breasts. The sight alone sends an almost painful jolt straight to my groin. She's all curves and porcelain skin, and she smiles as she runs teasing fingers across her own cleavage. Then she drops to her knees and slowly unzips my fly.

"God, Rose," I say, though it comes out hoarse. "What are you doing to me?"

"Don't you want this?" Her hand stills.

"I... Do you?"

She nods. "Of course." She slips her fingers inside my boxer briefs and draws out my cock, now fully erect and aching for her touch. She takes my length in her hand and smiles.

"You're so big."

I let out a low growl as she slowly licks the tip, working her way down like I'm her favorite treat. Then she wraps her hand around the base and takes me in her mouth, her green eyes fluttering closed. The sensation is exquisite, and the slow drag of her tongue and lips has me biting back a moan. It's almost too much—the tender suction, the gentle swirls of her pointed tongue around the tip.

"Fuck..." I curse under my breath. I'd like to thrust into her pretty little mouth, but I don't want to hurt her. I'm losing control. She's so damn confident, like she's done this a hundred times. Maybe she has.

Her free hand braces on my thigh, and she takes me deeper. Each pull and bob of her head sends sparks of ecstasy shooting through me. I thread my fingers into her messy updo. She engulfs me in wet heat, gagging a little but not stopping.

"Rose, seriously... Fuck."

She pulls back and looks up at me, wiping saliva from her chin. "Are you okay?"

"Don't ask me any questions. I don't even know who I am right now. But are you sure you want to do this?"

"I've never been more sure." She smiles and takes me again, grazing her free hand over her lacy bra as she does so. I'm hanging by a thread, every nerve stretched to breaking, every muscle tensed, every breath shallow and quick.

I'm not sure if I can hold on much longer. She's relentless, her mouth is so hot, and I'm spinning. My heart hammers against my chest as she ups the pace.

"God, Rose," is all I can gasp out as the pleasure builds, coiling tighter and tighter. My balls are about to burst. "I can't hold on..."

"I don't want you to." She pulls back and unhooks her bra, tugging it off and casting it aside. Her full and round breasts spill out, nipples peaked and hard like she's incredibly turned on, and I'm desperate to know how wet she is, but I'm so far gone. "Don't hold back." She licks my length again, running the tip of her tongue across my tip that's weeping precum, fondling her breasts at the same time.

I groan as she envelops me once more with her lips and hand. The warmth of her mouth sends shivers up my spine, and I fist her hair gently, rocking my hips against her. Her flat tongue glides up my length in a broad stroke.

"Aw jeez. That's so fucking good."

She flicks at me with the tip of her tongue. "You told me to be a good girl from now on… Is this good enough?"

"More than… You're a very good girl."

Her nipples seem to perk up even more, and she smiles, then takes me in her mouth again, her hand working in tandem, driving me closer to the edge. She takes me deep.

"Rose… Fuck." My voice is ragged, my body wound tight. I can feel every suck, every caress, magnified, as if my whole existence has narrowed down to this one point of contact between us.

Her eyes flicker up to mine, heavy-lidded and filled with an intense heat that could ignite the very air. Her cheeks are hollow as she draws me in.

I can't anymore—I don't want to. With a final surge of pleasure that obliterates every coherent thought, I come undone, my climax tearing through me like wildfire. It's fierce, uncontrollable.

"Fuck," I gasp. She sits back, holding her breasts beneath me as I spill my load over her. She smiles up at me, trailing her finger through the mess on her skin, then she gets to her feet, and she reaches up to pull me into another kiss. Her lips are soft and yielding against mine, and I taste myself on her.

"What the fuck?" I whisper against her lips. "That was incredible."

I can hardly believe what just happened—but much as I enjoyed it, I'm also pissed at myself for letting her do it. She should have come first.

But not to worry. I'll make it up to her.

# 9
## *Rose*

John Knighton's arms are wrapped around me, and he doesn't seem to care that the sticky warmth on my breasts is very likely transferring to his shirt. Then again, it's me who does his laundry, so I guess I'm the one who should be bothered, but I'm not. Not one bit. Freddie never cuddled me after sex or blow jobs. Once he was done, he rolled over and went to sleep or zipped up his trousers and left.

This is new—different.

Nice.

"I shouldn't have let this happen." John's voice is raspy.

"Hey." I tilt my head up to meet his gaze, my fingers tracing the lines of his taut forearms. "We both wanted it, didn't we? No regrets here."

He shakes his head, and my insides turn cold. He didn't want this? Have I overstepped completely? Made a fool of myself? "It's not that I regret it—it's just… you should've come first. That's how it's supposed to be."

An almost manic laugh bubbles out of me before I can catch it. The blood warms in my veins again. "I've never come at all. Well, not with a person, anyway. Freddie either liked watching himself come on me or taking me from behind."

"What a prick." John's eyes darken, his jaw setting in a firm line. "Even though I've just done the same."

"No. This is different. Because I wanted to do it... and you're still here."

He gives me an odd look like he doesn't get that there's any other option, then he nods. "If we're doing this..." His voice is low and growly. "Then we're doing it properly. Let's rewrite the script."

Before I can respond, he lets go of me, peels off his shirt with a swift, fluid motion, and tosses it aside. His muscular chest is a work of art, and my nipples perk up at the sight—along with my pulse. Raw power seems to emanate from him. A thought about his scars flashes through my mind: How did he get them? But it's gone in a split second.

"How will you...?" Before I finish, he places his large palms on my shoulders. My insides leap at the touch, and I can't remember what I was going to say.

Gently, he turns me around, so he's behind me. For a moment, I think he's going to bend me over the worktop and fuck me—that's how Freddie would have liked it—but he guides me toward the sink. He starts the water, then wets his hands and squeezes some soap onto his palms. A lather begins to form.

"May I?" He looks down at me, and I turn to meet his gaze, catching on what he's doing. He's going to wash me.

"Okay."

I almost faint as he moves in behind me again, then reaches around and cups my breasts, smoothing the lather across my hypersensitive skin. With gentle caresses, he washes away the evidence of his climax.

"That was a big load you blew." I turn my head and nuzzle into his chest as he continues to palm my breasts.

"It's all for you. You've been such a good girl, after all." He tweaks my nipples with a wicked grin.

"Ah." I let out a soft cry as he works the bubbles over my skin, tracing circles around my swollen breasts. My nipples are like rocks now, and every touch ignites something deeper inside me. This is such a stark contrast to Freddie's rough handling, to the way he'd use me and leave me feeling hollow.

John's fingers glide over me, soapy and smooth, leaving tingling trails up to my neck. His other hand sweeps my hair aside, and his lips find the vulnerable spot just below my earlobe. A shiver races down my spine as he kisses me, and for a moment, I'm dizzy with it.

"Oh, God... Mr Knighton." My voice is barely a whisper, but he hears me and huffs into my ear.

"I think under the circumstances, you should call me John." His hold on me tightens a little.

"Okay... John."

"That's better. Such a good girl." He doesn't rush, taking his time to clean every inch of my breasts, collarbone, and neck. When it's done, he takes a clean dishcloth from a drawer. The linen is soft against my skin, warmer than I expect, and he pats me dry with gentle strokes.

"Wow... That was very nice."

He raises an eyebrow. "We're not done yet. That was just the beginning."

"It was?"

"Yes," he murmurs and meets my gaze. There's a promise in his eyes, and something more—something like hunger. "I've barely even started yet."

Without warning, he hooks his fingers into the waistband of my cropped work trousers, easing them down my legs. The fabric pools at my ankles, and I step out of them, suddenly self-conscious in my plain pink cotton panties. These are so not sexy, but they're comfy for work.

"Comfort over style, right?"

"Right." He traces the damp outline on the fabric that betrays my arousal. I'm soaked through. His fingers slip beneath the cotton, skimming my sensitive flesh, and I gasp. My body responds instantly, my nipples pebbling under his gaze. I feel exposed, yet seen, as if he's discovering parts of me I never knew were there.

My hands grip the edge of the counter for support, and he runs a thick fingertip along my slit, drawing it up over my clit. I take a fitful breath.

"So wet."

"I know." My words are barely audible.

Suddenly, his arms are beneath me, and he scoops me up with such ease that it takes my breath away. He places me on the cool surface of the kitchen table. It's hard to reconcile the raw power of his body with the tenderness he used to wash me.

He leans in and kisses me, first on the lips, then down my neck. His mouth brushes over the top of my breasts, teasing me. Then he pulls back, his breath warm against my skin. He eases my panties down my thighs. Every touch ignites a trail of fire, leaving me breathless with need.

He spreads my legs, his gaze intense, and I'm laid bare before him. Shouldn't this be awkward? And maybe it is a little, but it's also thrilling. I know whatever he does next will be good... I can hardly wait. I need him—now.

He bends down, lowering his head and placing a kiss directly on my clit. I nearly die. But before I've even caught my breath, his tongue licks up my slit.

"Oh, God."

It's like a gentle kiss at first, but soon he's licking and sucking more rapidly. I arch my back and moan. Heat spirals within me.

"That feels... so fucking good," I manage to gasp. My hands move to my breasts, and I touch myself. I'm not sure if it eases or increases the burn inside me.

"That's a good girl," he murmurs against me.

I can't think, can't focus on anything but the waves of pleasure furling inside me as he worships me with his lips. I lean back on one hand, my fingers gripping the edge of the table, still touching my breasts with the other as he licks my clit with broad strokes.

I'm so close. I've never managed this with anyone—my vibrator is the only thing I've ever orgasmed on.

John slips two fingers into me and I gasp. They're thick, but I'm so wet they glide in easily. He finds the secret spot inside and rubs against me, and it's as if he's flicked a switch. A jolt of pure bliss zaps through me, setting every nerve ending alight.

"Ah, John!" I cry out. I'm going to come. It's about to happen. He pumps his fingers inside me, driving me further into madness while his tongue continues its relentless assault on my pussy.

"That's good. Come on my fingers," he growls onto me. "Show me how you'd like to come on my cock." His lips form an O over my clit, and he sucks mercilessly.

My orgasm hits like a tidal wave, ripping through me with such force that I scream. "Holy fuck. I'm coming. Oh, fuck." I grab his hair, gripping it tightly. My body shakes uncontrollably, my vision blurs, and for a moment, there's nothing but pure, white-hot intensity flooding my senses.

"Fuck, John! Fuck!" I shout again, clinging to his head as aftershocks pulse through me, leaving me spent and trembling.

He breaks free of my hold. "Wow, you really are beautiful." His voice is soft and close to my ear now. He's moved, and he's beside me.

I'm utterly overwhelmed, my heart pounding, my soul full. For the first time, I understand what it means to be seen and worshipped.

His arms envelop me, his strength palpable as he lifts me from the table where I've just shattered into a thousand brilliant pieces. My legs are still trembling, my body humming with the aftershocks of pleasure. He carries me, and the feeling of being so utterly cared for is new, strange, and intoxicating.

We reach the living room, and he sits down on the plush couch, pulling me onto his lap. He reaches for a warm throw draped over the back of the couch and wraps it around us both. It's soft and comforting, and I snuggle closer to him, craving the warmth of his body against mine.

"You okay?" he asks, his voice low and soothing.

"Yeah... That was unreal," I whisper back, my head resting against his broad shoulder.

"I'm still not finished with you."

"You're not?" I'm not sure I can take much more. I'm still in a bubble of contented joy.

"No. But I'll save it for another day."

"Something to look forward to." I smile against his hot skin. "I'll have to start bringing a change of underwear to work if this is on the lunch menu every day. You realize I'll have to wash my own panties before I leave? They're a bit wet. Otherwise, I'll have none to wear on the bus home."

He chuckles, and it vibrates through his chest and tickles my ear. "You could leave them here. I might keep them... as a souvenir."

"Don't get any funny ideas." I poke him lightly in the ribs. "You know, there are blokes out there who'd pay good money for a pair like that. Women auction off their worn panties to men on the internet."

"Is that so?" He arches an eyebrow, kissing the top of my hair. "I can't tell if you're being serious."

"Dead serious," I assure him.

"It's a mad world." He kisses me softly on the forehead, and we lapse into silence. It's nice just existing like this.

"Thank you, Mr Knighton."

"There's nothing to thank me for. You deserve all the pleasure in the world. And honestly, it was the most beautiful thing that's happened to me in a long time."

A sudden bang jolts me from the cocoon of warmth in John's embrace. He stiffens underneath me, his body coiling like a spring. "What was that?" I whisper.

"Car door." He disentangles himself from me and gently places me on the couch, then goes to peer out the window. His face turns white. "Shit. It's my mother. We've got to move—now."

Hot spikes prickle at the base of my skull, and we're both moving before I can process anything else. I dash back to the kitchen, grabbing for my clothes. My fingers are clumsy, fumbling with the fabric. John's already halfway out the door. "Lock yourself in the laundry room and stay there until I sort her out."

"Right." I dart into the laundry room, slamming the door behind me and twisting the lock just as I hear his footsteps on the stairs and his mother's voice filtering through the house.

"John? Hello!"

My heart hammers against my ribcage as I yank on my bra. Trousers and tunic follow in quick succession. As for the panties, well, they're a lost cause, aren't they? With a flick of my wrist, they join a pile of laundry waiting to be washed. No time to answer Mrs Knighton; I need to look like I've been working the entire time, though for now, I'm staying in here like John said.

I hop onto the work surface, perching there, trying to calm my racing pulse.

"John? Are you about?" Mrs Knighton's voice climbs higher in pitch.

I chew on my lip and keep quiet, staring blankly at the whirring washing machine. Everything feels surreal—the adrenaline, the rush, the way my body still tingles all over. If this is what revenge looks like, then Freddie better watch out. Because screw being cold; revenge is best served scorching hot, leaving you breathless and reeling. And John? He's rewritten the script entirely.

"John?" His mother calls again, more insistently this time.

I sit quite still, my mind a whirlpool of exhilaration and nerves. I'm not ready to come down from this high—not yet.

# 10
## *John*

I zip up my jeans and yank a shirt over my head. No point checking my reflection. What I see there these days never brings me anything to smile about. My heart's still racing as I nip back down the stairs.

"John! Where on earth have you been hiding?" My mother whirls around as I enter the kitchen. My eyes scan around. Please don't let there be any evidence of what just took place in here. Just in case my mother spots anything she shouldn't, I approach her and hug her, while chivvying her out of the room.

"I wasn't hiding. Just getting a clean shirt. I, um, spilt tea on the other one."

"Oh dear. You always were a messy boy."

Indeed. If only she knew. "Why are you here?"

"Just passing by," she says. "I wanted to see you."

"Well, let's go through to the living room."

Images from half an hour ago invade my thoughts; Rose sprawled across the kitchen table, laid wide open for me. I shift uncomfortably, as a pang of heat burns low in my belly. Bloody hell, I'm lucky Mum decided to drop in now and not then.

"Mind if I stay for the afternoon?" she asks. "I'd like to wait until Isabel gets back from school. It's been too long since I've seen her."

"Sure, Mum." I push the living room door fully open. "You can watch TV in here. I've got some work to finish up."

It's not a lie, but I also need her out of the way while I get Rose out of the laundry room.

"That's fine," she says. "I might read. There's rarely anything I enjoy on TV these days—too much drama and horrible stuff."

She wears her confidence like armour these days. Since Dad died ten years ago, she's become a different woman—stronger, sharper. But she still avoids anything that brings back memories of the dark days. The days when she'd vanish from her social circle for weeks at a time, hiding the bruises, the shame. She never talks about it, but I haven't forgotten. None of us has.

She goes directly to the couch and immediately tuts at the sight of the throw crumpled on the floor. "Oh, that must've slipped off when Isabel was playing here this morning," I mutter, knowing full well it was anything but child's play that dislodged it.

She picks it up and folds it neatly. "How's the new cleaner getting on?"

"Fine." I don't make eye contact as the word leaves my mouth. I have a strange sense that if I do, my mother will see the truth in my face and guess just how 'fine' Rose is.

Mum nods, apparently satisfied, and settles onto the couch. She opens her brown leather tote bag and pulls out a thick paperback book. "Right, you get off to work. I'll be fine with this."

"Great." I close the door and head down the corridor, past the kitchen and up to the laundry room door.

"Rose, it's me." I knock quietly.

The door opens just a crack, and she peers out. "Is everything okay?" She glances past me.

"Yeah, it's all fine." I step inside, closing the door behind me. "My mum's in the living room. Best not clean in there today."

She nods, then a wry grin curves across her mouth. "Wouldn't it be typical if I bumped into her today, on the day when I have no panties on?"

The image hits me like a punch, and I let out a low growl. "Do you have any idea what you're doing to me?" I tug at the collar of my shirt.

She smiles and cocks an eyebrow like she's in no doubt of her power over me.

"And you needn't worry about my mother." I lean in closer, barely restraining the urge to kiss the soft skin of her neck, and whisper, "She won't notice your lack of underwear. Me, on the other hand? Different story."

"Well, they're in the wash now, so if I can dry them in time, I might be respectable for the bus home."

I keep my eyes on her. "Yes, save being respectable for the bus."

Her focus flits to the door. "Are we… going to 'have lunch together' again?" She air quotes.

"I'd like to if you do."

"I'm cleaning your brother's house tomorrow."

"I forbid you to 'have lunch' with him." I mimic her air quotes. "Not that he'd be interested. He's married, and he prefers men."

She prods me on the upper arm. "I meant I could come over during my lunch break."

"I like it. And Jamie will be working, so he won't know if you take a bit of extra time."

"Will I need it?"

"Oh yes. Let's not rush. I'll square things with Jamie if necessary. And tell him I needed you to do something over here. It won't be a lie, will it?"

She giggles. "No. And to be honest, his house is always so tidy I never need to do that much. I'll make sure I get the laundry done first. That's what takes longest."

"Excellent. Well, I'll see you tomorrow then. Revenge will be served promptly at one."

Her laughter fills the little room. I dip in and place a kiss on her cheek before I retreat to my study.

Now, I have to get my work head on and focus. I settle at my desk, running a hand through my hair before I open my laptop.

Hours slip by with the whir of the computer fan as the only sound. Until I hear my mother's voice. Who is she talking to?

I check the time. Rose is usually gone by now, but I guess I kept her from her work for too long today. My neck heats.

What am I playing at?

But I don't want to think about that just now. I get up and open the door.

"Thank you for your work today," Mum is saying.

"Of course, Mrs Knighton."

I stride out of the study and along the corridor. Rose catches my eye, keeping her expression neutral as she buttons her coat. Good girl—but is she wearing her panties?

The front door bursts open, and Isabel tumbles in. She drops her school bag and races toward my mother.

"Granny!" she squeals, throwing her arms around Mum's waist.

"Hello, my darling," Mum coos.

Isabel turns to me, her bright blue eyes sparkling. "Daddy!" She jumps on me and hugs me too.

"Hey, beautiful. How was school?"

"Good! We're learning about jungle animals. I like the panthers. Do you know a panther is just a black leopard?"

"Um... I'm not sure I did, but I do now."

"Who's she?" Isabel points at Rose.

"Don't point." My mother takes Isabel's hand and lowers it.

"This is Rose," I say. "She's the cleaner who set up all your toys for you."

"Oh, cool!" Isabel doesn't hesitate, wrapping Rose in a hug as if they've known each other for years.

"Really, Isabel," my mother says.

"Oh... Um, hi." Rose gives her a little pat on the back.

"Will you play with me one day?" Isabel pulls back to look up at her with hopeful eyes.

"Maybe one day." Rose smiles down at her. "But I'm usually away before you come home."

"Rose is just leaving," Mum says. "So let her go."

"Bye, Rose!" Isabel waves enthusiastically as Rose slips out the door.

"Bye." Rose gives us all a wave.

My mother's eyebrows are raised in a silent reprimand. "Isabel, we don't hug strangers like that." She watches through the side window as Rose crosses the courtyard.

"Rose isn't a stranger, Granny." Isabel looks up at her grandmother with a stubborn tilt to her chin. "She makes my room nice!"

"Still, darling, we must remember she works here," my mother adds.

I look away, unable to meet either of their gazes. The reality of what I've done, the invisible line I've crossed with Rose today, is now etched into the forefront of my mind. I'm a lot more deserving of this reprimand than my daughter. I've blurred the boundaries between employer and employee—a boundary that should be as clear as an eight-foot fence.

# 11

## *Rose*

I shove the last of Jamie's shirts into the washer, and as it whirs to life, my thoughts drift to his brother. John. I'm seeing him later, which sets off a flutter in my stomach like a cage of butterflies trying to escape. It's a weird mix of nerves and excitement—nerves because I'm not sure what we're doing and excitement because I totally love the fact that we are.

It's just a casual arrangement between two people who've been wounded in a similar way, I guess. A good way for us to forget—as well as get revenge. Freddie might never know, but I certainly feel better knowing I'm having a better time with an almost stranger than I ever had with him.

And there's the rub. Who is John really? I feel like I've given a part of myself to him, but I don't really know him. Where did he get his scars? Should I dare ask? He seems trustworthy—a good man. A good dad.

But what if there's darkness there I've yet to uncover? Freddie seemed like a good guy when I first met him. The answers don't really matter though, because in a few weeks the other cleaner will be back, and John Knighton and I won't see each other again.

That thought doesn't cheer me as I grab the duster, ready to go around the surfaces, while the laundry cycles through. Jamie's house is quiet, save for the hum of the washer. It feels more modern than the lodge, probably because it's in a converted stable block, so everything inside is relatively new. I've only met Jamie a couple of times. He's a little like John facially—minus the scars, of course—though his hair is shorter and he's not as tall and imposing.

After the surfaces are done, I do the vacuuming, then finally I gather up the garbage bags and haul them outside to the trash can.

"Typical Scottish weather," I mutter under my breath, pulling my coat tighter around me as the cold November air bites at my cheeks. The trash can lid clatters shut, echoing in the empty driveway—then another noise catches my ear. It's coming from the garage. A sort of metallic banging, like someone dropped a toolbox. No one's in there, surely. Jamie works at the hotel and so does his partner, Chris.

Snooping isn't part of the job description, and I've already been caught poking my nose in where I shouldn't. Still... can't hurt to have a quick look, right?

Probably just a cat or something. I head around the side of the garage, looking for an entrance. My fingers fumble on the cold metal handle of a side door, half-expecting it to be locked. But no, it swings open with an eerie creak.

"Hello?" I call tentatively, stepping inside the dimly lit space.

My eyes take a second to adjust, and then I see a man sprawled out on the floor. He's tall, gaunt, with limbs that seem too long for his body. There's something vaguely familiar about him.

"Hello..." I say from the door. "Are you okay?" No response. I can see he's not okay, and my heart's racing. What's he doing on the cold concrete? Part of me thinks I should help him, but warning bells are going off inside my head. What if this is a trick? What if I go over to him and he grabs me? He looks a lot bigger than me.

"Hey! Can you speak?" My voice barely cuts through the stale, icy air, muffled by the thick dust and shadows clinging to the garage walls. The only reply is a low, garbled mumble—thick and slurred, the syllables slipping over each other like knotted string unravelled too fast.

Drunk? Maybe. But it's not like how Dad used to be—no shouting, no glassy rage in his eyes, no threats. This guy's quiet, slumped, and oddly still. My skin prickles. There's no empty bottle beside him, no telltale smell of booze—just cold, damp concrete and oil stains.

What the hell is he doing in here?

I inch closer, heart thudding against my ribs, breath catching with every step. If he's wasted, he could be unpredictable. Dangerous.

"Can you hear me?" I call louder this time. The man stirs, trying to prop himself up on trembling arms. He sways like a top about to spin out, then collapses again with a weak grunt, his limbs folding awkwardly beneath him.

He's shivering now—full-body tremors that shake him down to the bones. Something in me twists. This isn't just someone sleeping off a heavy night.

Then it clicks where I've seen him before. He's the man from the bus that I sat next to on my first day here. I've seen him now and then since. Always pale, thin, a bit unsteady. I pegged him as someone with problems. But now?

I inch closer, scanning him for clues. His breath escapes in short, misty bursts. Still no smell of alcohol. No bottles. No obvious signs of drugs. Just a strange, sickly pallor.

Something's not right.

"Hey, it's okay, I'm just going to..." I trail off, unsure how to reassure him—or myself—as I kneel down beside him. I reach out tentatively and press my fingers against his forehead; it's icy to the touch, like he's been lying here for hours.

"Oh God, you're freezing!" A chill pricks at the edges of my mind, and I yank out my phone, scrolling until I find the number for the lodge. I hit it, closing my eyes and looking skyward. Please, John, be home.

"Hello?" John's voice replies a little uncertainly. My number has probably shown up as unknown. Maybe he's panicking that it's someone calling about Isabel.

"Hey, John, it's Rose."

"Hi. How are you?"

"I need your help. There's a man on the ground in Jamie's garage. He's really cold and shaky. I think he might have hypothermia."

"I'll call an ambulance," John says. "If you can get a blanket over him. I'll be there as soon as I can."

"Okay, sure." I end the call and look back at the man. "I'll be back in a minute with a blanket."

I dash into the house, grab a soft, heavy throw from the living room, and rush back to the garage. I hope this throw isn't of sentimental value and that Jamie is okay with me using it.

Weird how your brain latches onto the smallest things in moments like this. Adrenaline, I guess.

"Help is on the way," I tell the man as I return to the garage. He hasn't moved an inch. His eyes flutter open, meeting mine with dazed confusion. I drape the blanket over him, tucking it around his trembling form.

I stay crouched beside him. "Hang in there, yeah?"

Where is John? Or the ambulance. Or anyone. I feel clueless and not sure what to do next.

Eventually, I get to my feet and check out the door. A few moments later, John's Tesla crunches into the driveway. He's out of the car like a shot.

"Ambulance is on its way," he says. "Though they could be a while. Edinburgh traffic." He grimaces. "Let's see this man." He passes me by and heads into the garage. His focus falls on the shivering man on the ground. John kneels beside him, his large hands gently attempting to assess his condition. "Can you speak?" he probes softly.

The man tries to answer, but it comes out as a garbled mess of syllables that don't form words.

"Maybe a hot drink would help," I suggest; I feel useless just standing here.

"Good idea." John nods, and I hurry back to the warmth of the house.

While the kettle boils, I peer out through the kitchen window. Jamie's car pulls up, and moments later, John appears at the garage door. They speak briefly before disappearing inside, out of sight.

I finish making the tea—two sugars, just in case—and head back outside with the mug in hand. But halfway across the yard, the garage door swings open again. John and Jamie emerge, supporting the man between them.

John, taller and broader, takes one side; Jamie, though shorter, has wedged his shoulder under the man's arm, bearing much of his weight. They move slowly, the man sagging between them, legs barely cooperating.

My heart leaps. He looks like he could collapse any second.

I hurry ahead and pull the front door open, bracing it for them to come through.

Between John and Jamie, they manage to almost drag the man into the living room and manoeuvre him onto the couch.

I set the mug on the coffee table as they wrap him in another blanket. Jamie catches my eye. "Would you mind making up some hot water bottles?" he says. "There's a chest at the end of my bed. I think there are a couple in there."

"Of course." I dash upstairs to look for them. As I open the chest, I hear voices at the door. Crossing to the window, I glance out and see the ambulance in the yard.

Back downstairs, I fill the hot water bottles, feeling the heat seep into my fingers, bringing life back to my own chilled skin.

When I return, the man is sitting up.

"Shall I give him these?" I ask the paramedic.

"Yes, thank you." He takes them and tucks them into the blankets beside the man.

John steps over to me as the paramedics talk to the man. "His name's Greg. Jamie recognizes him. He works at the hotel. I think he's coming round a bit now that he's back in the warmth."

"He definitely looks a bit brighter." I frown over at Greg, who is holding the mug of tea and nodding at the paramedics.

"Looks like he'll be okay." One of the paramedics gets to his feet after talking to Greg. "He just needs to keep warm. Probably best if he can be at home with someone around."

"Shouldn't he go to hospital?" I ask.

"No, keeping warm is really the best cure."

"Okay," John says. "We'll see him right."

I watch the paramedics leave with a little frown.

"Well done." John puts his hand on my shoulder. "You did the right thing. We'll make sure he's okay."

"Where do you live, Greg?" Jamie sits on an armchair, leaning forward on his knees. "We can get you home somehow."

Greg's eyes flicker away, and he shakes his head.

"I can give you a lift," John says. "The car has heated seats, and we'll make sure you keep nice and warm on the way."

His voice is so soothing, I would happily jump in his car and let him take me anywhere, but Greg just shakes his head again.

Seems weird. Why would he resist going home? I frown as thoughts come together in my mind. Why was he in the garage? And not at work? I haven't seen him on the bus for the last few days either. Is it possible he doesn't have anywhere to go? He certainly has the look of someone who's been sleeping rough.

"Is it because you don't have a home?" I ask. "Were you sleeping rough in the garage?"

He nods, and it's like something breaks inside me. Nobody should be so alone, so forgotten by the world. My heart crumples, knowing how close to this I came the night Freddie hit me.

"Oh…" John looks from Greg to me, then to Jamie.

Jamie gets to his feet. "What are we going to do?" he says aside to John. "I need to get back to work. And I'm not sure he can stay here on his own."

"I could take him into town. To Darius."

Jamie nods.

"Who's that?" I ask. And why does it sound a bit shady?

"He's a friend of mine. He runs a shelter. I'm not letting anyone be stuck out in the cold." John looks at Greg, who's still wrapped in the blanket with his fingers gripping the mug.

"And will he have space?" I frown.

"Darius is always good at finding space. He never turns people away, and he'll take care of you, Greg. He's a good guy. How does that sound?"

Greg gives a little nod. I guess he's kind of out of options. He doesn't seem to be very chatty—whether that's down to how he's feeling or just how he is, I'm not sure—but he definitely isn't giving much away. I'd like to know his life story. How nosey am I? I can't help myself, but it doesn't look like he's going to tell anyone anything.

Jamie checks his watch as John helps Greg to his feet.

"I'll refill the hot water bottles." I lift them and head for the kitchen.

"Why don't you go with them?" Jamie suggests, following me out of the door. "Or at least take some time for yourself. The house already looks good. I think you should take a breather. That must have been stressful finding him like that."

"Thank you; that's so kind." I smile at him as he leaves with a little wave.

Loaded with the two hot water bottles, I grab my coat and return to the living room.

"Jamie's given me some time off to come with you." I smile at John, and he catches my eye.

"That's good. Let's get you in the car." He puts his hand on Greg's back. "If we let him have the front for now, so he can use the heated seats."

"Sure." I exchange a look with John as he passes. We don't need words to convey how we're feeling. This isn't what we had planned for the day, but it's necessary. Greg needs somewhere to go, and I can't deny a burning curiosity in my gut. Why is John friends with someone who runs a homeless shelter? It seems very odd to me.

John drives, and the car soon heats up. Greg is as quiet as ever and John puts on the radio to cover the silence. As we get closer to the city, people hustle by with their shoulders hunched, breath misting before them. John takes a few side roads as he can't take the car into Princes Street, then takes another road that winds around behind the Haymarket.

"Here we are." John pulls into the tiniest space in front of an old Georgian style house. One so typical of Edinburgh. It's worn, but not how I imagined a homeless shelter to look. Nothing on the outside says that's what it is. It looks like a normal townhouse to me.

John helps Greg up the steps to the door. I fiddle with the iron railing as I wait behind them. John rings the bell. We stand there for what seems like a long time before the door opens.

"Ah, hello. I got your message." A man moves onto the doorstep. He looks around the same age as John, with rough stubble, short, tousled hair, and kind of shabby clothes. But he's handsome, and his blue eyes are so bright and piercing they seem to be X-raying all of us.

"Darius." John pats his shoulder.

"You must be Greg." Darius's gaze moves to him.

Greg nods, shifting his weight a little awkwardly.

"I didn't have time to explain it all in my message, but he needs to keep warm." John explains the situation.

"Of course." Darius puts his hand on Greg's shoulder. "Come on in, son. We'll get you somewhere warm to stay."

I trail behind as they usher Greg inside, and I look around. This place defies my expectations. It's cosy, more like a slightly shabby old B&B than a hostel.

"This place is nice," I hear myself say, though I didn't mean the words to come out.

Darius gives me a gentle smile. "Sorry," he says. "Are you Greg's girlfriend? Do you need a place too?"

"No, no. I'm John and Jamie's cleaner. I um…"

"Rose Darwin," John says. "She found Greg in the garage and made sure he was okay."

"Apologies," Darius says. "My focus was so much on Greg when you arrived I didn't inquire about you. Thank you for your kindness. You've saved this young man." His eyes are so intense I have to look away.

"I didn't really do much."

"But you did something, and that's enough."

John raises his eyebrows at me. "Well, if Greg's okay here, we should leave you to it."

"Of course." Darius gives us both a smile, then turns to Greg. "Are you okay if they leave? I can show you around the house and get you something to eat."

"Yeah." Greg nods, raising his eyes to me. "And thanks."

"No worries," John says.

He and I leave the way we came, and I look back over my shoulder. Darius is chatting to Greg as he opens a door.

"What is this place?" Just one of many questions I have.

John closes the main door behind us, and we head back to the car. "I told you. It's a homeless shelter."

"But how do people find it?"

John indicates to me to get into the front seat of the car. I hop in and click the belt.

"It's word of mouth. Darius runs it, not the council or charity, or anything like that."

"Who is he? And how do you know him?"

John's gaze remains fixed on the road ahead as he pulls across the cobblestones away from the shelter. "It's a long story," he says. "And not wholly mine to tell."

"Fair enough," I murmur, though my curiosity isn't so easily shut down.

"So…" he begins, breaking through my thoughts, "do you want me to drop you somewhere? I don't know where you live, but I'm happy to drive you there, wherever it is."

I consider it for a moment—the idea of going back to the shithole I call home does not appeal one bit. I've just seen a homeless shelter that's in better nick than my apartment. "If I've got the day off… I'd rather spend it with you."

Something flickers across his face, and he nods. "I know just the place we can go for 'lunch'." A smile tugs at the corner of his lips as he air-quotes. Those sensuous lips. I know how much damage they can do.

John's hand lands on my thigh, and the city blurs into the background. His touch is warm and assertive, sending a jolt of anticipation through me. All my curiosity about Darius and the shelter is wiped out as John's fingers inch upwards, teasingly slow, until they press against me, right where I ache for him the most.

"Are you wearing panties today?" His voice is low, almost a growl, and so damn sexy it should be illegal.

"You'll have to wait and see." My breath hitches as he continues his torturous exploration.

Concentration locked on the traffic, he manoeuvres expertly with one hand while the other dances dangerously close to the edge of my control. I throw my head back, a silent moan trapped in my throat, and shift my own hand to the bulge straining against his trousers.

"Christ, Rose…" He groans as I trace the outline of his erection, revelling in its impressive size. "Not here, or you'll put me off the road."

"Then hurry up and get us wherever we're going," I manage between shallow breaths, "because I'm starving for your cock, and I can't wait much longer to feel you inside me."

This man. Tender with a stranger one minute, wild with me the next. How do I stop myself falling for that?

John's grip tightens on the steering wheel, knuckles white, as we speed toward our mysterious destination.

# 12

## John

Pulling up to the boutique hotel named the Taybury, I slide the car into a space that's marked private right next to the two disabled spaces by the entrance. Rose arches an eyebrow and glances at me.

"Are you allowed to park here?" she asks.

I raise an eyebrow. "Sure I am. The owner can park where he likes."

"You own this hotel?"

With a nod, I get out of the car. Rose gets out on her side, and I walk around to meet her.

"I thought you owned Ardencairn." She looks up at me.

"I do. But it's part of a chain. I have a few in the city and others in different parts of the country."

"I didn't realize." She glances around as we climb the wide stone steps. In the summer, the pots on either side of the door have huge floral displays in them, but November brings the Christmas trees. Two short, rather stubby trees flank the door; glowing white string lights shine from them.

Inside, the lobby buzzes with muted conversations and the clinking of china from the adjoining restaurant. I head toward the reception desk, where a woman with immaculately bobbed hair looks up from her computer. I open my wallet and show her my ID, feeling a bit like a cop from a TV show. Not all the employees know me, so it's safer to prove who I am before any awkward questions arise. These days I imagine most of them have heard the story of the fire at the Gladstone, so when a big guy with a scarred face appears at the desk, they probably guess it's me. But maybe not—if they listen to all the rumours, they'll know I very rarely go out these days. Even now, I feel eyes watching me. They're pretending not to, but whispers have started. People wonder how I got them. I can't hear anything in particular. The tone, however, is either along the lines of 'poor guy, I wonder what kind of accident he had' or 'what trouble must he have been making to have had that done to him'. Neither really fits what actually happened.

"Good afternoon, Mr Knighton. How may I assist you today?" The receptionist smiles at me now that she's studied my ID and had a moment to match my unblemished photo to the scarred face in front of her.

"I need a table for a business lunch," I say without looking at Rose. "And do you have a room available? I want to stay in the city tonight."

"Of course, Mr Knighton." She taps away at her keyboard. "Let me check. We have a penthouse suite available. Would that work for you?"

"Definitely."

"Okay. Let me pop that through for you and activate your key. Then I'll ring through to the restaurant and get you a table." The receptionist hands me the key card, then lifts the phone and speaks to someone in the restaurant. "Your table will be ready shortly. If you'd like to just go through, someone will meet you."

"Thanks." I pocket the card and turn to Rose, adjusting my cuffs. I'm in a work shirt and sweater, which isn't what I'd like to wear out for lunch. But it'll do, especially as Rose is still wearing her cleaning uniform under her jacket. "Shall we?" I gesture toward the restaurant.

"Will they let me in dressed like this?" Rose asks, clearly channelling my thoughts. That bond she talked about the other day might be real.

"They'll do as I tell them." Though my heart dips a little. I can tell she's uncomfortable.

I lead Rose through an arched doorway into the restaurant. A server greets me by name.

"We'd like a private spot," I say. "Neither of us is dressed for dining. We had to attend to an emergency and came straight from there."

"Of course, sir." The server leads us to a table by the window. The restaurant is filled with screens of flowers and fairy lights and there's one close to our table. "We can adjust the screen slightly, so you're not overlooked."

Rose takes off her jacket, and I hold out the seat for her. She sits with a smile. The server has moved the screen by the time I sit down, and I catch Rose's eye. She's giving me an almost appraising look.

"Do you like it?" I signal for the server to return.

"Yes, it's stunning."

I order a bottle of Puligny-Montrachet—something crisp and light, but with depth. Once the server leaves, I lean back and let out a long breath. "Well, we've got all day... and night," I tell her. "No need to rush, though if you want to go home after lunch, that's up to you."

"No... I'd rather stay with you, but what about Isabel? Don't you have to get back to her?"

"She's back with her mum tonight." The words stir a dull ache in my chest. "I hate the thought of her with Lydia, especially if Freddie might be around."

"Are they living together now?" Concern flickers across her face, and she bites down on her lower lip.

"I don't think so. Isabel told me he stays at his own house because he works so late."

"That sounds like Freddie." A wry smile tugs at Rose's mouth, but it doesn't quite reach her eyes. "Always staying out late. Expected me to wait up for him, no matter what. He liked his..." She glances around, then whispers, "Pre-bed blow jobs."

I ball my fists under the table. "He treated you like shit."

"I realize that now." Rose sighs, staring out of the window. "But when I was living it, I thought that was what life was. If I wanted the lifestyle Freddie gave me, I thought I had to play along. Now, I get how stupid I was."

"It's not stupidity. I'd call it survival. You did what you had to, but that doesn't make it right."

She nods and glances at the menu. "This all look delicious."

The server returns and we order.

"I've never tried them," she says after I order the pan-seared scallops.

"You can try some of mine."

"I'll try anything of yours," she says quietly as the server moves off.

I cast her a little wink. "Patience."

The server returns with our wine, and once we both have a glass in our hand, it's easier to chat about mundane things, small talk to pass the time, but surprisingly pleasant.

"I'm the middle child." Rose gives a dry laugh. "Stuck between my older brother, who thought he ran the place, and my little sister, who learned early how to get what she wanted with a pout and a well-timed tantrum."

She takes a sip, eyes flicking to mine, then away again. "My brother used to scrap with anyone who looked at him sideways. He was always in trouble at school, always swearing he'd be a big shot one day—though of course that never happened. My sister is mouthy, clever, and dangerous when she wants something."

A pause. The air shifts slightly.

"But my mum died when I was eleven. After that, things just... fell apart. Dad drank more than he worked. There wasn't much money, not that there ever was, and the house was always full of shouting. I kept my head down and tried not to be a problem."

She swirls her wine, eyes distant. "I came here for university—to get away. I needed to breathe. They all still live up north, in the back end of nowhere. I visit sometimes, but we don't have a lot in common now."

I watch her for a second, taking in the tight set of her shoulders and the calm way she says it all, like it's old news. But pain like that doesn't go away. You just learn how to carry it.

"You've had a tough time."

"Everyone has issues, don't they?"

With a wry smile, I nod. "Yeah, that's true. What did you study?" I'm curious now. How did someone who came here for university end up cleaning for an agency?

"English and philosophy."

"And did you graduate?"

She nods and takes a sip of wine. "But I've never used my degree. I met Freddie and got a job working for his parents. Then... Well, after our split, I looked at graduate jobs, but I felt underqualified for them all."

I shake my head. "Sounds more like you lost your confidence. You should keep applying. Something will come up."

"I guess. I just panic that Freddie's parents will have blacklisted me somehow."

I take a swig of wine and shake my head. "They do have a lot of influence, but it's not universal, and there are people who won't care about their opinion. People like me."

"Do you know the Blackwoods?"

"I certainly do. And I know all their dirty tricks. The fact Freddie is now with Lydia doesn't surprise me one bit. I'm sure it's all part of their schemes to get their hands on my business."

"Wow." She swirls the wine around the glass. "I had no idea."

"That's why Freddie's gone into politics, I expect. They want him influencing people from the inside. But don't let it put you off applying for jobs. Chances are, you'll be fine."

"Yeah. I need to look again."

The pan-seared scallops arrive, along with Rose's honey roast chicken. I cut a little from one of the scallops and hold the fork across the table to Rose. She opens her mouth and takes it with a seductive look that makes my groin twitch.

"Mmm. They're good." She nods, dabbing her lip with her napkin.

"I'm glad you enjoyed it." I lean back a little to check around the screen that the server has moved off. "And there's plenty more to enjoy later."

Rose looks up from her food with a smile but narrows her eyes a little as she switches her focus to the screen. "Is this really to hide our clothes?"

"Why? Would you rather do something indecent behind it?"

A cheeky grin tugs on her lips. "I would, but that's not what I meant."

"What then?"

"Are you... Well, are you hiding your face from people?"

I scoff and eat a scallop. "Maybe." My gaze drifts out the window to the city street beyond. "Since I got these..." My fingers drift up to touch the side of my face, tracing the lines of my scars without actually making contact. "I find it difficult. People are always staring, and I don't like it."

"I bet. And how—"

The server glances around to ask us if everything's okay.

"It's all good, thanks." I give him a nod. "If the Gladstone was still open, we could have gone there. It's closer to the city centre." Though I'm not sure I ever want to go there again.

"Do you own that too?" Her brow creases with a quite adorable frown.

"Yes, sorry, I thought you knew that. It's shut down for investigations after the fire."

"Good," Rose says sharply. "I don't want to set foot in there ever again. No offense to your hotel, and I'm sorry that it's losing you money, but that place has nothing but bad memories for me."

"Same here." I take a sip of wine.

"Fucking Freddie," Rose mutters. "I never thought he could get any worse, but you think he only went after Lydia to get to you?"

"At least to get to my money. Lydia wants a cut of the business—the business she had no hand in building. But the courts might insist. She's banking on that, anyway. Then I expect Freddie will find a way to have it signed over as his own."

"God, I hate them." Rose's eyes darken. "How come people like that get away with shit all the time, while honest people suffer?"

"I wish I knew." My fist tightens around my knife.

Rose reaches across the table to take my hand. "Nothing we do right now can stop their little tricks, but we can definitely make ourselves feel better."

"How true." I smile, a real one, and it feels like the first genuine smile in a while. We leave our half-finished plates, skipping dessert for an even sweeter treat.

We make our way to the elevator and up to the fourth floor. At the end of the corridor, I unlock the door and hold it for Rose. She steps into the room ahead of me, her gasp audible as she takes in the opulent space.

"Wow, look at this place." Her eyes flit over the high ceilings adorned with intricate mouldings. The plush carpet underfoot mutes our footsteps as she wanders toward the floor-to-ceiling windows and looks out over the gray street. The daylight is fading, and in an hour or so, it'll be dark.

"Even with Freddie, I've never stayed anywhere this grand." She turns to me, her eyes sparkling.

"It's all about who you know." I tug off my sweater and toss it over the back of a leather bucket chair. The suite is decked out with a lavish king-sized bed draped in satin sheets; a chandelier twinkles over the room, and the sitting area has a fireplace that flickers to life at the touch of a button.

"It's beautiful," Rose says, and I can tell she means it. Maybe it's not just the room she's talking about, but the moment. It definitely feels beautiful to me.

"Only the best for you." I wrap her in my arms, pulling her close until there's no space left between us. Our lips meet with an urgency, and I cradle the back of her head. My tongue touches hers, and I taste the wine on her, sweet and intoxicating. Her body presses against mine, sending a surge of desire through me.

"Oh God," she murmurs against my mouth, her hands finding the hem of my shirt and tugging it upward.

"Let me." We break apart, and I peel the fabric over my head and drop it to the floor. Her fingers are eager as they trace the lines of my chest. This is part of me I don't mind her seeing. But she doesn't stop there. Her fingertips continue upward, along my shoulder, up my neck and across my scars. Her touch is so gentle it nearly undoes me.

"Beautiful," she whispers.

"You're the beautiful one." I undo the buttons of her tunic and prise it over her head. Her delicious soft skin makes me want to touch her everywhere. Dipping in, I place a kiss on her neck, tugging down the straps of her lacy pink bra as I do. She leans her head to the side, her blonde hair cascading over her shoulders, and moans.

My heart races with desire. Rose's fingers fumble with the waistband of my trousers, and I capture her hands in mine.

I brush soft kisses across her knuckles. A strange warmth floods me from the inside out. For the first time in what feels like forever, I want to make a real, deep connection. I'm not even sure why. Letting go of her hands, I step back and unbutton my trousers. "Take yours off." I indicate her trousers with my eyes.

"Okay…" She goes to tug them down. "Shouldn't we shut the curtains?"

"Let's not. I don't care if the whole world sees what I'm going to do to you. I especially hope Freddie Blackwood is watching. Then he might learn exactly how to treat a woman."

With a smile, she pulls down her trousers. I growl when I realize she's not wearing any panties. "You naughty girl."

"I only did what I was told."

Her smile makes me smile too, and I drop my trousers and boxer briefs, kicking them off. My cock is hard as steel and bobs up like it's locking in on its target. She drops her focus to me, and I know what she's going to try to do. She's programmed to suck every time she sees a stiff dick, and much as I like the idea, it's not happening. Not until I have some fun with her. Not until I have her screaming in ecstasy, crying my name.

I erase the distance between us with a single step and softly palm her breasts through her bra until her nipples are diamond hard. Then I lift her up. She squeals, but I silence her with a kiss and lay her down on the bed that dominates the suite. It's large and plush, a bed you could lose days in—and I intend for us to start right now.

As I hover over her, I trail kisses along her thighs, the skin there soft and warm. She shivers under my touch, a response that sends a thrill right through me. Pulling back, I take one of her dainty feet in my hand, and, meeting her gaze, I rub it along the length of my cock. The friction and the sight of her, so willing and beautiful, make me even harder. Christ, I never thought it was possible.

"Oh my God, John," she gasps, reaching out to me.

"Patience," I murmur, though my self-control is hanging by a thread.

My mouth finds the tender skin of her inner thigh, and as I kiss closer to her heat, she moans, "Please, I want you inside me."

"We can't," I breathe out. "I don't have any condoms... but I can still make it good for you."

"Do we need them?" she asks. "I'm on birth control. And after Freddie did the dirty, I got tested, and I haven't been with anyone since."

"Neither have I." I look into her eyes. "And I took the tests, too. I didn't know where Lydia had been."

"Then there's nothing stopping us. I want to feel all of you." She sits up and takes my length in her hand, stroking it with her thumb. I lean in and kiss her, pushing her gently back onto the pillows. Then, I kneel between her legs. She's so tiny, I easily lift her hips, bringing her sweet spot to my mouth. She hooks her legs over my arms, and I kiss her clit until she's whimpering. Lowering her back onto the bed, I trail kisses higher up her body, my lips grazing past her belly button. The tip of my nose edges toward the hem of her lacy pink bra. I unhook it, pulling the fabric aside to reveal her breasts in all their glory. They're perfect, round and full. Her nipples are rosy and peaked. I lean in, drawing one into the heat of my mouth, teasing it with a flick of my tongue. Rose gasps, and her fingers thread through my hair, holding me to her as I lavish attention on her other breast, feeling her body tense and relax. She moans and gulps for air.

"God, you feel amazing," I murmur against her skin.

She wraps her fingers around my cock, stroking it like she's trying to move it closer to where she wants it. "You're so big," she says. Her touch sparks me like a powder keg.

Got to keep control.

My lips find hers in a hot, claiming kiss. Our mouths move together, hot and desperate, every brush of our tongues stoking a white-hot fire between us.

With a growl, I pull away, trailing kisses back down her belly until I hover above her clit. It's a moment of pure anticipation, both of us waiting for the touch that'll unravel us. Then I dive in, my tongue finding her sweet spot. She tastes like heaven, all honey and heat, and I feast on her, drawing circles and flicks, driving her to the edge.

"John! Oh my God." Her voice crescendos, the sound vibrating through my skull. Her hips buck against my face, urging me on, and I double my efforts, wanting—no, needing—to hear her come undone.

"More, please, more..." she pleads, and I oblige, giving her everything I have.

Her climax builds, her moans increase into a high-pitched squeal of delight. And then she crashes over the edge into ecstasy. Her thighs clamp around my head, nearly squeezing the breath from me, but I don't care. I relish the power of her orgasm, knowing I'm the one who's brought her to this state of bliss.

"Fuck, John..." Her words are barely coherent, and I lift my head, watching her come undone. How incredible that this gorgeous woman has such a reaction to me. The sight of her, flushed and panting, is one of the most amazing things I've ever seen.

She smiles at me through half-lidded eyes.

"You're amazing," I say, and I cannot help but marvel at my luck. Revenge mission or not, here I am, John Knighton, wounded and scarred, with the most unbelievable woman in the world.

# 13

## Rose

The afterglow of my orgasm wraps around me like a warm blanket. Lying back on the vast bed, I try to focus. Has John just called me amazing? He can say that when he's just given me the most mind-blowing climax of my life.

"Thank you," I breathe out, still reeling from the comedown. My body's not used to this. "That was… incredible."

He looks down at me, the corners of his lips twitching into one of those rare smiles that transform his usually serious face. "My pleasure," he says. "And you're the incredible one."

My hunger for him hasn't subsided; it's insistent, throbbing with every heartbeat. "I still want you," I whisper, my hands wandering to my breasts, cupping them, and soothing them. They feel swollen, achingly sensitive. I then drop one hand to his cock and stroke it. "I need you inside me."

John's eyes darken, and he leans in and kisses me. "And you can have me." He shifts, sitting up between my legs. My fingers move back to my breasts, and I touch them, letting out little sounds of need. His gaze locks on my self-caress, and I watch as he takes hold of himself. His cock is huge, and he taps it against my clit. "You ready for this?"

"God, yes." My body craves him.

He runs his thumb along my slick folds, spreading the wetness there. "Love how wet you are for me," he murmurs. The sensation sends a shiver up my spine, and I can't stop the whimper that escapes my lips.

"I'm desperate for you."

"Good girl." A slight smile tugs at the corner of his lips, and he positions himself at my entrance, pausing for a moment, still toying gently with my clit. Slowly, ever so slowly, he inches into me, stretching me deliciously. "So tight," he says. "Christ."

His fingers tease my clit again, circling it gently, coaxing my body to relax and accommodate him. As he slides home, I arch toward him and gasp, the sensation overwhelming yet perfect. "You okay?" he asks.

"Yes," I manage to say, my smile broadening even as I pant. "I just love how you fill me up." And it's true; I feel him everywhere, each inch of him like a brand, marking me in the most intimate way.

"Good. And I love your tight little pussy." He gently thrusts into me, and the sensation is unbearably good. I arch my back, reaching up to caress my own breasts, their sensitivity heightened to torturous levels. His gaze locks onto mine, sea-blue eyes intense and focused.

"You're incredible," he breathes out, his voice rough. "Taking me so well, like a good girl."

A moan escapes me as he thrusts harder, deeper. The room seems to spin, my senses sharpening on the singular point of pleasure where we're joined. With two thick fingers, he rubs my clit, faster and faster. It's too much, and yet it's exactly what I need. I feel dizzy, lost in a whirlwind of sensation.

"Oh God, that's so good," I gasp, barely recognizing my own voice. He pumps harder, more urgently, driving into me with low guttural groans. The sound of our bodies slapping together is so loud, I'm sure people must be able to hear us. The curtains are still open too, but I don't care who sees now. I'm too far gone, and if people want to witness the most incredible orgasm, then who am I to stop them?

John's body looms over mine, so protective and safe. I'm cocooned from the world outside—even if they're watching, they can't get me. When he bends down to kiss me, I'm enveloped by his presence, his scent, his warmth. It's a moment of pure intimacy that makes every sensation multiply.

The pressure builds to an excruciating crescendo, the thrusting, the clitoral stimulation and the kissing swirling together in a perfect storm. My body's trembling on the brink, about to tumble into oblivion.

"I'm going to come," I scream, breaking the kiss.

"That's a good girl," John encourages, his voice firm and commanding. "Come for me."

Pleasure hits me like a tidal wave of release that crashes over me, leaving me gasping, quivering, shattered in the most exquisite way. The orgasm is monumental, ravaging my senses until I'm nothing but a bundle of raw nerves, left breathless and floating in its wake.

John's arms encircle me, cradling my trembling body. I'm still quivering, every nerve ending singing from the seismic climax that has just rocked me to my core. My breath comes in ragged gasps, but as the aftershocks subside, I curl into his embrace.

"Thank you," I whisper against his chest, my lips hovering close to his heart. I press a kiss there.

"No need to thank me," he murmurs, his voice a low rumble that resonates within me. "It was a true pleasure."

Slowly, I gather myself, returning from the dizzying heights of ecstasy. I find his cock and grip it. He's still hard. My own mighty orgasm pushed everything from my mind. With newfound strength, I release his cock and push against his broad shoulders, nudging him onto his back. His eyes hold a flicker of surprise, quickly replaced by heat as I shift downwards.

I take him into my mouth, savouring the taste of him, the pulsing heat, the dripping precum. He's so ready to blow. My tongue swirls around his length, drawing a deep, guttural groan from his lips. His hand finds my hair, fingers intertwining with gentle firmness as he surrenders to the sensation.

"Fuck, Rose..." His voice is strained as he watches me work on him.

My arousal flares anew at the sound of my name on his lips, spurring me on deeper. I can feel him at the back of my throat, and I fight the urge to gag, focusing instead on the power I wield over him. I'm well practised in this art, and I take him again, in and out, saliva filling my mouth. He groans again. It would be easy to suck him off from here, but I'm hungry for more. I want him inside me again.

Pulling back, I wipe my chin and straddle him. I position myself above him and slowly, oh so slowly, I sink down, taking him inside me inch by exquisite inch. My eyelids flutter shut, overwhelmed by the fullness. "Oh, this is so good." I lean my head back.

"Look at me, Rose."

His command snaps my eyes open, and I meet his gaze. It burns hot, tearing through me like a flame.

He starts moving beneath me, each thrust driving us both closer to another precipice. Our eyes remain locked, a silent conversation passing between us. His scars are an unspoken part of his history, a weight he carries, but I can ease his pain and he's easing mine. Together we have this.

"John. Fuck me," I breathe out, a plea, as the tension builds again.

"Stay with me," he responds.

I raise my hands to the soft waves of my hair, lifting them from my neck and tossing back my head. My hips bounce up and down on him, and his cock hits every nerve end inside me. I glance at the window. It's getting dark, and streetlamps are coming on. We're too high up for anyone to realistically be able to see us, but I can't help wishing Freddie was down there looking up, seeing what a real man can do.

John's large palms roam over my breasts. "Look at me," he says again.

I turn back to him, moaning as the rough pads of his fingertips roll my nipples, sending jolts of electric pleasure through me. I can hardly contain the surge of desire threatening to consume me.

"You're so beautiful," he murmurs, then grips my breasts and pounds into me.

My hand slips to my clit, and I frisk furiously at it. The pressure builds rapidly, a torrent of sensation rushing through me, and I know I'm close to shattering all over again.

"Ah, God, yes!" I cry out as the climax crashes into me, wave after relentless wave. Beneath me, John bucks his hips, his hold on my breasts tightening. His growl vibrates through me as he reaches his own peak, filling me deep. I clench around him, taking everything he's got.

We collapse together, our limbs tangling. He still has a hand on my breast, and he palms it absently. I nestle into his broad chest, relishing the solid comfort of his embrace. I can't get over how safe he makes me feel. He might look scary, and I barely know him, but there's something so trustworthy about him.

"Sweetest revenge ever," I say.

"Mmm, very sweet indeed."

Snuggling closer, I let out a contented sigh as he strokes my hair. A rush of emotions hits me hard. It's so unusual for me to feel anything after sex—other than completely dissatisfied. I want to stay here, cocooned in John's arms, far beyond today or tomorrow. It's terrifying and yet, it feels so right.

I burrow deeper into his embrace, and his arms tighten around me reassuringly. We stay quiet like this for some time. I'm not counting minutes—or time at all. I could probably sleep like this and not wake until the morning.

"You realize we're both lacking in the clothing department?" John wakes me from my dopey state.

"Oh yeah. That's annoying."

"Let's go shopping," he says. "It's not too late."

"No way can I afford that."

"My treat."

"I can't let you do that." I bite my lip. "You shouldn't have to—"

"It's fine," he cuts in. "I'm not doing it because I have to. I want to. You won't owe me anything." The warmth in his eyes makes me believe him. "I'm going to take a very quick shower." He moves off me. "I would invite you to join me, but I think we should save more fun for after we have clothes."

"So we can take them straight off again?"

"Exactly." He snaps his fingers and points at me.

I giggle and lie back under the covers for a moment, listening to the taps coming on. When John comes out, he towels himself dry, and I take my chance for a quick hose down before putting my cleaning tunic and trousers back on. Once my coat's on, it isn't too noticeable, but the trousers are cropped at my ankles and I'm in white trainers and bare feet, so it's freezing when we step outside.

Thankfully we're not too far from the shops. John holds my hand as we practically run toward the bright lights, now and then catching each other's eyes and laughing.

He guides me toward an expensive-looking department store with grand display windows and Christmas trees already twinkling inside.

"That looks far too expensive." I shake my head at it.

"It's not. Now, come on. You can have anything you want."

My eyes widen as they sweep over the racks of clothes, and I run my fingers over the sumptuous fabrics. A few months ago, Freddie's money would have bought me anything I wanted, but now I know what it's like having barely a penny, it feels odd.

"You deserve it," he says. "You work hard. Look at this as an early Christmas bonus."

"I think I had that this afternoon."

"That wasn't a bonus, just part of the revenge pact." He gives me the tiniest wink as I weave through the racks.

"What am I dressing for?" I ask.

"Dinner tonight. And choose whatever nightwear you fancy..." He raises an eyebrow, reminding me that he'll be taking it off as soon as he can. "And whatever you need to wear tomorrow."

"Okay." I select a cocktail dress with an emerald sheen that reminds me of my own eyes, a slinky pair of black jeans that promise to hug every curve, and a cosy sweater—that'll be useful back in the apartment as the heating is always going off. John's patience never wanes; instead, he helps me pick some incredibly sexy lingerie. I wouldn't touch stuff like this normally—even with Freddie, I didn't bother. And now I'm glad. John knows how to appreciate me in it.

"Wow," he murmurs under his breath. "I can't wait to see you in that... and help you take it off."

John grabs some items for himself, and we finally exit the store, his arms laden with bags. Of course, he won't let me carry them. Such a gentleman.

"Thank you." I stand on tiptoe and press a quick, grateful kiss to his lips.

His response is immediate and hot, even though it's brief.

"Maybe we shouldn't do that in public," he says. "Not everyone knows about our pact. And you never know who might be about."

"Oh, yeah."

Suddenly, I remember why we're here, doing all this. Freddie and Lydia... our exes. It's not about us—it's about them. Or at least, it was supposed to be. But something else has woken inside me, and I can't quite catch it or pin it down, but it hurts my chest every time I think about being somewhere without John.

# 14

## *John*

Chandeliers gleam in the grand lobby of the Taybury Hotel as Rose and I make our way past well-heeled guests mingling near the reception desk. My hand finds the small of her back, and she looks up at me and smiles. When our eyes meet, the connection is as strong as ever. Would we feel it if we were just two random strangers and not bound by the connection between our exes?

I think back to the first time I ever saw Rose with her bleeding nose. Back then, I was still married, so I didn't look at other women closely, but I'm pretty certain I would have found her attractive if I had. Would she have returned the thought? She certainly wouldn't now. These scars don't exactly make me look like a catch. *Nope*. It's the trauma bond we have to thank for bringing us together and making us feel close when we don't really know each other. We just understand each other better than most people.

The same table we had earlier is ready for us again, and the screen is still in place. The server ushers us toward the hidden corner and holds the seat out for Rose before I can do it.

"Thank you." Rose slips into her chair, stunning in her new green dress that clings in all the right places. Her blonde waves tumble over her shoulders, giving her an almost elfin glow that's radiant and effortlessly captivating.

I lift the leather-bound menu, though I already know what's on it after all the lengthy discussions we had getting it right. "I already know what I want." I glance at Rose with a slight curl of my lip, then up at the server.

"Steak, rare." I keep my eyes on Rose. "You can have whatever you like, of course, but I can recommend the salmon."

"That's perfect." She closes her menu with a soft snap. "Saves me having to decide."

"And a bottle of champagne." I hand my menu to the server.

"Of course, sir."

I interlink my fingers and rest them on the table. "I hope you don't mind me suggesting that. I just wanted to get the order in quickly before it gets busy in here."

"Hungry, are you?"

"Starved."

"But no, I don't mind at all."

"Good." I reach across the table and brush my thumb across the soft skin on her hand. She shivers, and I pull back, smiling. I love how responsive she is, even to the lightest touch.

Rain begins to patter against the window, the droplets catching in the glow of the streetlamps outside. In here, it's warm and cocooned—our own little bubble, tucked away from the rest of the dining room behind the screen draped with flowers and fairy lights.

"John?" Rose's voice pulls me back to the present. She's watching me with her sharp green eyes. "It's good how easy this is between us, isn't it?"

"Yeah." I nod.

"Proper no-strings arrangement."

"Absolutely."

The server arrives with the champagne, and as he uncorks and pours it, my mind drifts. I've never done the no-strings thing before, and there's something liberating and refreshingly simple about it. But still, a flicker of unease twists in my chest. I can't quite put my finger on why.

When we have our champagne, I raise my glass, then clink it on the side of hers.

"To revenge," she says with a smirk.

I take a sip and look out of the window. "Sweet revenge."

Rose chats as we wait for our food. She's a natural talker and tells me a story about breaking a vase at one of the houses she was cleaning. I listen and smile, watching her facial expressions. I can only imagine she'd be happier out and about with a group of similarly aged people, but she's doing well entertaining me.

When the food arrives, she takes a break from her monologue to eat, and I take a moment to look through the screen and see what's happening in the main dining area. Over Rose's head, I can see the door and a steady stream of people coming in and being led to tables. Great to see business booming.

"The salmon is delicious." Rose does a chef's kiss. "Thanks for recommending it."

"I thought you'd like it." Taking another sip of champagne, my eyes fall on the door again, only this time, I catch sight of a face I recognize. I crane my neck, peering over Rose's head.

"What are you looking at?" She whirls around, trying to follow my gaze.

"It that Freddie at the door?" I hiss through clenched teeth, the old familiar anger surging up like bile. The man has the audacity to come here. Is this where he brings his 'sponsors' to dine? My restaurant?

"Freddie? Here?" Rose sits up high to look, then turns back to me and blanches. "What the fuck is he here for?"

"No idea." But I want nothing more than to march over there, to grab him by the collar and show him what happens when you mess with John Knighton. "I'll have him thrown out. Or better still, I'll introduce him to my fist. He deserves it after what he did to you."

"No, John." She reaches across the table and takes my hand. "Don't do anything that'll get you into trouble. You're a better man than him. Keep it that way. There are other ways to get revenge." She raises an eyebrow at me.

"Hmm." Much as I like how we've been getting revenge so far—it's definitely been a boost to the ego—it hasn't hurt Freddie enough. And seeing him here is making my skin crawl.

From our hidden vantage point, I watch as Freddie and his entourage are ushered to a secluded table on the far side of the restaurant. It's too far to overhear anything, but the group's body language screams schemes and secrets. Something tight clenches behind my ribs. How often has he used my restaurant to plot God knows what?

"I wish I knew what he was up to," I mutter, more to myself than to Rose. A flicker of relief cuts through the tension. At least Freddie's here and not anywhere near Isabel.

"Let them plot," Rose says. "We've got better things to be doing."

The rain taps a steady rhythm against the windows now—almost like sleet. The heat in here, however, is overpowering. I try to refocus on my plate and ignore Freddie, but Rose's foot, now divested of its shoe, is wandering up my leg.

"Maybe Freddie heard us earlier," she says, her voice low. "Or maybe he felt our avenging energy all the way across Edinburgh."

I chuckle, though the burn in my gut hasn't fully subsided. "With you, I'm starting to believe in psychic powers."

My hand sneaks under the tablecloth, finding her foot. Her skin is soft, and as I massage it, drawing it closer, her toes find the firm outline pressing against my trousers. For a moment, she circles me with her toes, and I forget to be angry. In fact, I pretty much forget everything.

"Upstairs?" I suggest.

She giggles, and it's an adorable sound that makes me harder. "We're making a habit of abandoning meals for more... carnal feasts."

I brush her arch with my thumb. "I've got an appetite for something that's not on the menu."

She smiles. "Dessert in bed?"

"Yes, please." We stand up at the same time and I adjust my trousers before we slip out from behind the screen. As we move through the restaurant, I glance back toward Freddie's table. He and his cronies are engrossed in a hushed conversation.

"I wouldn't care if he saw us," I murmur in Rose's ear.

"Then you better make me scream loud enough for him to hear."

My blood thrums and heads south again.

"Consider it a challenge gladly accepted."

The moment the room door clicks shut behind us, Rose pounces on me, grabbing my neck and pulling me down to kiss her. She's so much smaller than me I could easily break free, but I don't want to. I want to return her kisses. The frenzied patter of rain against the windows matches my racing heart. The thick curtains can stay parted. If people can see in from the dark, then good. I want every shadow and light to witness us.

"You make me feral," Rose pants, pulling back a little. Her hands find the hem of her dress, but I stop her with a firm grip on her wrists. Tonight, she's mine to unwrap like a precious gift.

"Patience." My fingers trace the curve of her collarbone before sliding the straps of her dress down her arms. The fabric whispers to the floor, pooling at her feet like emerald waves.

I cross my arms over my abs and tug off my shirt; the air cools my heated skin. Rose steps closer, unbuckles my belt and unzips my trousers. The sensation of being freed from confinement is nothing compared to her touch, warm and sure as she wraps her hand around me.

"Fuck." The word rasps out as pleasure jolts through me. She's got a way of holding me that could make me come undone in seconds if I let it.

"Like that?" Her thumb swipes over the head of my cock, spreading the pre-cum that's beading there.

"Exactly like that."

Her strokes are slow, deliberate, coaxing more of the ache from deep within me.

"Good girl." But I'm not going to let her give everything to me. No. This is about her too. Her needs and desires matter. I can wait. With a firmness that makes her gasp, I drop to my knees and take hold of her hips, pushing her against the wall. I dip my head to her pussy. Her scent is intoxicating, a mix of her sweet perfume and the deeper aroma of her arousal.

"Oh, God…" Her voice quivers as I part her thighs, my hands sliding up the smooth skin, pushing her panties to one side. Her hips rock forward as I press my mouth to her, teasing her open with the barest touch of my tongue.

"Please," she whimpers, and I don't need telling twice.

I lick a broader stripe up her centre, tasting her, savouring her. Her fingers tangle in my hair, urging me on. But I stop and remove her panties. She moans and kicks them off her ankles impatiently. Then I return my mouth to her, finding her clit and circling it with the tip of my tongue. She lets out a sharp cry, her body trembling.

"Not sure that was loud enough for Freddie to hear," I say against her.

"Then make me come," she challenges, pulling me back in.

I suck gently, then firmer, drawing more delicious sounds from her lips that crescendo into squeals. She clenches her inner walls as I slip two fingers inside her, thrusting in time with the flicks of my tongue. She's close, so close, her entire body wound tight.

"Oh, fuck, John, I'm—" Her sentence ends on a scream, the sound piercing the room, drowning out even the rain. It's music; it's victory; it's everything I want. And still, I don't stop. Not until she's shaking, spent, and still calling my name on repeat.

I get to my feet and gather her in my arms, her legs wrap around my waist, and she clings to me like I'm the only thing anchoring her to this world. Her heat against me is inviting, and I could take her like this.

"Are you ready?" I whisper in her ear.

"Yes." She nuzzles my neck, her teeth nipping me.

Holding her with one hand, I use the other to angle my cock, then with a gentle nudge, I push my way into her hot cunt.

"Oh my God." She lets out a whimper as her slick walls clench around me, sucking me into her depths.

I grind into her, holding her lightweight body, but I'm hardly moving compared to her. She's hammering against me, her hips bucking so fiercely I'm scared I drop her. I shift my arms from around her back to under her thighs, so that her knees are hooked over me, then I cup her ass.

She squeals and starts bouncing again.

"Oh, fuck," she gasps. "More. Harder, please."

"Anything for you," I grunt as I pump into her, each stroke hitting deeper. The slap of skin on skin mingles with the sound of rain on the window.

She meets my every move, her breasts springing up and down as she bounces. I move her up against the wall and release one of my hands. Her leg instantly wraps around my back. Using my free hand, I run it over her nipples, watching her. She smiles dreamily as I touch her.

She tightens around me, and I know she's close.

"I need to come," she moans, bucking her hips, but the wall prevents her moving too far.

"And you will." I drop my hand to her clit and use my thumb to circle it until she's whimpering and breathing in little fits.

"I need you... Kiss me, please."

I oblige, pressing my lips against hers. She opens her mouth to me and our tongues meet, hot and needy. When she tightens again and cries out, I move away from the wall, thrusting hard.

"Come with me, Rose," I urge, the familiar coil of release building deep within me.

"I am," she screams. Her nails dig into my shoulders, and she bucks against me, her body shuddering in my arms as her orgasm rips through her. It triggers mine, and I pour myself into her, deep and hot. I let out a primal groan that I hope everyone hears—especially Freddie Blackwood.

As our breathing slows, I hold her against me, feeling her heartbeat against my chest. She drops her head onto my shoulder, and I relish the weight of her.

"Wow," she murmurs, her voice a soft whisper that sends shivers down my spine.

"Wow indeed," I agree.

Slowly, I lower her onto her feet. She's still a little shaky. She glances down, swiping her fingers over her inner thigh where a trail of cum is dripping from her. "Looks like you've made quite the mess again, Mr Knighton."

"It's all for you," I reply with a grin.

"Well, I am the maid... I'm good at cleaning up." She raises her finger to her lips and licks it. "You taste good."

"So do you." I lean in and kiss her. "But I'm not letting you clean up my mess all by yourself. Shall we take a shower?"

"Yes, please."

I scoop her up again because she still looks about as stable as Bambi. Soon, hot water cascades over us, steam rising around our entwined bodies. I take the soap and lather it over her curves, my hands exploring every inch of her. I can't imagine ever tiring of her beautiful body.

She glances up at me with wide eyes. "You've missed a spot." Her gaze falls to her shaved pussy.

"Is that so?" My hand slides between her thighs, and she responds immediately, parting her legs.

"Right... there... Ahh..." Her breath hitches as my fingers find her clit.

"Naughty girl." My thumb circles her sensitive nub.

"Am I not your good girl anymore?" She circles her hand around my arousal.

"I think you're making up for it now."

We fall into a rhythm, both rubbing and stroking, driving each other to the edge once more.

"Say my name," I command.

"John!" she cries out, her inner walls fluttering against my fingers as another climax hits her.

"Fuck yes." I follow her over the brink as pleasure courses through me, my release spilling over her and mingling with the water at our feet.

We stand under the spray, panting, washing away the evidence of our lust. But even as the water cleanses us, I know that what's happening between us can't be washed away so easily. This is more than just physical; it's something deeper, something more even than revenge, something that's taking root in my very soul.

"You're incredible, Rose. I don't think I've ever had so much back-to-back sex like this." I'm so damn hot for her.

She smiles, leaning into me, her blonde hair plastered to her face from the water. "So are you, John. So are you."

Later, the hum of the city outside is a distant whisper against the soft rustle of sheets as I pull Rose closer, our naked bodies fitting together like two perfect pieces of a puzzle. I gently tease my fingers through her hair.

"Today," I murmur, my voice barely above a breath, "has been... amazing."

Rose's eyelashes flutter against my chest, making me twitch. "Mmm, it really has, hasn't it?"

I nod, feeling a warmth spread through me, one that has nothing to do with the physical heat of our entwined bodies. I've built walls around myself for so long, but she seems to walk right through them as if they're made of mist.

I lean in, kissing her forehead gently, allowing myself this moment of peace. It's strange how someone who walked into my life out of nowhere has become my anchor, my storm, and my calm all at once.

We lie there, curled up in the afterglow, and I realize that I don't want to close my eyes, afraid that I might wake up to find this day was just a dream. But the steady rise and fall of her chest against mine tells me this is real—she is real—even if it's only for a brief moment in our lives.

# 15

## Rose

The city whooshes past the Tesla, all gray clouds, shimmering pavements, and spray from the stop-start vehicles at the traffic lights. A gloomy cloud has descended on me too, as we get ever closer to my dingy apartment.

I don't really want John to see where I live. I don't suppose he'll mind, but compared to the luxury he's used to, it makes me feel awful. None of the friends I made when I was with Freddie know where I live—but, come to think of it, none of those people would want to be my friend now.

Thank goodness I have Sienna. She keeps me sane.

"Why don't you just drop me off here?"

The line of traffic is barely moving anyway in the morning rush. It's still quite a walk to the apartment, but probably quicker than trying to get there in the car. "I can cut through the houses this way, and you can join the bypass to get back to Ardencairn."

"Are you sure? I don't mind taking you to your door." John looks over and smiles a little. I don't look too closely. Something tells me if I do, I won't want to leave him at all.

I unbuckle my seatbelt. "No, really, it's fine. It'll take me two minutes." That's a stretch. It'll be nearer fifteen, maybe more.

His eyes search mine, and I hold my ground. Then he indicates and pulls in at the side of the curb. A car horn blares behind us. John ignores it. Everyone in this city gets road rage the second they get behind a wheel, so it's nothing new or surprising. I lean over and plant a soft kiss on his cheek, feeling the rough stubble graze my lips. "Thank you. For everything—the hotel, the clothes..."

"It was my pleasure." His hand brushes against mine. "All of it. I'll see you back at Ardencairn next week."

I nod, smiling, though my chest tightens. I don't want to leave him. With one last glance at his beautiful face, I open the car door and step out into the damp air. The door closes with a solid thud, and I make a run for a nearby office block that has a long covered area at the front. That'll keep me dry for a moment or two.

An odd sensation washes over me—like I've left something important behind. Shaking off the feeling, I hurry back to my reality, to an apartment that feels a world away from the luxury of the Taybury Hotel.

Tucking my hands into the pockets of my new coat, I try to tell myself it's all fine.

It was just a pause from normal life—to have some fun, to feel like we're getting a bit of revenge. People have reactions like this to big stuff.

When my mum died, my brother went full-on psycho. He damn near killed himself pulling a crazy stunt—jumped off a bridge in the middle of the night. Like we didn't already have enough going on. No wonder my dad hit the bottle.

By the time I reach the grimy staircase of the apartment, I'm soaked through. The door creaks open, revealing Sienna sprawled at the little table with a drawing pad and pencils.

"Where have you been?" She glances around, pushing her glasses up her nose.

I flop into the armchair across from her and kick off my boots. "Aw man. I should have messaged, sorry, but I've had an absolutely mental couple of days. Yesterday morning, we found a guy with hypothermia in the garage of the house I clean. John and I took him to a shelter in town."

"John?" Sienna's brow furrows in concern. "Is he the hot boss guy?"

"The very same." I lean my head back on the couch and look at the ceiling. "Then… Well, John took me to a hotel, and we stayed the night there."

"What?" Her voice pitches higher, and she sits up straighter. "What for?"

"What do you think? We spent the day and night together."

"You mean you were…"

"Shagging him, yeah."

"Rose!" Sienna's shock is as palpable as the sudden warmth flooding my cheeks, but I laugh it off.

"Why not? YOLO and all that. It's nothing serious. We're just enjoying the ride."

She shakes her head at my bad pun. "Just be careful, okay? Don't get burnt by this."

She says it lightly, but the words hit like a punch to the gut. She has no idea how that phrase guts me. *Burnt.*

It's not just a metaphor for me. I watched our house burn to the ground with my mum still inside it. She'd gone back in to save our dog. Neither of them made it out.I don't even remember the flames clearly—just the sound. The screaming. The smell of smoke in my throat. It's like my brain has filed the worst of it away in some locked room I'm not allowed to enter. But now and then, something slips through. Certain words. A siren. The alarm that went off at the Gladstone that night.

And now this.

I force a smile, nodding as if her comment was nothing. But my hands are cold and clammy in my lap.

"That's not going to happen," I say, waving off her concern. "I told you about the weird connection—you know, Freddie dating John's ex. We agreed to have some fun. For revenge... and to make us feel better."But even as I say it, a knot of unease tightens in my chest.

I stand, needing to move, and begin unpacking the bag of new clothes John bought me. My fingers trail over the soft fabric of a top as I fold it carefully.

Keep busy. Keep moving.

"Nice stuff." Sienna watches me with wide eyes.

"John bought it for me. We didn't have anything with us—just what we were wearing. And for me, that was my uniform."

She raises an eyebrow. "Isn't it a bit risky, letting him buy you things? I mean... what does he want in return?"

"Nothing," I say quickly. A strange longing claws at my chest—warm and unwelcome. "It's not like that. He's kind, that's all."

Still, my thoughts drift to his scars. How did he get them? It's odd how it doesn't seem to matter now... but what if it *does*? What if it's something terrible—something unforgivable?

Then again, it's not like this is forever.

I press my hand to my chest as my heart flickers with something painful.

"Missing him already?" Sienna eyes me.

"A bit." But that's an understatement. My whole body and soul feel empty without him.

That weekend, I hunch over my laptop, poring over job applications. I swear the blank boxes are mocking me. I might have a degree, but my experience is zero. But John thinks I can do it. My heart does a pathetic little flutter at his name, and I squish it down with a mental stomp. This is about me, not him, even if it's his words that have got me finally looking.

The words *Assistant Manager* stare back at me from the screen. I take a breath, my fingers hovering before they clack away, detailing every tiny scrap of responsibility I've ever had. I hit *submit* before I can talk myself out of it, and then, like ripping off a plaster, I do it again for another, equally terrifying role.

"Nothing ventured," I whisper, but the rest of the saying feels lost in the void of the too-quiet apartment. Sienna has gone out, and the other two are still in bed.

This is how I spend the weekend, only venturing out for a quick run when the rain finally goes off, but it's too cold to stay out for long.

Monday rolls around quickly. Normally Monday mornings make me groan and grumble, but today I can't wait to get to Ardencairn to see John.

I get on the busy bus and stand, leaning my head on the pole. As we reach a stop and a few people get off, someone taps me on the shoulder.

"Hey."

I look around to see Greg towering over me. He's still gaunt and skinny, but he's some height.

"Oh, hi."

He grips the seat back for balance. "I just wanted to say thanks."

"That's okay." I smile. He's a little rough looking—like someone who needs a bit of TLC. "Are you staying at the shelter?"

"Yeah." He nods. "Darius is cool. He's been so helpful, y'know?"

"That's good." Though I don't voice the thought that I found him a little scary too. In an inexplicable way—a bit like John, really. Someone with power who you wouldn't want to cross.

"Thanks to you." He glances down and scuffs his shoe against the floor. "It means I can keep working; keeps me going, doesn't it?"

"Sure. That's what matters." The bus lurches forward, and I grab the rail. Maybe we're both moving forward, in our own ways.

When we get off the bus, Greg takes the path to the main hotel while I head around the side toward the lodge.

"Take care," I call as I go on my way. He gives me a somewhat shy nod. The cold air nips at my cheeks as I hurry through the grounds. They look dismal in the November weather. I can't wait to see John, to tell him about the jobs I've dared to aim for. It feels like I'm shedding an old skin, stepping into something new, terrifying and exhilarating all at once.

The gravel crunches underfoot as I head in through the gate. The Lodge looms ahead; its mix of old stone and modern extensions looks austere in the dim morning light. My heart does this funny little skip as I get closer.

But as I head toward the door, a sleek car rolls up the driveway. My pulse quickens, but not in the way it does for John. I watch to see who it is. When the car stops, Vanessa Knighton steps out. She's all poise and grace, her silver-streaked hair impeccable, and her clothes expensive looking.

"Good morning," she greets me as she puts up an umbrella, even though it isn't actually raining, just damp and a little misty.

"Morning." I clutch my bag tightly. "How are you today?"

"Very well," she replies, glancing around. "I wasn't sure if you were still here or if the other lady was back yet. Have you heard anything about her?"

"No, not a thing." I plaster on a smile, hoping it looks genuine. Inside, I'm wilting a bit. There's no chance now of catching John alone, not with his mum here. I don't dare imagine the disapproval in her gaze if she knew what John, and I have been up to. She might drop dead.

"I'll leave you to work," she says, and my heart sinks a little more. "Don't want to get in your way."

"Thanks." I give a small nod, my earlier excitement draining away. No sharing my news with John, then.

Not yet anyway.

I head straight to the laundry room and put on a load of washing. Somewhere in the house, John and his mother are talking.

Once the washing is on, I get the dusters and polishing cloths and start going over the surfaces in the living areas. As I pass pictures of John and Isabel, I smile, and my mind flips back to the happy times we had.

His voice—deep, resonant—is coming from the study down the hall. Oh God, I'd love to have him whispering in my ear again. Being in the house with him is good—better than being in an apartment miles away from him—but it's not as good as being in his arms.

A familiar heat curls in my belly as I remember how his hands mapped every inch of me, like he was charting new territory. I shake my head, running the duster over the wooden surface.

Isabel's room is next. I take extra care arranging her plush toys, lining them up for a tea party again. The little elephant with the frayed ear goes in the centre. He looks like he needs some attention.

"There you go; you're the guest of honour." I give him a pat on the head before standing back to admire my work. My eyes catch the family photo by the bed, and I feel a pang of something... guilt? No, not quite—it's odd, cleaning up a life I'm only brushing past. In another life, I'd like to get to know Isabel better, maybe join her in one of these tea parties like she asked me to, but I know that can't happen here.

A dull ache settles in my chest. I never had tea parties like this—even before Mum died, our family functioned on stress. My childhood wasn't made of moments like these. It was ruptured in too many places to hold that kind of softness.

Finally, I push open the door to John's room. It's neat, almost spartan, but there's a warmth to it too. I smooth out non-existent wrinkles in the duvet, dust the shelves, and the dresser. I'm stalling, caught between doing my job and wanting, desperately, to feel close to him again.

As I head downstairs, Vanessa's voice floats up to me. Surprisingly, she's still here and it sounds like she's still talking to John. That's annoying because I want to talk to him, but that doesn't seem likely anytime soon. Maybe I should just remember my place and get on with my work. In a couple of weeks, John won't be in my life anymore, and I'll have to deal with it, so this is practice.

But also completely miserable.

# 16

## *John*

I flick through the blueprints on my desk. Today was supposed to be devoted to my golf course design for the new course to the south of Ardencairn, but so far all it's been is one long conversation with my mother. There's no stopping her this morning. She's been through a whole agenda already and doesn't seem to be letting up at all.

"And what's happening with the insurance claim for the Gladstone?" She raises a neatly plucked eyebrow. "And have you made sure there isn't a way for Lydia to sneak in and take it?"

"It's all with the lawyers." I make a mental note of where I've left off and push back from the desk, getting to my feet. "Lydia has already staked a claim to the Gladstone. When the case comes to court, we'll see what happens. There's nothing more I can do in the interim."

"It's all very depressing."

"I agree, but stressing out over it won't help. That's why I want to focus on the projects we can control and that are making money." I stride toward her and put my arm around her.

"The Gladstone was your father's first hotel." Mum presses her lips together. She rarely brings him up—none of us do.

"It was the start of his money," she goes on. "But money didn't bring him the happiness he thought it would. It only made him greedy. And with the greed came the bad moods."

"Yeah... I know."

She glances at me, her expression softening. "I've always worried you and Jamie might follow that path, but I count myself lucky. You've both stayed grounded. Especially with everything you've been through these past few months—you've handled it with strength." Her gaze lingers on my scars.

I rub a hand along my cheek, down to my jaw. It still feels strange that I don't have more flashbacks to that night, or that thoughts of The Gladstone don't send me spiralling. The scarring, the surgeries, even the physical pain—they don't cut as deep as Lydia's betrayal. Or the memory of that woman trapped in the fire, and how close she came to dying if I hadn't pulled her out.

"It's frustrating having our flagship hotel sitting empty." I pause, jaw tightening. But not as annoying as Lydia shacking up with Freddie Blackwood. The bitter flicker of revenge still burns low in my gut.

"Come on." I gesture toward the living room. "Let's sit down."

My mum nods and moves ahead, lips pursed in that familiar way that tells me she's still chewing over our conversation.

I fold myself into an armchair and lounge back. There's no point in attempting to work if she's this desperate to chat.

She walks to the window, then perches on the couch, her hands clasped tightly in her lap. "You've been cooped up here too long. You need to get out more."

"What are you talking about?" I frown at her. "Where do you want me to go?"

"Nowhere particular. But you're always here. It's like you're afraid to be seen in public." Her tone's gentle, but there's an undercurrent of steel there.

"I had a life-changing accident." I look away from her.

"I'm aware, and no one is more saddened than me to see my beautiful boy so scarred. But something tells me it's not that."

"What do you mean?"

"It feels to me that you're more afraid of facing Lydia than of having people see you with scars."

"I have faced Lydia. I see her frequently when I drop off Isabel." Too frequently, though she's hit on a truth I thought I'd kept well hidden from everyone but Rose.

"I don't mean her in person as such. But facing up to people's questions about her... or meeting people who know she's with Freddie Blackwood and feeling inadequate."

A shiver of unease travels down my spine. She makes a good point. Perhaps that is what I'm avoiding. If I go back to the society evenings I went to previously, I'll be alone, while Lydia and Freddie will be swanning around, gloating.

"Well, you'll have to see them in Paris next week. There's no getting away from it." She takes a seat on the couch, adjusting the cushion behind her back.

"Paris?" I blink, momentarily thrown.

"The Global Hotel Investment Forum." She folds her arms. "You got the invitation weeks ago."

I touch my cheek unconsciously, fingers tracing the ridges of healed skin. "I'm not going." My chest tightens at the thought—Lydia and Freddie, mingling with the industry elite, their laughter echoing in opulent halls while I lurk on the fringes on my own. "You're right. I don't want to face Lydia and Freddie alone."

"Oh, John," my mother chides gently, yet there's an edge to her voice. "They shouldn't get the satisfaction of thinking they've driven you away."

"Maybe." But I won't parade myself in front of them for their sport. "Jamie could go in my place."

"He would have, but he'll be in Belize with Owen. Have you forgotten?"

I rub my forehead. "No, I haven't." Though it had temporarily escaped me.

Mum frowns. "You shouldn't be alone here, stewing in your own worries."

"I won't be alone; Isabel will be here. Which is another reason I can't go. If Lydia is away, Isabel will need to be with me."

"Darling, you know I love spending time with her. I can take care of her, no problem. We'll have a wonderful time."

"Not this time." I shake my head. "You're welcome to spend time with her, but I'm not going to Paris."

After a moment's silence, she nods, resigned. "Alright, John. If that's what you want." She checks her watch. "Goodness, the time. I should be off." She rises, drifts over and kisses my cheek. "See you again soon."

"Bye, Mum." I give her hand a little squeeze. I lean back and sigh. Of course, I should go to Paris and not care about meeting Lydia and Freddie, but a blockade in my mind won't let me see a way of doing it that isn't painful.

I return to my study. The scent of furniture polish hits me as I step inside, and my gaze lands on Rose in her black uniform with her blonde hair piled high in a messy bun.

"Hey." She gives me a huge smile. "How are you?"

"Happy to see you." I return her smile, though I can't muster her level of enthusiasm. My head is too full of irritating thoughts.

"Aw, that's sweet." She sets the duster aside and holds up her hands. "You'll be proud of what I've done."

"And what's that?"

"I applied for some jobs at the weekend. Proper ones."

That brings my smile out and I look into her beautiful eyes. "Well done. I'm sure you'll get something a lot better than cleaning this house. Even though you do a good job."

"Why, thank you." She fake curtseys. "Oh, and guess what? I saw Greg on the bus. He was really grateful we got him to Darius's shelter."

"Darius is a good man. He'll see him right."

She watches me for a moment, head tilted. "Have you known him long?"

"We were at school together, so yes. He's had a tough life, yet he chooses to devote himself to doing good." I slump into my seat with a sigh. It's not my place to tell her Darius's story, but he's not had it easy. Right now, I feel the same. My insides are squirmy with the knowledge I should go to Paris, but the resistance within me is too strong.

"Are you okay?" Rose's voice is soft and stacked with concern. "You seem... off. Has something happened?"

I drum an uneven rhythm on the desk. "I suppose it has. My mother gave me quite a lecture this morning. It wasn't easy listening, and she made good points."

"Do you want to talk about it? I'm happy to listen."

I lean back and steeple my fingers. "The Global Hotel Investment Forum is on in Paris next week. It's something I always attend—and should attend. But Freddie and Lydia will also be there, and I can't face it." I glance up at her. "My mother reckons it's them I'm afraid of and not being seen with my scars. Maybe she's right. Because the thought of seeing them makes me sick—especially if I'm on my own."

Rose steps closer and leans on my desk. "I might be overstepping here, but if you wanted... I could go with you." She hesitates, biting her lip. "We could pretend to be a couple. Wouldn't that be the best revenge?"

My head snaps up, eyes locking onto hers. "Are you serious?" The beginning of a smile tugs at the corners of my mouth.

"Absolutely." She raises her eyebrows. "If you want to. I can request my annual leave. And if you let my boss know that you're away and won't need me here that week, she'll probably approve it."

"Perfect." I already feel lighter, bolstered by the prospect of having her by my side. "Let's do it." I open my arms to her, a wordless invitation, and she doesn't hesitate. She sits on my lap, curling into me like she belongs there. And she does. Or I really want her to. I hold her close, my hands tracing the curve of her back, and the warmth of her body seeps into mine.

"Imagine their faces," I murmur against her hair, the soft strands tickling my nose. I've gone from not wanting to go to wishing it was right now in the space of a few minutes.

Rose lets out a low chuckle, her breath warm on my neck. "It'll be brilliant." She lifts her head to meet my gaze. Her eyes are alight as she cups my cheek in her hand. Our lips meet, softly at first, but I've missed her too much to let this moment go, and I push open her mouth with my tongue. She links her fingers at the back of my neck as we make out deep and slow.

My body reacts, desire coiling in my belly, and my cock is rock solid. She shifts, grinding down against me. I grasp her bottom, kneading it as she rocks over me.

"Oh God, John." Her movements become more frantic.

I take hold of her tunic top and yank it off. She stands up and swiftly strips off her trousers and panties.

"I've missed you." She leans over me and unzips my trousers. I shift a little to free myself, and Rose straddles my lap.

"Likewise. I've thought about nothing else all weekend."

She takes hold of my cock and guides me inside her. Her eyes lose focus as I fill her deep.

"God, yes," I groan.

She starts to ride me, setting a punishing pace that drives every coherent thought from my mind. I hope this chair can take it. She leans down to kiss me again, and it's a mess of teeth, tongues and raw need. All finesse has gone. This is urgent and desperate.

I glide my hands up her body, grazing her breasts through the lace of her bra, then settling my palms on her back.

She bucks her hips rapidly, moaning, until she snaps, and tenses around me. Her legs shudder, and she gasps for air. I thrust upward into her hot wet pussy, and an orgasm rips through me. I spill my load deep inside her.

Rose rests her forehead against mine and smiles. "That was just a warm up. Just wait until we get to Paris."

# 17

## Rose

I'm quite literally above the clouds, looking down on their mass from a clear sky. It's strange to think that down below is a cold, dreary November day. The plush leather of the first-class seat cradles my body; even the simple action of reclining it feels decadently smooth. I glance at John in the seat next to me and smile.

"Champagne?" He lifts an eyebrow. He doesn't wait for my response before signalling to the attendant, who promptly brings over two flutes of bubbling liquid gold.

"Cheers." I clink my glass gently against his, taking care not to spill a single drop of the precious elixir. We both take a sip, and I watch as he relaxes into his seat, the corners of his eyes crinkling ever so slightly.

"I've never flown first class before." I glance out of the window again. "In fact, I've only been on a plane once. It was a holiday to Spain with some girls from uni, and we were squeezed in like sardines. We found the cheapest deal we could and went for it. I wanted to go to the Caribbean, but the prices were about fifty times more than my budget."

He places his hand on my knee and squeezes. "Well, you don't need to worry about that this week. My girlfriend deserves the best." His gaze meets mine, and he winks. "And she'll have it."

"Ooh, thank you." With a grin, I raise my glass to him and take another sip, the bubbles fizzing against my nose. "Does that mean you're taking me to Barbados after this?" I joke, but it would be dangerously easy to get used to this kind of luxury—I need to remember it's just a part I'm playing for the next couple of days. Nothing more.

John chuckles. "You never know what I might do." He checks his phone. "But one thing at a time. I've got a couple of seminars to attend. They'll probably bore you to tears, so make the most of the hotel—or go explore Paris."

"Sounds great." Though I'd prefer it if I could explore with him. But that's not my job. I should be thanking my lucky stars I'm getting a free trip to Paris. When I told Sienna, she nearly fainted. She's still not got a proper answer out of me about what I'm doing—maybe because I don't know myself.

Normally, plane rides seem to go on forever, and I find them agonizingly slow. But this one is the opposite, and before I know it, the plane cuts through the clouds, inching closer to the city of love.

"I've always wanted to visit Paris." I peer out of the window. "I mean, it's the most romantic city in the world, isn't it?"

"It has that reputation, yes." John lifts his glass to his lips. "And I'm sure we'll find a way to make it pleasurable."

That word, spoken in his low rasp and slipping from that sensual mouth, sends a shiver right through me—completely inappropriate for a plane ride. What the fuck am I doing? Sitting in first class, jetting off to Paris with a man who stirs up feelings I've no business entertaining. I'm teetering on the edge with him—one misstep and I could be falling. But I can't let that happen. As easy as it would be to lose myself to John Knighton, I'm more likely to crash and burn. This is meant to be simple. Just an arrangement. He's not even divorced yet, and who knows if he'll ever be ready for more? It's not like I'm long-term material for someone like him. I'm probably just a pleasant distraction. Shame I'm finding it hard to see him the same way.

Later that day, our taxi stops outside a huge hotel in the centre of Paris. It's like something out of a fairytale. I can't quite get over the fact that I can see the Eiffel Tower from here. My head is still buzzing from the champagne, or maybe it's just the proximity to John, but there's an electric current thrumming under my skin. A shadow lies beneath the buzz, though; something I'm scared to name in case it pops my happy bubble. But it's there, lingering just out of reach. Unavoidable.

And soon it rises to the surface.

Freddie Blackwood. The real reason I'm here, I suppose. The revenge I wanted felt sweeter from a distance. Now, I'm not sure I want to see him again at all. I'd prefer this trip to be playing out with just me and John, *sans* the issue of the exes!

"Wow." I breathe out as we get out of the taxi. The building rises before us, all elegant stone and intricate detailing around the many windows.

John pays the driver and takes my hand, leading me into the opulent lobby, adorned with gilded mirrors and marble floors. Crystal chandeliers glitter above. "Just wait until you see the room." He approaches the desk. "This hotel is an inspiration."

I stand back and listen as John converses with the receptionist. He speaks French. I may just have creamed my panties. Who would have thought that voice could get any sexier? But the French rolls off his tongue smoother than velvet.

We're whisked up in a luxurious elevator, and John rakes his eyes over me. I'd pounce on him in a second, but he gives me a little headshake and raises his eyes momentarily to what I recognize to be a security camera.

"I'm not that bold." He raises an eyebrow and steps closer. "Because I know how these things work, and you never know who might be watching." The powerful scent of his sandalwood cologne hits me deep, reminding me of the heat we've shared, but also comforting me. It's like the scent of safety.

The doors open, and John guides me down a hushed corridor lined with plush carpets. I wheel my case behind me. John stops in front of a door and taps the keycard against it.

"Après vous." He gestures, and I step into the suite.

"Oh my God." My jaw might just have hit the floor. "This is..." Words fail me. The suite is bigger than my whole apartment.

"You like?" His brow furrows slightly.

"I love!" There's a decadence here that makes me want to explore every inch—the plush king-sized bed, the elegant sitting area, the fresh roses that perfume the air. But it's the French doors that beckon me with the view over the city beyond them.

Pulling them open, I step out onto the balcony. It's freezing cold, but I don't care. I need to see this. In the near distance, stands the Eiffel Tower, majestic and utterly breathtaking. I lean against the railing, gazing out.

"Look at the view." No doubt I sound like an idiotic tourist, but who cares? This might be my one and only visit here, so I want to make the most of it.

"It's nothing compared to you." John comes out behind me and puts an arm over my shoulder.

I laugh, rolling my eyes at the compliment but secretly loving it. "It's cold, though."

"Come inside." John leads me back in. "You can see almost as much from inside, and it's much warmer." He positions one of the recliner seats a little closer to the window, but neither of us sits down.

"Thank you. For saying yes to this trip." His eyes lock onto mine.

"Thank you for bringing me. No matter what happens with Freddie and Lydia, at least we have this." I turn my eyes back to the view.

"Yes, we do." He takes a deep breath before closing the French doors.

The air is crisp now and still a little cold from the door being open, but I know it'll soon warm up. If not, I'd be willing to spend the rest of the day in that bed getting cosy—either under the layers of covers... or with John.

His hand slides round to my side, pulling me closer, and I wrap my arms around his neck. For a moment, we just look at each other. Then our lips meet in a kiss that's soft and lingering, a silent conversation between two souls. If only this was real, it would be perfect. John tugs me closer, and I tilt my head as the kiss deepens. My heart leaps, and the carnal urge for skin-on-skin contact burns low.

When we part, breathless, the city lights shimmer around us as the sky darkens.

"You are so beautiful," he says. "I can't get enough of you. I'm an addict. Maybe I should try rehab."

I smile, but when we're done here, I'll definitely need therapy to get over this.

"I'm on the same drug." My heart races, and it's not just from the kiss. Maybe I'm not on the same drug at all. He's here for revenge and sex, but it's become so much more for me.

"And very soon we'll both be high." Slowly, he pushes my tan-colored jacket from my shoulders. As he leans in and places kisses along my collarbone, the jacket falls to the floor, leaving me in my ditsy-print short dress. The colors are autumnal and great for the season when teamed with ribbed camel tights and brown knee-high boots, but it's all about to come off. John undoes the buttons at the front of my dress, still kissing me.

The urge to touch him is so strong, and I reach for the buttons of his shirt and open a couple. He stands back and shucks off his suit jacket, then crosses his arms across his front and pulls off his shirt, revealing the defined muscles of his abdomen and chest.

"That's better." I grab his waistband and tug him back to me, moving my hand lower, until I feel the bulge of his erection. I rub over him with my palm. He's so big and my lower belly spasms at the thought of him inside me.

His hands move back to my dress, and he slides it off my shoulders and lowers it down. He takes his time, watching me with hunger blazing in his bright blue irises. My dress slips down my legs and pools at my feet.

"Step out," he instructs.

I comply, and he tilts his head, raking me over with his eyes.

"Beautiful." The word feels like a caress against my skin. He moves closer, glides his fingers inside the waistband of my tights, then slips them down. He follows, kneeling as he pulls them off my feet. I steady myself on the French door handle as I step out of them completely.

John levels his head at my pussy, grasping my hips with his big hands, then using his lips and his tongue, he plays with the triangle of lace covering me, teasing me through it. I grab his hair and try to hold him in one place. "More," I mutter.

He smiles up at me. "Anything for my good girl." He gets to his feet and gently eases me back onto the recliner. "What do you want?" he whispers as he kneels again, his fingers tracing a path of fire along my inner thighs.

"I want you."

"And I'm here. What do you want me to do?"

"Make me come... please." I lie back with a moan on the plush cushion. The Eiffel Tower looms in the distance through the window, its lights twinkling like stars. This is surreal.

John's head dips between my legs, and a gasp escapes me as he pulls my panties to the side. The warmth of his mouth is incredible, and when he sucks gently on my clit, a bolt of pleasure shoots through me. My hands find purchase on the arms of the chair, gripping tightly as his fingers slip inside me, moving steadily. A crescendo builds deep in my belly.

"God. John. I. Please." The words come in little fits. The city blurs before my eyes, the iconic silhouette of the tower now just a hazy backdrop to the sensations that are coiling tighter and tighter within me.

John's tongue is like fire, sending heat through every nerve end in my body. My breasts swell and ache, and my bra is too tight. I tug it down and my breasts spill out, nipples pebbling with need. I run my hands over them to soothe them. At the same moment, John ups the pressure, and I can't hold back the orgasm that rips through me. My body arches off the lounger as waves of intense pleasure crash over me. It's almost too much, the way he doesn't let up, drawing out every last tremor until I'm spent and boneless, my heart thundering in my chest.

"Oh, fuck." My head rolls to the side, and I see the city lights twinkling all around as I try to regain my breath.

John leans over me and kisses his way up my body, rolling his warm palms across my breasts. "Are you okay?"

"More than." I reconnect my eyes with his and smile as I sit up. John moves back a little, giving me space, but I don't want him away from me. I need him close.

With his back to the French doors, he watches me with those deep eyes, and I shuffle to the edge of the seat. Unclipping his waistband, I push down his trousers and boxer briefs, freeing his cock and running my hands up the hard shaft.

"Christ, Rose," he groans as my mouth envelops him. I take my time, savouring the taste of him, the weight of him on my tongue. I used to hate the monotony of this with Freddie. It was a chore—something he expected. Something I did with the ever-fading hope that one day he would return the favor in some small way.

But this is different. It doesn't feel transactional or something that I need paid back. I want to give John pleasure because it makes me feel good too. *He* makes me feel good.

With each stroke, each flick of my lips, I feel him unravel a little more.

"Fuck..." His hand finds its way into my hair, guiding me without forcing. And I give myself over to him, knowing that in this moment, we belong to each other.

"Oh hell—" His words cut off with a sharp intake of breath. "Let's stop for a minute."

I pull back and wipe the edge of my lips with the back of my hand. "Why?" I look up at him.

"Because I want to be inside you." He lifts me up from my knees, and I love how strong he is. It's like I weigh nothing as he scoops me into his arms. "You're my girlfriend, after all. For the next few days, I'm going to treat you exactly the way my girlfriend should be treated."

I curl into his shoulder, resting my forehead on the crook of his neck and running my fingertips over his chest. "Sounds like I'm going to be spoiled."

"Oh, I'll ruin you all right."

"Do it," I breathe out. His hands, large and capable, hold me tight as he sits in the recliner, taking me with him.

"How would you like to do this?" He cups my face, gently kissing me. "Tell me what you what."

"Pretend that you love me." Fuck knows where those words came from, but it's exactly what I want.

He huffs out a little laugh that lands on my neck. For a moment, I hold my breath. Have I killed the mood with my idiocy?

"You're my girlfriend. Of course, I love you. Let me show you how much." He lies me back, and my heart pounds ever faster. He did just say those three little words, didn't he? In his super sexy voice. I've melted so completely that I feel like nothing but a puddle of warm liquid. "I love you so much, my beautiful girl." He strokes his hand down my cheek as he moves on top of me.

My insides furl with need. "Oh God…" I can hardly breathe. Everything that felt amazing before is now even more intense. This is what it's like to be loved, utterly and completely. I trust him so deeply I'm willing to abandon my soul to him.

Slowly, he enters me, nudging deeper, and I spread my legs wide to accommodate him. The sensation is overwhelming, intimate, and intense. I love how deep he is; how he fills me. He moves slowly, and I savour every second, every breath, every whisper of skin against skin. His thrusts are tender, an exploration rather than a conquest, and every time he pulls back, I feel the anticipation curl inside me, building toward the next release.

"My beautiful girl," he murmurs, leaning in and kissing me, "you feel incredible."

I can only moan, my fingers digging into his shoulders. The city lights dance outside the window. I let my head fall back, drinking in the feel of him with this dreamy backdrop. My body responds to his every touch, and when he wraps me firmly in his arms, still thrusting slow and deep, my insides coil tightly.

"Oh, fuck," I gasp. "This…You—"

"It's all for you." He kisses me again. "You make me feel alive in a way I never have before."

I reach up and draw his face down to mine. I want to tell him I love him too, but when he said it, it was because I asked him to pretend. If I say it now, it'll sound needy and pathetic. So, I'll show him instead. I pour all my feelings into it. It's a promise, a silent vow in the heart of

Paris. He quickens his pace a little, and I rub my clit against him as he thrusts; sensational sparks burst at the contact.

"Fuck, Rose," he whispers against my lips. "This is insane."

"I know." My own emotions threaten to overwhelm me. "Just be here with me."

And he is. Fully, completely. There's nothing else but us. I cling to him, my nails digging into his back as we move together, the sensations building, spiralling.

This isn't just sex. No, he's making love to me under the twinkling lights of Paris. He's unravelling everything that's gone before and rewriting it.

Still holding me firmly with one arm, he gently strokes me with the other, gliding his palm over my breasts, tracing patterns of desire along my skin. He works his fingers lower, shifting them between us and working on my clit as he continues to thrust.

Now I can feel him on the inside and the outside. Each caress adds to the stimulation until I know I'm about to burst.

"Come for me," he breathes into ear. "It's all okay." His raspy voice is enough to send me tumbling over the edge.

Another orgasm pulses through me like fire racing through dry grass—sudden and consuming, stealing the breath from my lungs. My body clenches around him, and I cry out. "Oh, fuck."

"God, Rose..." John's voice is strained. He drives into me more urgently until he jolts and stiffens. His warm seed floods me, and I clench around him again as a blissful aftershock hits.

I close my eyes, and John leans his head on my shoulder, breathing heavily. Neither of us moves. I don't want to. This is a happy place, and I love it. I wrap my legs around him, holding him, preventing him from moving.

"I hope Freddie and Lydia are next door," I murmur. "I hope this was the soundtrack to their evening."

"Indeed," John replies.

"God knows why Lydia chose Freddie over you. You're so much more."

"Control." John kisses my neck. "She wanted a bigger role in the running of the business. I wasn't against it, but I didn't agree with all her suggestions. She's very money orientated, and I didn't like some of her proposed directions. They compromised too much just for the sake of making a quick buck. But instead of discussing it, she got angry with me and took her bad feelings out on our personal relationship. She distanced herself from me and blamed me. It's hard to balance a relationship when it's both personal and professional. I'm not saying I was blameless, but in the end, she decided that divorcing me would be the best way to get the businesses she wanted. And I strongly suspect Freddie was part of that. I guess he persuaded her, but I doubt he has her best interests at heart."

"He won't. He and his parents are always looking for ways to expand their empire."

"I know." John kisses me softly. "They're very influential and have many contacts." He lets out a sigh, and I increase my grip on his muscular back, holding him as close as possible.

*I love you.* The words swirl through my head, silent but unrelenting. I love him so damn much it's painful.

Maybe it's the city of love I have to blame for all these feelings—Paris weaving its magic around my heart. Because falling for this man could destroy me. He's already undone me in ways I can't explain, and soon enough, when this little arrangement ends, he'll break my heart too. So I have to make the most of this... while I still can.

# 18

## *John*

Straightening my tie in the mirror, I catch sight of Rose behind me, brushing out her hair. "I hope you'll be okay on your own today. I can arrange a car if you feel like going for a drive around the city." The seminars at the Global Hotel Investment Forum aren't exactly her scene—truth be told, I'm not sure any part of my world is. It's tonight's event where I'll need her to shine.

"No, it's fine. I'd like to walk around. I think it'll be easier. And I want to ride the Metro. It's compulsory when you come to Paris."

I let out a low chuckle and turn to face her. "That's the spirit." I move closer until there's no space left between us and swipe a stray curl of blonde hair from her face. She looks incredible—glamorous but effortless, with her long hair loose around her shoulders. A soft cashmere turtleneck hugs her slim frame, tucked into a short, tailored skirt that shows off her shapely legs. Her tan coat is draped over one arm, and sleek, knee-high leather boots add just the right amount of city polish. Paris suits her. "Sounds like you'll have a great time exploring the city. If you want to use the spa, just give them the room number. I should be done by four, and then dinner at seven. That's when we'll have some fun."

"You bet." She reaches up and adjusts my tie, even though I'm sure it was perfectly straight before. With a little tilt of her head, she studies me, and my chest tightens. "I'll miss you, though," she murmurs before pressing her lips to mine.

I cup her cheek and kiss her back before breaking away with a reluctant sigh. "I'll miss you too."

Moments later, we head through the lobby together. I walk Rose to the door, placing my hand on her lower back as we make our way through some scattered groups of people.

"I'll see you later." I lean in and give her a peck on the cheek. There's no reason for me to keep up the pretence here, but I want to kiss her. And more. She's taken over my world—I can't think about anything else.

As I glance up, my eyes link on a woman at the other end of the lobby. My heart flips. It's Lydia. Well, thank fuck, I did keep up the pretence then, because she's watching—not directly, but I know we're on her radar.

She's as beautiful as ever, like a painting come to life, her raven-black hair cascading over her shoulders like a dark waterfall, her eyes sharp and calculating even from a distance. But it's a harsh, cold beauty compared to Rose's softness and warmth.

My hand finds Rose's waist, pulling her against me in one swift motion. She giggles, then our lips meet, and I kiss her like there's no tomorrow. And really, there isn't. Not for us in the real world. It's a passionate, deep kiss, partly for Lydia's benefit but more as a silent proclamation that I belong wholly to someone else.

"What was that for?" Rose grins as I pull back, her expression a little dazed.

"Lydia's over there," I murmur into her ear, just loud enough for her to hear over the growing buzz of the conference crowd milling around us. "I wanted her to see."

Rose's soft laugh is almost lost in the low conversations around us. "Of course." She pushes onto her tiptoes, her arms curling around my neck, and pulls me in for a hug. This, if anything, looks even more intimate than the kiss. I wrap my arms about her, pulling her close, and together we stand in a tight embrace. It fills me with the oomph I need to get through this.

"Have fun, my beautiful girl," I whisper and pull away.

"And you." She gives me a little wave before backing out the door and blowing a kiss. When she's outside, she turns and walks away, looking confident and carefree in her long boots and tan wool coat. I watch her disappear into the stream of people outside.

Now I've got to get to the conference room and avoid Lydia if I can. I keep my gaze fixed forward; my shoulders squared. As I cross the foyer, I sense that Lydia is watching me, her eyes on me like icy pinpricks down my spine. Let her look. Let her wonder who Rose is. That's why I brought her here after all.

I head directly into the conference room, not turning toward Lydia, and move through the crowd, giving polite nods where necessary.

"John, hello," someone says, and I'm pulled into a conversation about investment opportunities with some acquaintances. I talk and listen, but part of me is elsewhere, imagining what Rose is doing now and hoping she's okay on her own.

As I chat, I glance back to the door, and my gaze falls directly on Freddie Blackwood. What a bastard. He strolls in like he owns the place, and I ball my fists. After what he did to Rose at the Gladstone, I'll never stop wanting to rearrange his face. I take a seat with my acquaintances, casually observing as Freddie makes a beeline for Lydia's table. Their heads dip together, conspiratorial whispers shared between them. The sight irks me, but I don't let it show. Instead, I smirk to myself. Just wait until they see Rose and me together. I can't wait to see the look on their faces.

"Quite the turnout this year, isn't it?" a fellow hotelier says.

"Indeed." My focus still trails Freddie and Lydia as they whisper together. "Plenty of new blood looking to sink their teeth into the market."

"Speaking of new, who was that lovely lady you were with earlier? Quite a stunner."

I frown a little. Has everyone been watching us?

"She's... my new girlfriend."

"Excellent."

Why, then, do I hear unspoken words of judgement? *Isn't she too young for you? What's a gorgeous girl like her doing with a broken man like you? Has your divorce even come through yet? You didn't waste any time, did you? And isn't that your ex-wife just over there?*

They don't need to be said aloud. I can feel them on the lips of everyone here. I reach for the carafe of water and pour some into a glass, not because I want it particularly but because I need to have something in my hands. I feel like I might smash something otherwise.

The seminar drones on all morning, a relentless march of slides and the occasional murmur of approval. But it's all white noise. I just can't concentrate, which is so unlike me. I tap out a message to Rose.

*How's it going? xx*

I hit send, then wait... Impatiently. It's a strange sensation, this flicker of excitement mixed with concern, like I'm a schoolboy waiting for a note to be passed back in class. I glance at the phone repeatedly, but it remains silent.

"What are your thoughts on the projected ROI for resort investments?" a woman at my table asks.

I muster a reply quickly. All the while glancing at my phone. Why doesn't Rose respond? The worry in my gut builds. Could something have happened to her?

The moment the seminar breaks for lunch, I march out of the room, bypassing the networking crowd, ignoring the beckoning scents of the catering, and head straight to my room.

Once inside, I prowl out onto the balcony, the chill November air biting at my skin. Paris sprawls before me, the rooftops glazed with icy raindrops under a sullen sky. I lean against the railing. "Where are you, Rose?" I mutter into the void, willing my phone to come alive with her response. But it stubbornly refuses, leaving me to pace in silence.

I thumb the screen and shoot off another message. My gaze snags on the Eiffel Tower, its iron lattice somehow stark against the graying sky, and I wonder if she's looking at it too from down there somewhere.

I head back inside and order room service. While I wait for it to arrive, I dial Mum's number. She picks up after the third ring.

"John, darling! How's Paris?"

"Could be worse." I slip into the recliner. "How are you and Isabel?"

"We're just fine. Isabel's been drawing a lot. She says she's making a surprise for you."

A smile tugs at my lips. "That's great. Tell her I can't wait to see it."

"Will do."

"I assume everything's fine?"

"Don't worry about us. We're managing splendidly."

"Thanks, Mum."

"And how about you, dear? How is the conference? Have you seen Lydia?"

"It's going fine, and, yeah, I saw her, but we didn't talk."

"Probably for the best. It's very awkward for me to know what to say when Isabel mentions her."

"Just keep it neutral. I don't want to vilify her to Isabel." It isn't my place to screw up their relationship. Lydia will probably manage it all on her own, like she has with me.

"I suppose."

"I better go. I'm glad everything is fine. Speak soon, Mum."

"Take care, John."

The line goes dead, and I'm left to my thoughts again. The longing for Rose swells like a wave, threatening to pull me under. I've never been one to need people, but damn it if she hasn't burrowed her way into my very core. I don't think I'll ever be the same again.

# 19
## Rose

Paris is beautiful, even if the weather is a little grim. I'm being a proper tourist, soaking in all the sights and sounds and getting lots of photos.

"Mademoiselle, regardez!" A street artist calls out to me, his easel displaying an impressive sketch of Notre-Dame. I flutter my hand at him, grinning, and he winks back, a sparkle in his eyes.

"Maybe later," I call back, already distracted by a charming patisserie window crammed with rainbow macarons. This place is magic.

I duck into the patisserie and check my phone for messages. I never have the notifications on as they drive me mad, but I'd like to send John some of my photos. When I open the message thread, I spy a whole string of messages.

Oops, John must be wondering what the hell is wrong with me. I just assumed he'd be too busy to text me.

I message him back quickly while I wait in the line.

*Sorry for the radio silence. Been dashing here and there. It's amazing. Just getting macarons. They look so good. Will bring you some. xx*

Slipping the phone back into my bag, I look at the glass cabinet in front of me. What a feast of sweet treats.

When I leave with my little box of macarons, I check my phone again and realize it's already past one o'clock. There's no way I'll make it to the hotel for lunch, as John suggested in one of his messages. I weave through the bustling Parisian streets, dodging tourists with their noses buried in guidebooks and locals striding by. If I'd known he wanted to meet for lunch, I wouldn't have strayed so far. He must be missing me. I feel the same, but he'll just have to wait!

*I won't make it for lunch. I'm too far away. I've booked a spa treatment for three, so coming back for that. Can't wait to see you after.*

I send it off along with some pictures.

Before I pocket my phone, it buzzes with his reply.

*No worries, looking forward to our evening. Enjoy your spa time. See you soon, beautiful xxx*

Nibbling on a macaron, I head back toward the metro station, my eyes catching glimpses of shops I'd love to visit another time. Will that ever happen? It seems unlikely I'll be back with John anyhow.

I take a seat on the Metro and send a message to Sienna along with some photos. She knows I'm in Paris, but I haven't filled her in on everything about John. Sure, she's aware we hooked up at the Taybury, but I'm not convinced I can explain the rest without sounding unhinged. What would she think—me, getting involved with a forty-two-year-old single dad, scarred, and a history even I don't know the whole of?

Putting it like that makes me wonder why I'm interested. But the pull is undeniable. I can't seem to stop... even though I know eventually I'll have to.

Her reply flashes up on my screen, and I open it with a smirk.

*Seriously! What the hell is going on? Stop teasing me and tell me why you're in Paris. If this has anything to do with Freddie, I'll be flying over there to drag you away from him.*

Bless her for being so protective. But what will she make of the real story?

*I am here because of Freddie, but not for the reason you're thinking! No way am I getting back together with him. I'm here for payback!!*

*Sounds mental, doesn't it?*

*John and I decided to get a little revenge on Freddie and Lydia, John's ex. They're in Paris for a conference, and John was invited too. We're pretending to be a couple to rub them up the wrong way.*

I shake my head as I send it, knowing how wild it sounds. What will she make of it? I don't have to wait long to find out.

*What the hell?*

*Are you insane?*

*When you say pretending to be a couple, what does that mean exactly?*

*As in holding hands in public... or what?*

*Do you have to kiss him? Shag him? Is this legit?*

I laugh—how can I help it? She's sweet and funny at the same time. I appreciate her concern, but she doesn't know how into John I've got. And I'm not sure I want to tell her. I know she won't want me hurt, and it's obvious that's where this is going.

*Let's just say it's another hookup... this time with Parisian benefits. He's a nice guy and I like him, so it's not a hardship, and he treats me better than anyone I've been with for real.*

And it's no lie.

Sienna's replies ping in fast and furious again.

*Bloody hell!!*

*Sounds like you fancy him for real!*

*Do you?*

*Where does this end?*

Ha! Good questions. Ones I'm not sure I can answer. Or more like I don't want to. That would mean analysing this situation, and I can't do that—not yet.

*I like him, yeah. Not denying it. But it ends when we get back.*

That's the cold, hard truth, and I have to remember it.

I make my way from the Metro station to the hotel, and I slip inside. The warm lobby is a welcome respite from the chilly air outside. A glance at my watch tells me there's still time to kill before my spa appointment, so I head upstairs and dump my bags, grab my bikini and make a beeline for the pool.

The tranquillity of the rippling water instantly calms me, the jacuzzi bubbling invitingly at the far end. A few other guests lounge nearby.

Sinking into the jacuzzi, I let out a contented sigh; the jets massage my cold muscles. My mind drifts to John and what it would feel like if he were here with me. The thought sends a delicious shiver down my spine, and I close my eyes, imagining us alone, his hands running over my skin, his lips plying me with kisses.

The warmth and the bubbles cocoon me, and I can almost feel his phantom caress as he slides my bikini bottoms to the side and rubs his thick fingers over my clit. His other hand slides off my bikini top and cups an aching breast.

A splash in the pool beyond makes my eyes jump open. It's just someone fooling around, but it's enough to remind me I'm not alone and I really should stop this fantasy from playing out before I get myself into trouble.

After a good half hour, I emerge, dry myself off and change into a luxurious hotel robe, before heading toward the spa. The gentle scent of essential oils and soft ambient music trickles out to meet me. As I wait in the reception area, I look around, and my heart drops. I freeze and look away. Lydia is heading this way, her heels clicking on the tiled floor.

Shit.

My mind races for an escape route, but there's none. The corridor is narrow, hemmed in by tall potted plants and artful sconces, so I can't go past her, and I can't get past this desk either, not unless I barge into one of the private massage rooms, which would be ridiculous.

There's one person in front of me checking in. If they would just hurry up.

"Excuse me." She speaks behind me, and I look around. "I hope you don't mind me saying so, but I saw you this morning, and I feel like I know you from somewhere. Have we met before?"

My pulse quickens, but I keep my expression neutral as I turn to face her properly. Of course, *I* know who *she* is. I remember the first time I saw her—at the Gladstone with Freddie—watching me with cool calculation and casual disdain. Turns out she was either working on stealing my boyfriend... or he was already halfway through stealing her. Hard to tell, really.

Now here she is, peering at me like she's trying to place me. Clearly, she's not got there yet, which honestly doesn't surprise me. Freddie probably didn't tell her who I was. Not when apparently I was nothing more than his sex toy.

"Uh, possibly."

"Mademoiselle?" the receptionist says, and I'm delighted to have an excuse to turn away from Lydia.

"J'ai un rendez-vous pour un massage, pour Rose Darwin." Hopefully I got the French right.

"C'est parfait. Veuillez entrer dans la salle deux, s'il vous plaît."

I look at the doors behind the desk and move quickly toward room two, not looking back at Lydia. A serene voice greets me as I enter the private massage room. The masseuse—a woman with kindly eyes—instructs me to undress and ushers me to the table draped in fresh linen. She leaves me, and I take off the robe and lie face down, resting my head on the cushioned cutout.

The door clicks shut, plunging the room into quiet. Soft music mingles with the faint sound of the masseuse moving about, preparing oils that soon release their calming aroma into the air. Her hands begin moving across my tense shoulders, kneading away the knots of stress that have probably increased tenfold since seeing Lydia. We weren't supposed to see each other alone. I don't want to see her until I'm with John and she's with Freddie. Then John and I can really show them who got the better deal—even if ours is fake.

I groan. Oh God. It's all fake. None of this is real. What the fuck am I doing?

"Relâchez-vous, Mademoiselle." The masseuse presses on my tense shoulders, and I let out a sigh, letting the sensation wash over me. Yet, even as I do, my thoughts drift to John, how his strong, capable hands would feel gliding over my skin. I imagine his touch, tender yet assured, sending ripples of pleasure through me.

For a fleeting moment, I wish it were him here in this dimly lit room, not the masseuse. I wish I could turn my head and find his ocean-blue eyes staring back at me.

But reality pulls me back. Pleasant as this is, it's all just part of a game, and one I don't know how to win. Even if we make Freddie and Lydia squirm, it doesn't change the long-term outcome for John and me. All the decisions we've made to get us here have been flawed. We've been hellbent on revenge when we should have been healing. And perhaps we could have done that for each other without reference to Lydia and Freddie.

But it's too late to turn back now.

# 20

## *John*

I lounge back in the plush recliner in the room, looking out over the city. It's gone four now. The seminar finished early, but I assume Rose is still at her spa treatment. Hopefully she's enjoying it and getting some relaxation before this evening. The dinner is at seven, but we can mingle before that, which gives us a couple of hours to relax and get ready.

The door clicks open, and I twist my neck around, leaning on the back of the lounger to see better. Rose ambles in, her skin glowing and pink with a post-spa radiance.

"Hey." I shift forward on the recliner. "You're looking good."

"Thank you. But don't get up." She comes over and sits on my lap, wrapping her arms around my neck and kissing my cheek. "Miss me?" Her eyes sparkle, and she grins as she tips her face up to mine.

"Of course I did. How could I not? I've been clock-watching all day."

"Same. Though I didn't notice quite so much in the morning. Paris is so beautiful."

"Not as beautiful as you." I lean down and capture her lips with mine. It's a soft and soulful kiss. I close my eyes as her hands clasp at the back of my neck, her fingers playing with the hair at the nape.

"Guess what?" She pulls back.

"What?"

"I saw Lydia at the spa. She spoke to me."

I furrow my brow, certain this isn't good news. "What about?"

"She said she'd seen me this morning and thought she recognized me. She asked if we'd met before."

"But you haven't, have you?"

"I saw her at the Gladstone... the night Freddie hit me. He was talking to her. But I don't think she really registered me."

"Well... I saw both Freddie and her at the seminar, though I kept away from them." I hold Rose close, a surge of protectiveness rising inside me. "And we can't avoid seeing them later."

"Are you sure we're doing the right thing?" Her eyes are still locked with mine. They're wide and almost pleading.

"What do you mean?"

"I don't know exactly. Maybe I just don't want to reduce myself to their level."

Bending in, I kiss her on the cheek. "We're not. You and I aren't having an affair. Both of them cheated on us. We're not like them. Maybe it's low coming here together just to spite them, but to be honest, even if they were out of the equation, I'd be happier here with you than I would be on my own."

She lets out a little laugh on a sigh, curling into me. "Then I'm glad I'm here."

"Me too. But I won't force you to do anything you're uncomfortable with. If you'd rather not see Freddie tonight, I'm fine with that. We can stay here. No way am I going to push you into a situation like that if you don't want to."

"You're so sweet."

"It's not sweetness, though you're kind to say so. It's just human decency."

She traces a finger around my collar. "I do want to go. This whole thing is an experience for me. I wonder why Lydia was at the spa. Wasn't she at the seminar?"

"She was, but we wrapped up earlier than expected."

"If I'd known, I wouldn't have bothered with the spa. I'd have come back here."

"I'm glad you went. You deserve some me time."

Rose bites her lip and sighs. "I do want to go to the dinner, but I am a tad nervous about seeing Freddie again." She looks away and sighs. "I can't deny it. It was easier planning all this when we were far away from him, but now he's close, I'm anxious."

"Aw no, beautiful." I hold her tight, tilting her chin up so she has no choice but to meet my gaze. "Let's just stay here. I don't want you to be anxious."

"No, I want to face him. I'm going to be brave." She smiles at me. "I just want you to stay with me."

"Of course I will. Where else would I go?"

"I don't know, but Freddie used to always abandon me at events. Do you remember seeing me at the Gladstone? Before you found me in the corridor? I saw you in the event room. You looked over at me."

I nod. Even then she caught my attention, but I was a married man and made sure I wasn't looking too closely. "I remember."

"That was when I was looking for him. He was always going off, leaving me to fend for myself."

"I most certainly won't be doing that. You're my girlfriend, and we'll be together all evening. If Freddie so much as breathes in your direction, I'll bring him down so fast he won't know what hit him."

"Thank you." She melts into me even more. "That makes me feel a lot better."

"Nothing's going to ruin tonight for us," I assure her, rubbing her shoulder. "We're the ones who'll spoil their evening, if anything. We'll give them plenty to talk about, that's for sure."

She smiles and kisses me on the cheek. "Yes, we will."

My breath catches as I take her in—the delicate fabric clinging to her figure, the way it accentuates her curves, the soft waves of blonde hair twisted into a messy updo. It takes every ounce of willpower not to cross the room and take her right there. She smooths the front of the dress and turns sideways in the long mirror, admiring herself.

"Do I look okay?" She has a doubtful expression.

"No, you don't." I flatten my lips to prevent myself from laughing.

Rose pulls back from the mirror, her expression falling. "I don't?"

"You don't look okay. You look bloody incredible." I move in behind her and put my arms around her. "Irresistible, in fact."

"Thank God." She grins. "You had me worried."

"You don't need to worry. I, on the other hand... Well, I'll be fighting off competition all night. Everyone's eyes will be on you."

"You think?" She worries her bottom lip between her teeth.

"I know. You could stop every heart in the room."

She blushes, and it's a sight that never fails to stir something deep within me. Crossing the room, I retrieve a small velvet box from my jacket pocket and hold it out to her.

"What's that? Are you proposing?"

I let out a short laugh. "No, not quite." I flick open the box to reveal a necklace, the diamonds catching the light and twinkling.

"Oh my God, John. You didn't have to do that. Why…? I—"

"You deserve it. It's a thank you for coming here with me. For making me feel alive again."

"I don't need thanks for that."

I take the necklace and move behind her, my fingers brushing the nape of her neck as I fasten the clasp. "It'll be like a lucky charm."

"Thank you so much." She turns to face me. "You really are too good to me."

"Nothing's too good for you." I fix my bow tie, then hold out my elbow.

Arm in arm, we head out of the room toward the elevator. We smile at each other as it descends.

We barely have a second to get out when I feel Rose tense beside me. Following her gaze, I spot Lydia and Freddie mingling among the crowd, their heads close together in conversation.

"Hey, it's okay." I give her a reassuring squeeze. "Let's keep away from them for now. If the opportunity comes up, we'll speak to them, but I'm not going to force it."

She nods, inching closer until her side is pressed firmly against mine. I drape my arm around her shoulders. Tonight, she's mine, and she's protected.

We mingle and chat with people. It's easy to introduce Rose as my girlfriend, and I don't even care about the barely disguised looks—whether sceptical or impressed, I don't care. With her at my side, I'm buoyed up. Wherever Freddie and Lydia are, I can't see them as we take our seats for dinner, so I don't let it bother me. Rose and I sit close, chatting as much to each other as to anyone else.

When the meal is done, we leave the room, heading through a grand archway into a ballroom. And that's when we see them again. Freddie and Lydia are inside already, and Freddie's gaze snaps to us as we enter. The gears turning in his brain are almost visible as he registers me. Then Rose.

"I think we've been spotted." I put my arm around her. "But we don't need to go near them."

"Let's do it." Her eyes narrow. "That's why we're here, after all. Look at his face. He can't believe it."

She has a steely expression. This must be like a virtual slap for Freddie, and she's relishing the delivery.

"Okay. If you're sure."

The hum of conversation around us fades to a dull buzz as I watch Freddie's eyes widen with the slow grind of recognition. Lydia, all poised grace next to him, follows his gaze and... there it is—the moment it clicks. Surprise flickers across her polished features like a crack in fine china, and I can't help but find a twisted satisfaction in it.

Rose's grip on my hand is vice-like, and she almost hauls me through the cluster of guests.

"Good evening." I plaster on a fake smile as we reach Freddie and Lydia. Freddie's eyes narrow first at me, then at Rose.

"What are *you* doing here?" He looks her up and down with unconcealed disdain. What a fucking prick.

"Wow, your manners leave a lot to be desired," I say quietly, but loud enough for him to hear.

Rose smiles broadly at me, then looks at Freddie. "I'm here with my new *man*." She places an emphasis on 'man', her eyes never leaving Freddie's.

"But—"

Lydia doesn't get to finish as Rose goes on. "John's a real man who knows how to treat women properly." The jab hits its mark; I can see it in the way Freddie's jaw tenses. "Unlike some people."

Lydia raises her chin and sniffs, her jaw tense as she looks from Rose to Freddie, studiously ignoring me.

"God knows what you're on about." Freddie's words are laced with venom. "You always were too immature and badly bred for me. No doubt you and your man..." He looks me up and down. "Are made for each other. Obviously you've discovered her one and only skill," he says aside to me. "She's made to suck."

I raise my eyebrows, feeling Rose's fingers tighten in mine. "Clearly, you don't know her at all. Rose has a lot more skills than that. But I'm glad she didn't waste them on you. And it's rather depressing that you decided instead of treating her right, you'd abuse her. I know all about what you did to her, Freddie. And I'd be quite happy to let everyone else know too."

Lydia's gaze darts between us, confusion morphing into concern. She obviously doesn't know his true colors, and this is as good a way as any to warn her. If he tries to deny it, I have Rose as the expert witness. I don't think Lydia, for all her faults, will ignore the testament of another woman.

"Trust me, if you ever lay a finger on Rose again—or if you go anywhere near my daughter—you won't have another second to regret it."

"John—" Lydia starts, but Freddie cuts her off.

"I'll get you back for this. Both of you."

"Try anything, and it'll be the last thing you do." I keep my arm securely around Rose and turn my back on Freddie and Lydia, leaving them together. Lydia is furiously whispering something to him.

As we weave through the clusters of guests laughing and conversing, I feel Rose melting slightly into me. The clink of glasses on a silver tray catches my attention, and Rose plucks two flutes of champagne from a waiter's grasp.

"Here." She passes one to me.

"Cheers."

Our glasses meet mid-air, the sound crisp and satisfying. "We got our sweet revenge."

"We did." I take a sip of the fizzy champagne, the bubbles tickling my throat. "And hopefully Lydia gets the message that he isn't a safe person to be around. I'd rest a lot easier if I knew there was no chance of my daughter coming in contact with him."

"That would make me happy too."

I dip in and kiss her cheek. "Let's drink to a tentative mission accomplished."

# 21

## Rose

The champagne is good. Maybe it's just the Paris effect, or maybe it's because I've finally told Freddie what I think of him. My revenge. As the adrenaline wears off, I lean into John, letting him take the weight from me.

My pulse races, and I let out a long, slow breath. I can't believe I actually got the words out, and it felt good. But something else creeps in, and I can't quite pinpoint it.

"Are you okay?" John says.

"Yeah." I chug some more champagne. "You don't think he'll really try anything, do you? To get back at us?"

"I doubt it. He's a politician. All mouth. But if you're worried about it, we'll figure out a way to keep you safely away from him." John tightens his hold on my shoulder. "He's got no power over you, not anymore. If he tries anything, I swear I'll bring him down."

"You're right. I know he loves to open his mouth and let his belly rumble. And if he does something petty like has his parents blacklist me, it's no more than I expected, anyway."

"Don't worry about that. I know just as many people as them and if they blacklist you, I'll make sure no one believes it. They'll be discrediting themselves if they try it."

"Thank you." His words comfort me, but there's still a niggling worry that I've poked a sleeping bear. "I trust you."

His eyes lock onto mine, fierce and protective. "You're safe with me. Always."

I let out a shaky breath and offer a small smile, warmth spreading through my veins.

"Let's get some air." He leads me away from the bustling energy of the room.

Tension slowly ebbs from my shoulders as we retreat to the lobby. The door beside the one we just came out of leads into the spa area. I half wish I could go back there just to lie down in some peace and quiet.

"When I was having my massage earlier, I imagined you were the one giving me it." I glance at John. "Not that it really worked. You have the magic hands."

His eyebrow arches. "Oh? What kind of massage were you getting?"

"Just a normal one. Nothing like the type I'm sure you'd give me."

He watches me for a moment, his expression hovering between amused and uncertain.

"Wait here a sec." He nods toward a plush seat in the reception area.

"Where are you going?"

"Not far. I just need to speak to the receptionist."

I perch on the edge of the seat, fiddling with the hem of my dress as he goes up to the desk and talks to the woman on duty. Before long, he's making his way back, a small grin playing on his lips.

"Come with me," he says.

"Where to?"

"For your private massage."

"My what?"

He waves a keycard in front of me. "This is the key to our own private massage room."

I let out a laugh. "How on earth did you get that?"

"Let's just say it's all about who you know." John leads the way down the dimly lit corridor, past the potted plants. We pass the now abandoned check-in desk, and John slaps the keycard to the door of the first massage room.

We slip into it, the scent of essential oils lingering in the air. This isn't the same room I was in earlier, but it's pretty much the same design with the muted natural colors, the greenery and the Venetian blinds.

"I can't believe you got us in here."

John smiles as he goes to a shelf. He fiddles with something, and ambient music plays gently through the speakers, instantly relaxing me. Then he turns to me with that look—his hungry eyes tell me he's got plans and I'm at the centre of them all.

"Come here," he murmurs, and it's not a request—it's an invitation. One I accept without hesitation. Our lips meet almost instantly, and I wrap my arms around John's neck. His hands fall on my hips, and he draws me closer. I lose myself in the heat of his lips.

Very gently he eases down the wide straps of my dress. The silk slides over my upper arms and my breasts. I wriggle it over my hips and step out of it, standing before him in just my black lace panties. His appreciative gaze travels over me as he rips off his tie and discards it. Then he tosses off his jacket and, with deliberate slowness, unbuttons his shirt.

He skims his fingertips along a shelf of small bottles of essential oils, opens one, and pours a few drops onto his hands. After replacing the bottle, he moves in close again. A dark and musky scent with a hint of jasmine curls around me. His warm palms slide over my shoulders, the slickness of the oil making every touch feel decadent. Then he trails one hand down, cupping my breast and making my breath hitch. I let out a soft moan, my back arching into his touch. His thumb brushes over my nipple, slow and deliberate, teasing it to a hardened peak. Every nerve in my body sparks to life, heat coiling low in my belly. He continues with my other breast. The air is filled with the heavily perfumed aroma.

"Lie down on the table for me." John guides me toward the massage bed. "Face down." My skin tingles all over, thrumming with need as I take my place on the plush surface. Just lying like this is relaxing, but when John's large hands touch my back, slicking the oil across me, I can't suppress a sigh. His touch is firm yet gentle, kneading away the tension in my shoulders and back, while it builds increasingly between my legs.

"Is this okay?"

I hear the smile in his voice.

"Very okay... Your hands are perfect."

He chuckles, and the sound vibrates through me. As he works his way across my shoulders and down my spine, each stroke sends sparks of pleasure dancing under my skin. Every callus on his palms, every finger pad pressing into flesh, owns me, claims me.

I close my eyes, letting myself just exist in this moment.

John replenishes the oil on his hands, then glides over the curve of my ass. His fingers gently tease my slit.

"So wet." He nudges my knees, prompting me to lift myself onto all fours, and I comply willingly, feeling the cool air of the room kiss me where the warmth of his touch had been. Freddie used to like taking me doggy style, so I'm used to it. I glance over my shoulder, watching as John's eyes darken with desire, his gaze fixed on the most intimate part of me now vulnerably presented to him.

"So perfect." He's still dressed from the waist down and doesn't seem in any rush to take off his trousers. Instead, his fingers start caressing my pussy. I drop my head to the pillow and moan as pressure coils inside me.

I twist, expecting him to slow down, to give me a breather, but he's relentless. A hand slides between my legs, then upward. He holds my ass cheeks, and he makes out with my wet cunt, sending shockwaves through my system.

"Fuck!" I can't stop myself from bucking.

The slick pressure makes my mind go completely blank, and I can't hold back, can't pretend to be anything but his.

His hand squeezes my ass, keeping me spread for him. He's ruthless and relentless, the warm wetness pushing inside, a finger flicking over my clit. I gasp and grind against him, every nerve alive and begging for more. John works me over until I am a puddle of needy, desperate sounds. I can barely breathe, barely think. My whole body is buzzing, alive, alight.

His voice rumbles against me, deep and devastating. "Don't pass out on me, Rose."

I manage a half-laugh, more breath than sound. "Your fault." I should have known he'd do this properly.

"Damn right it is."

I laugh again—giddy, breathless, buzzing. But then his mouth returns to my pussy, and my voice is a whimper, a plea, a scream. He tongue fucks me with filthy sounds and an obscene hunger that matches my own. He makes it last forever and no time at all until I can't stop. "I'm coming. Fuck. I'm coming." An orgasm, hot, long and delicious, tears through me. Stars burst around me, and I cling to the massage table.

"Fuck, John!" I cry out as waves of bliss envelop me. John strokes his hands over my back as I come down from my high, but I'm not nearly done. There's more in me, but I need him to release it. "Take me like this, please. I want you inside me."

"Greedy girl."

"You make me hungry."

"Anything for you."

I hear him taking off his trousers, then his hands are back on me, gliding over my oiled-up hips, then steadying my ass as he presses the blunt tip of his erection against my pussy. I breathe heavily as he pushes inside me, filling me deep. "Oh God. You're so big. I love it." I love *him*—though I dare not say it.

"Beautiful girl." He wraps his arms around me from behind, leaning in so I'm flush against his chest. His hands roam over my breasts, teasing my nipples. He thrusts gently inside me, hitting exactly the right spot.

Then he slides his fingers down to where our bodies are joined. He pumps harder, his pace relentless, each thrust driving deeper, stoking the fire within me. His fingers find my clit, and he taps it, circles it and rubs it while he continues to move inside me.

"Oh yes... like that." I rock my hips, meeting his with equal fervour. The delicious friction of our bodies, the way he fills me so completely, it's everything I've fantasized about and more.

He tightens his grip on me, the strength in his arms making me feel cherished and possessed. There's something raw and primal in the way we move together.

"Fuck, Rose... You're too good." His voice is strained, his breath hot against my neck, and I can tell he's close. I am too, seconds from shattering once more, ready to fall into the abyss of pleasure with him.

"Please don't stop." My entire being is focused on the exquisite sensations he's drawing out of me, a connection that runs deeper than flesh.

This is where I'm meant to be—in the arms of a man who makes me feel incredible.

The pressure builds, waves of heat increasing inside me, and John quickens his pace, his movements more urgent. Each thrust drives us higher until we're not just two bodies, but one single pulse of energy.

"Rose," he pants.

"John!" I cry out as my orgasm hits so intensely I stop breathing. I'm blinded by white light.

John bucks inside me and groans. "Fu-u-u-ck."

Gradually, the world comes back into focus, and I suddenly register the soft music still playing in the background. I stay quiet for a moment, just breathing, then John lies alongside me, and I curl into his arms.

"Did that live up to your fantasies?" he asks.

"Exceeded them by hundreds of miles."

He lets out a low chuckle. "Let's not fall asleep here. I know it would be nice just to curl up now, but we don't want to be caught here in the morning. Let's clean up and go back to the room. We might even want to try round two."

I trace a circle on his broad chest. "There's no 'might' about it."

We clean up—both each other and the room, then grab our clothes and return to our suite via the lobby, where John returns the keycard to the massage room. I'm sure the receptionist can smell the massage oil, and no doubt she can guess what we were doing, but she says nothing.

When we're back in the room, we slip between the cool sheets of the bed and sink into a long, languid kiss before we make love again, and I say make love, because that's what it feels like to me. It's soft and loving, though I still come hard. My clitoral 'workouts' have been incredible since meeting John.

Afterwards, we settle into a tight snuggle. His skin against mine is warm and reassuring. I run my fingertips up his neck and onto his cheek, where it's marked by the scars. He's never volunteered any reason for them, and I've never wanted to ask, but I'm curious. And now I trust him, I'm not afraid to know the reason.

"How did you get the scars?" I murmur, my fingers brushing lightly over his chest.

He goes still. For a moment, I think I've pushed too far, but then he exhales slowly and turns to face me, pressing a gentle kiss to my forehead.

"You don't have to tell me," I add quickly. "I just wondered... Was it a fight?"

"No." His arm tightens around me. "I thought you already knew."

"How could I?"

"I suppose you couldn't." He sighs. "It happened that night at The Gladstone. I always had it in my head that you were there, that you'd heard—but of course you wouldn't have. You'd left by then."

"What do you mean?"

"There was a fire."

"Yeah, I know."

"I went back in. People weren't taking the alarm seriously, and I was still hoping it was a false alarm. But no, the fire was real. It was in the kitchen, and a member of staff was trapped."

"Oh my God, who?"

"One of the kitchen workers." He pauses, the breath catching in his throat. "I couldn't leave her. So, I went in. Got her out—but not without... well." He gestures vaguely to the scars I've come to know so intimately.

A sharp sting rises behind my eyes. My chest tightens. I can barely speak for the rush of emotion—admiration, awe, and something deeper still. This man didn't just survive; he risked everything for someone else.

"That was so brave of you," I whisper.

"Brave or stupid, I'm not sure," he replies with a half-smile. "But she lived. That's what matters."

Exactly. The moment slices deeper, brushing the raw place inside me that never quite healed. My mother. Lost to fire when I was little. No one got to her in time. I blink hard, swallowing the lump in my throat.

"You saved someone," I say softly, my voice thick. "Not everyone gets that ending."

His brow furrows, as if he senses there's more behind my words, but I lean in, pressing my forehead to his, breathing him in. The man lying beside me bears scars, yes—but they're the kind that come from courage, from sacrifice. And suddenly, I feel even more drawn to him—wound to wound, fire to fire.

"You could've died too."

"Maybe," he says. "But dying for something worthwhile doesn't scare me as much as living, knowing I didn't even try to help her."

My breath catches. That... that hits something deep. I swallow hard, blinking at the ceiling for a second before the words come—quiet, but steady.

"My mum died in a fire."

His head turns sharply, eyes fixed on mine. I keep going, the words unspooling.

"I was ten. There was a faulty plug in the living room—we didn't even realize anything was wrong until smoke started pouring out the windows. My brother, my sister and I—we got out. Dad too. We were all standing on the street, watching the flames, screaming for Mum."

John doesn't speak, just strokes my arm gently, grounding me.

"She came out at first. But she—" I stop, swallow again. "She went back in to get the dog. We watched her go back inside."

The silence that follows is heavy as I try to find the words to explain the memories I've kept squashed for so long.

"She never came out again."

Tears prick my eyes, but I blink them back. I don't cry about this. Not usually. But with him, lying warm and steady beside me, it's different. Safe.

"I always wondered if she regretted it, even for a second. If she knew it was a mistake and tried to turn back. But we never saw her again. Just... smoke."

John pulls me closer, his hand cradling the back of my head as if shielding me from the memory.

"Christ, Rose. This is awful. I'm so sorry."

"I've pretty much blanked it out. I don't really tell anyone. The last person I told was Freddie, and he didn't even care. He just brushed it off, so I did too."

John keeps me close. "Talk to me whenever you need to. It's not something you have to hide. Your mum was brave," he says softly. "Just like you."

A small, broken laugh escapes me. "I'm not brave."

"You are. You've lived through that. And you're still here. Still standing. Your mum didn't make it, but she was doing what she thought was right."

"I know." I press my face into his shoulder, letting his quiet strength hold me. "I just wish she'd cared more for us than our dog. Though we were all screaming about him being stuck. I guess she just thought she would grab him and get out again."

"Adrenaline pushes you to do crazy things. I went in to save the woman in the kitchen without thinking about how my daughter would survive if I didn't come out again."

He rubs my shoulder gently. Maybe he's right. Maybe surviving is its own kind of courage. I nestle closer, the heat of his body a soft cocoon of comfort. All this time, part of me feared that his past was shadowed with something dark, something he might be trying to escape from. But now, knowing the truth, I see him in a different light.

He's so much more than just a businessman, a father, or a lover. He's brave and selfless. I lean up and press a soft kiss to his lips.

He returns it with a depth that's like a balm to my soul. "If you want to talk about this, now or ever, I'm here."

As I settle into his embrace, I feel safe, cherished, and utterly connected to this man. It's a sensation that's both new and intoxicating.

His hand finds mine, fingers intertwining as if to say without words that we're in this together. As I close my eyes, listening to the steady beat of his heart, I no longer feel the need to hide any part of myself from him. I only wish I could stay like this forever.

# 22
## *Rose*

I trudge through the fallen leaves that have made their home on the gravel path leading up to The Lodge at Ardencairn and pull my scarf tighter. It's November, so the weather doesn't surprise me, though it's chilly enough to take my breath away, freezing my lungs every time I breathe in. Maybe it's not only the weather numbing my bones. My survival instincts have kicked in. This is my last day cleaning here. Weird to think I've been to Paris and back since this time last week. But that's done. Now I'm just the cleaner with a job to do. I don't want to make this weird for John—bad enough I spilled my history to him, though I can't fault how understanding about it he's been.

We both knew the deal from the start, and I don't want to be the one who changes it now.

The house is quiet when I go in. That's nothing new. John is often in his study when I arrive, but something about the stillness makes me shiver. This house has always weirded me out. Its odd design makes it like a rabbit warren, and no matter how much I scrub it, it always feels dingy. Shame John can't get the planning consent he needs to alter the building. I can fully understand why he'd like to rip it down. It sucks that anyone would want to keep a place like this. It's hardly a historical masterpiece.

"Hello?" My voice echoes through the empty hall. John's study door is closed, and it doesn't open. Maybe he doesn't want to be disturbed.

I set to work. No point putting it off. That's why I'm officially here. I'm just the maid. I have no claim on this house or its owner. A bang from somewhere in the house makes me jump, and I almost drop the cloth I'm wiping the surfaces with. John is talking, and it sounds like he's upstairs. Is someone up there with him?

My brain plays hundreds of scenarios before I can stop it. Nearly all of them involve John and other women. But do I have a right to complain? I'm not really his girlfriend. If he's got company, then that's his business. My heart hasn't got the memo though. It sags and hurts like hell.

A moment later, the kitchen door opens, and he comes in. "Morning." His greeting is warm, but there's tension in his frame, like something's bothering him.

"Hey. Is everything okay? I heard a noise upstairs? Were you talking to someone?"

"Yeah." He runs his hand through his hair. "Isabel's not feeling well, so she's off school. I shut one of the doors and it slammed louder than I meant to. I was just apologizing to her."

"Ah, I see." My heart has suddenly leapt. That's so much better than the thoughts I was having—not that I wish the poor girl to be ill. "Can I go and see her? I mean, if you're working, she might want company. Or is she asleep?"

"She's wide awake, and I'm sure she'd love the company. I told her to rest, but I imagine she'll be up playing with her toys already."

"I won't let it interfere with the cleaning, but I'll duck in and see her."

He smiles and watches me. "I don't care if you ditch the cleaning. I'd rather my daughter had your attention. You're exactly the kind of loving friend she needs right now."

Loving friend. If I'm honest, I'd like to be a lot more to John than a loving friend to his daughter, but I'll take it.

"Before you go..." He pauses, his fingers drumming against the countertop. "I need to tell you something."

"Okay." I press my lips together. This sounds ominous.

"I understand this is your last week here." He clears his throat, avoiding my gaze for a split second before meeting it again. "The other cleaner is coming back. You won't be doing Ardencairn anymore. I just had a confirmation email from your boss."

"Yeah. I know." I nod, trying to mask the pain knifing through me.

"I think... Well, given the circumstances..." His voice is soft enough to lift my spirits a notch. "I—"

"Daddy!" a voice yells from upstairs.

John lets out a faint sigh and steps into the hallway. "Coming in a second."

"Should I go?"

"You can. If you really don't mind."

"Of course I don't." I smile at him, and I know what he's thinking—how carefree we felt in Paris. How natural and easy. Not this odd, strained sensation.

"Thank you." He nods and puts his warm palm on my shoulder as he passes. For a moment, we catch each other's eye and my heart trembles, aching to be close to his. Where it belongs—right beside him.

But Isabel is the priority just now. I only met her that one time before. And I promised I'd play with her sometime. Maybe this is the day, though perhaps she shouldn't be playing if she's ill.

At Isabel's door, I knock softly. Her room is dim, curtains drawn, and she's sitting up in bed, frowning.

"Hey." I smile as I peer inside. "Do you remember me? I'm Rose."

Her frown disappears almost straight away, and she smiles. "I remember you. You're Daddy's friend."

It's my turn to frown. Is that what John told her? Or is she just forgetful of my role?

"Yeah." No point in arguing or trying to explain myself. "How are you feeling?"

"I've got a cough." She demonstrates with a very unconvincing one. "And Daddy says I have a temperature, so I had the yucky medicine."

"Ooh, I like it. I still take it when I get a sore head. It's much nicer than pills."

"But you're a grown-up. You're not allowed."

I chuckle. "That's the fun of being a grown-up. You can do that kind of thing if you want."

"That's naughty." She grins. "You better not drink my medicine."

"I won't. Do you still feel too hot?"

"No. Just hungry... and bored."

I settle onto the edge of Isabel's bed. "Well, I could get you something to eat and then maybe we could play something quiet—or I could read you some stories."

"Okay. I'm not *that* hungry. Maybe I could have a story first."

"Of course you could. Which story would you like?"

"On my shelf there's the one about the little bear who doesn't like the dark. That's my favorite one."

I head over to the shelf and lift it up. It's obviously a favorite, as it's well-thumbed. She shuffles across the bed to make room, and I sit in beside her. As I open the first page, she leans her head on my arm. She's so openly trusting and loving. It reminds me of John. He's obviously more guarded initially, but once you're in, he has so much love to give... Though it's not for me. And I need to remember that. It's odd to think this little one is also part of Lydia. She looks a lot like her, but from what I can see, she seems far warmer.

"The darkness all around," I say in my best baby bear voice.

Isabel listens intently, occasionally pointing something out in the pictures—which really are very cute. When it's done, I close the book and look down at her.

"Will you still come visit, even if you're not cleaning here anymore? Daddy said this was your last week here."

The question stings, reminding me of what I'm losing. "Maybe. I don't really know yet."

"Why not?" She settles back into her pillows with a sigh.

"Well, I'll have to work somewhere else."

"But if your daddy's friend, won't you—"

"Hello ladies."

We both look around to see John leaning against the doorframe, arms folded, watching us. There's warmth in his eyes, almost to the point of being fiery.

"How's my little invalid?" He raises an eyebrow at Isabel.

"Okay now. Can I play?"

"I suppose so. Just don't make too much of a mess."

"And can you play with me, Rose?"

"For twenty minutes. Then I should do some cleaning. Is that fair?"

"Yep." Isabel throws off her cover and jumps out of bed, looking as fresh as a daisy and not at all unwell. I catch John's eye.

"Thank you," he mouths silently.

A wave of affection crashes over me, and I nod, sending him a smile of my own. He gives me the tiniest of winks as he retreats from the room.

I move onto the floor and sit with my legs crossed as Isabel digs out a box of dolls. I start dressing one, trying to keep my mind here and not chasing John. But it's not easy. We're in some weird limbo, and I don't like it. Not one bit.

# 23

## *John*

The clock on the kitchen wall tells me it's creeping toward six in the evening. The day's been long, and Rose is still here. She doesn't need to be. I told her I was happy for her to leave the cleaning for the day and spend it with Isabel, but she's still working, perhaps making up for the time she spent with my daughter.

"Rose." I head into the living room. "You don't need to do this."

"I know." Her eyebrows lift, and she smiles at me. "But it's not like I have anything else that pressing to go home to. I'm happy being here with you."

"Then put the duster away. Come and have some dinner. Stay if you want." I keep it casual, though my pulse kicks up a notch.

Her lips part before she nods. "I'd like that... but... is it sensible?"

"Probably not." I rub the back of my neck. "But you only have a short time left here and—"

"I know. And I want to stay. Isabel's great." Rose smiles, and something warm uncurls in my chest. I'm not sure if she mentioned her just to change the subject or if liking Isabel is related to her wanting to stay, but either way, I'm happy she is.

"You've definitely made her feel better. She's just finishing watching an episode of that strange TV show she likes, and then she's coming for food. Come and join us."

There's no harm in that. Isabel likes Rose and is probably too young still to make too much out of it... Though I don't think I want her to know that Rose is sleeping over—in my bed.

Rose tucks a loose strand of hair behind her ear. "Can I help with anything?" She follows me into the kitchen. "I might be an epic kitchen maid, but I'm not a chef. Still, I'm willing to give it a go though—if you want to risk it."

"Let's not," I say. "You relax. I've got this in hand."

She tugs the clip from her hair that's keeping it in the messy updo and shakes her head about, freeing her mane of blonde locks. My hand freezes at the oven door and my eyes drink in just how beautiful she is.

Isabel saunters in behind Rose and I force my eyes back to the oven.

"You're still here," Isabel says to Rose.

"Yeah. I'm staying for dinner."

"Cool." Isabel grabs her around the waist and hugs her. She's always been an affectionate girl. Yet another reason for me to want to make sure Freddie is kept far from her. I hate to think of my beautiful little girl trying to win his affection, and what his reaction might be.

"Right, let's sit, my beauties."

Isabel giggles and looks at Rose. "If we're beauties, he's the beast."

"He certainly is." Rose waggles her eyebrows at me.

"Not funny." I put the steaming casserole dish on the table. A while back, I might have felt sensitive about being called that after what happened to my face, but I know what Rose is driving at. And how can I deny it? She brings out the animal in me, making me want to ravish her.

As we eat, the conversation flows. Isabel chatters about her school friends and the bizarre shows she watches—though Rose seems to agree with her taste. I'm sidelined as they discuss characters I've never even heard of before, but I don't mind. It makes my chest swell to see them getting on like this.

"Rose," Isabel pipes up as she scoops the last of her pudding, "will you read my story tonight before bed? You can help me read my new books. Dad won't like them."

"Of course, I'd love to," Rose answers.

"Why won't I like them?" I raise an eyebrow at my daughter.

"You know," Isabel giggles. "They have kissing parts."

"Do they?" I frown at her. "And are you sure these books are appropriate for your age?"

"Yes, Dad." She rolls her eyes. "Everyone in the class reads them, but I need help with some of the words."

"I can do that." Rose smiles at her. "Girlie book club it is."

"And you can tell me if it's appropriate after." I raise my brows at her.

She and Isabel look at each other and smirk.

I clear up while Rose goes upstairs with Isabel. Sounds like Isabel is doing a fashion show. "Remember to have a shower," I call up the stairs.

When I head up some forty minutes later, I lean on Isabel's bedroom doorframe, watching Rose and Isabel sitting on the bed with their noses in a book. Rose has changed into a casual sweater and jeans—I assume they were in her backpack. Her head is close to Isabel's as she reads aloud, getting almost every word right. If she stumbles, Rose helps her.

I leave them to it, going into my room and dressing in my sweatpants and a t-shirt. Before I shut the curtains, I look into the darkness beyond. Lights twinkle all over the estate, and usually I draw comfort from them, but there's an uneasiness on me that I can't quite explain.

The muffled sound of Isabel and Rose chatting settles me for a moment, and my mind races ahead, taking a path into an unseen future. My heart warms at the thought that this could be normal life for me and not just a few days of stolen pleasure.

Rose pokes her head around the door a few moments later. "Isabel is looking for a goodnight kiss."

"Okay."

"And so am I," she says as I pass.

"You'll have to wait until later."

I go to Isabel and sit with her, cuddling her and letting her chatter. She's a good kid for going to sleep early and not making a fuss. She's always been an early riser no matter when she goes to bed, so getting her down nice and early makes sense, especially as she's possibly still not a hundred percent well yet.

"Good night, my love." I kiss her forehead and pull her covers over her. She already looks sleepy and content as I back out of the room and close the door.

When I get back to my room, Rose is sitting on the bed. "Hey." She smiles at me. "Everything okay?"

"Yeah." I run my hand through my hair. "I always feel a bit strange leaving her in her room like that."

"What do you mean?"

"I don't know exactly. It's hard to explain. It just feels wrong leaving your kids to fend for themselves overnight. My instinct is that she should be here with me, so I can fight the monsters if she needs me to."

"You're so cute." Rose gets off the bed, comes over and wraps her arms around my neck. "But think of all the things we couldn't do if Isabel was in here."

"Yes, that's true." All my senses home in on her. Her floral scent fills my nostrils, and her soft curves press eagerly against my body, igniting a surge of desire low in my belly.

My hands roam over her back, her waist, her hips, relishing the feel of her feminine form through the layers of her clothes. I ache to explore every inch of her creamy skin, to touch and taste her most intimate places until she writhes in ecstasy again. The days of these guilty pleasures are numbered, so I need to take my time and savour each moment.

Rose's slender fingers thread through my hair, tugging me even closer as her tongue tangles with mine. I groan low in my throat as arousal pulses through my veins.

We stumble further into the room, arms wrapped tightly around each other, bodies straining to get closer. My knees hit the edge of the king-sized bed, but I barely register it, too lost in the heat of Rose's mouth, the scent of her skin, the maddening friction as she rubs against me.

"I want you," she whimpers between deep, drugging kisses. "I need you." Her smoky eyes blaze with blatant need.

"I'm yours," I rasp, my voice rough with lust. "Every inch of me." My hands tremble slightly as I reach for the hem of Rose's soft sweater.

Slowly, reverently, I peel it up and over her head, unveiling the red lace of her bra. She takes my breath away.

Her hair tumbles around her flushed face in tousled waves, and her eyes glitter with unmistakable desire. "This needs to come off." She plucks at my t-shirt.

I grin and whip it off in one swift motion, tossing it aside carelessly. "Better?"

She lets her hungry gaze roam over my bare chest and abs. "Much," she purrs appreciatively, trailing her fingertips over my heated skin. I shudder at her feather-light touch.

Impatient now, I pop the button on her jeans and lower the zipper tooth by tooth. Rose wriggles her hips to help me shimmy the jeans down her slender legs. Christ, she's a vision in just her matching panties and bra—all creamy expanses of soft skin and womanly curves that I can't wait to map with my hands and mouth. I'll never tire of them.

"Stunning," I murmur, drinking her in. "Absolutely bloody gorgeous."

Color blooms across her cheeks at the compliment. Emboldened, she hooks her fingers in the waistband of my loungers and slides them over my hips. My cock is throbbing and bulging against my boxer-briefs.

I pull Rose closer, groaning at the exquisite feel of all her bare skin finally pressed against mine. I crash my mouth to hers, our tongues meeting in a feverish tangle. Her nails score lightly down my back, urging me closer.

Rolling my hips, I grind my painfully hard erection against her core, the friction sparking jolts of electricity through my body. Rose whimpers into my mouth and arches up to meet my thrusts, her breathing ragged.

"Please." She runs her hands over the bulge in my boxers. "I need to feel all of you."

I unclasp her bra and slide it down her arms, my mouth going dry at the unveiling of her perfect breasts. Dusky pink nipples pucker for my attention. I palm the supple mounds, flicking my thumbs over the sensitive peaks until Rose cries out sharply.

She fumbles with my boxer briefs, shoving them down impatiently. I do the same with her panties, leaving us finally, blissfully naked. Skin against skin. Nothing between us but heat and yearning.

Rose draws my face to hers, her lips a hairsbreadth from mine. "You're so fucking hot," she breathes.

I pick her up and gently toss her onto the bed, her golden hair fanning out around her like a halo. "You're the hot one, beautiful."

She looks up at me with her captivating green eyes, equal parts trusting and hungry. I'm nearly undone at the sight of her spread out before me, ready and wanting.

I press slow, worshipful kisses along the elegant line of her neck, across the delicate bones of her shoulders, and over the full contours of her breasts. Then, I take one pebbled nipple into my mouth, my tongue coaxing a shiver from her. She fists her hands in my hair.

"Oh, God," she mewls, arching into my touch. "Lower..."

I rub my palms over her skin, relishing her abandon. "I want to worship every inch of you."

But I oblige, blazing a path of open-mouthed kisses down her quivering belly. I nip playfully at her hipbones before settling between her parted thighs. The scent of her arousal floods my senses, heady and intoxicating.

"Christ, you're so wet for me already," I groan appreciatively. Rose's skin blooms with color. "Good girl."

I lift her hips and bury my face in her glistening folds, lapping at her essence like a man starved. Rose nearly bucks off the bed, a strangled cry tearing from her throat. I grip her hips firmly, holding her in place as I feast on her honeyed flesh.

I alternate long, bold strokes of my tongue with teasing flicks over her swollen clit, stoking the fire in her veins. Rose is moaning brokenly, her thighs trembling around my head. Liquid heat coats my chin as I delve deeper, thrusting my tongue inside her channel.

"Oh God, John, don't stop!" She grabs fistfuls of the duvet. "I'm so close..."

I lie her flat on the bed, shuffling back, and double my efforts, sealing my lips around her clit and suckling hard. At the same time, I thrust two fingers knuckle-deep into her molten core, curling them just so. Rose shatters with a wordless scream, her walls clamping down on my digits as I work her through her release.

Gradually, her spasms subside, and she collapses bonelessly into the mattress. I crawl back up her body, and she makes a contented humming noise and drapes her arms around my neck, drawing me down into a warm, languid kiss.

She licks her own taste from my tongue, sighing into my mouth. "That was incredible," she murmurs dreamily. "You just keep doing what no one's ever done before."

My heart swells with masculine pride, but also with a profound sense of connection. Loving Rose is about so much more than physical pleasure; it's a deep merging of minds, bodies and souls.

"You're exquisite," I breathe against her lips.

Rose smiles, her eyes luminous. "We're good together."

"That we are." We lose ourselves in slow, sensual kisses, hands roaming and caressing as the embers reignite into flames. And though I'm painfully hard and aching to be inside her, I don't want to rush.

"I need you," Rose moans, her hips grinding against my erection. "Now. I want to feel you inside me."

"God, Rose, I need you too," I groan, my control slipping. "Tonight is all about you. Whatever you want, it's yours."

Her eyes flash with mischief as she pushes me onto my back, straddling my hips. "Then lie back and enjoy the show, Mr Knighton."

She moves down my body and takes my cock in her warm, wet mouth, her tongue swirling around the tip before she takes me deeper. I grip the sheets as she bobs her head, her hair spilling around us like a silken curtain. Her green eyes sparkle, and she lowers her mouth even further, until I'm practically in her throat.

"Fuck," I gasp, my toes curling. "That's deep. Slow down a bit, beautiful."

She lets me pop out of her mouth. "Oh, I think not," she purrs, her voice husky. "I want to make you feel as good as you just made me feel."

And, bloody hell, does she? She takes me back into her mouth, this time slower, her lips sliding along my length, her tongue flicking over the weeping head of my dick. My hips buck involuntarily as she teases and torments me with her mouth. I'm on the precipice of losing control when she pulls back, and I let out a groan of protest.

"I can't take it anymore. I need to be inside you."

She grins, a devious glint in her eyes. "Okay, let's have some fun."

Rose straddles me, her slick folds teasingly close to my aching cock. My hands find her hips as she eases herself onto me, using her hand to guide me inside. "Fuck." I inhale as she takes all of me and gyrates like she's dancing. Her hands go to her hair, and she tosses it out, her beautiful breasts peaking before her. I raise my hands and touch them, eliciting a moan from her.

Then she starts to move. Every rock of her body sends shivers up my spine; every roll of her hips has my heart racing faster. She rides me like a pro, grinding down on me like she's desperate... And maybe she is. I know I am.

"I need to come again." She moves even faster, rubbing her clit against my pubic bone. "With you inside me this time."

"Look at me," I urge, and when she does, I see the need in her eyes.

I sit up so we're close. It's intimate. And I like it. Our hips start to rock in a slow, sensual rhythm, each thrust a deliberate invitation to linger in this moment. Rose's nails rake delicious trails of fire down my back, urging me on as she moans my name like a prayer. I bury my head in her shoulder as I thrust deeper.

Her scent, a heady mix of passion and sweet perfume, fills my senses, intoxicating me, as her breasts press against my chest, nipples hard and peaked.

"Oh, God, John," she pants, her nails digging into my back. "I-I'm so close. I need you to kiss me."

My mouth touches hers, and our tongues mate as I deliver further deep thrusts.

"Oh, help, I'm—" She breathes into the kiss, then cries out and spasms around me as her climax hits. Her body tenses, and she shudders uncontrollably, but her eyes are still on me.

"Oh, fuck!" I follow her over the precipice, a powerful orgasm ripping through me and I spill deep inside her. For a moment, we're still, letting all the aftershocks subside. I hold her close, then we collapse together, her on top of me, both of us panting and spent.

She makes a whimpering sound. "Will you spoon me?"

"Sure."

She rolls onto her side, and I snuggle in close behind her, moulding my body to the curve of her back. The silky warmth of her bare skin pressed against mine from head to toe is pure bliss. I nuzzle into the nape of her neck, breathing in the floral scent of her hair.

She sighs contentedly and wriggles her bottom against my now semi hard dick. I don't think it ever goes down fully when she's near. "Mmm, are you ready for round two already?" She reaches back to stroke my hip.

"I always want you." I nibble the sensitive spot below her ear. "But this is still the aftermath. And I'm happy just holding you like this. Being close to you."

"Me too," she whispers with a contented sigh. "Would you... um..."

I wait for her to finish, but she doesn't. "Would I what?"

"I just wondered if you'd put yourself back inside me? I want to fall asleep still connected to you."

Wow, no one's ever asked me to do that before. My heart swells with emotion. "Sure." I position myself at her slick entrance from behind. "There's nowhere else I'd rather be."

Slowly, I push forward, gliding into her welcoming heat until I'm buried to the hilt, our bodies joined as one. We both release shuddering sighs at the exquisite sensation. I wrap my arms securely around her, one hand splayed across her stomach, the other seeking out her fingers and interlacing them with my own.

Cocooned in our embrace, I've never felt such profound peace and belonging. The rest of the world falls away until we're the only two people in existence. As Rose's breathing deepens and evens out, I allow my own eyes to drift shut, lulled by the hypnotic rhythm of her heartbeat against my chest.

Confident she's asleep, I press a featherlight kiss to her temple and whisper my deepest secret into her hair. "I love you, Rose. You really were made for me." This bone-deep feeling of utter rightness tells me so. But if I want to keep her with me, I have to summon the courage to tell her while she's awake... and brave her response.

# 24

## *John*

The bed is empty; the space beside me cold where Rose should be. I reach out, half hoping to find her still there, but my hand meets only the rumpled sheets.

Where is she? Has she just gone to the bathroom? Or has she run out of my life? That's not a scenario I want to find myself in—not yet. If she wants to leave, we'll do it properly and not before I've put some cards on the table.

The faint sound of movement downstairs makes me sit up. It could be Isabel. She always gets up early, but hopefully it's Rose.

I throw on a pair of sweats and a t-shirt.

"Daddy..." Isabel's voice calls from her bedroom door.

"Morning." I cross the hallway to her. "Are you okay? Feeling better?"

"I've still got a sore ear and a cough." She fakes a little cough to prove her point.

"Well, you can stay home with me again until you're better. We don't want you spreading bugs around the school. You're going back to Mummy's later. I'll message her and tell her you're here and not at school."

"Is Rose still here?" she asks.

"I... Um... It's her day cleaning Uncle Jamie's." Which makes sense now as to why she's up. She's got a real sense of duty.

"But why does she have to go?" Isabel pouts, her chin jutting out stubbornly.

"Because Jamie's house won't clean itself." Though inwardly I feel exactly the same as Isabel.

"Can't she just stay here? With us?"

"That would be nice, but I'm not sure. She was only helping out while our regular cleaner was recovering from a broken ankle."

Isabel looks down, kicking at the carpet with her toes. "But I want her to stay."

I squat down to her level, meeting her gaze. "I know you do. And maybe... maybe she will come around again, yeah?"

"Just as our friend?" There's a glimmer of hope in those bright blue eyes.

"Can't promise, sweetheart. But we can ask her next time we see her, okay?"

"Okay," she concedes, wrapping her arms around my neck for a hug. "I'll miss her."

"Me too," I confess into her hair, the scent of strawberries reminding me of Rose's shampoo. "Breakfast? Are you well enough to eat?"

"Yes."

Any faint hope of Rose still being about are extinguished when my phone buzzes, and I see a message from her.

*Thanks for last night. At Jamie's today. See you tomorrow for my last day. :( XX*

"Are you okay, Daddy?" Isabel gazes up at me.

"Yeah, yeah. Fine." I force a smile as I usher her toward the table. "Now, what's it going to be—pancakes or cereal?"

"Pancakes!"

"Good choice." I set to work on breakfast, focusing on the task at hand rather than the absence of the woman who has taken up residence in my heart.

Isabel doesn't seem too ill, but a day off school won't harm her. She's clingy though, wanting my attention, so there's no point in trying to get any work done. She's more important. So I spend the day cuddled up on the couch with her, watching her girly shows on TV, reading and playing board games with her. I arranged with Lydia for her to pick her up here later, though I'm not relishing the prospect of seeing my ex.

She arrives half an hour before we arranged. When the doorbell goes, I expect a delivery driver, so it's a shock when I open the door to see Lydia.

"You're early."

Before Lydia can answer, Isabel barrels into her. "Mummy!"

Lydia raises an eyebrow. "You don't look ill to me."

"She's a lot better now. But she's been very tired for the past few days. I think the bug has sapped her of energy."

"And no doubt you've got it back just in time for me." Lydia gives her a long-suffering look. "Why don't you run up and get your stuff? I need to speak to Daddy for a minute."

I fold my arms. This sounds ominous—no doubt she's going to berate me for keeping Isabel off school when she seems fine now.

Isabel dashes upstairs, and Lydia comes into the hall, fidgeting with her fingers and looking around with a slight frown. She never liked this house—something we had in common. She got fed-up waiting for the planning consent. And with hindsight, I should have had the whole place redecorated instead of holding out for something that might never happen.

"What do you want to talk to me about?"

She hesitates, then looks up at me. "I've left Freddie."

"Have you?" I raise an eyebrow. Whatever I expected her to say, it certainly wasn't that.

"Look, I know I've made mistakes." Her eyes search mine. "But Freddie... he was manipulating me. The claims I made on the hotels, they were his idea. His way of keeping control over me."

I nod slowly. "That's what I thought, but I was quite sure you wouldn't have believed me if I suggested it."

"Yes." She twists her fingers together. "He's a manipulator, and I'm really mad at myself for being taken in." She rubs her forehead and sighs. "I'm dropping all claims for part of the business. I want to start over. For Isabel's sake."

"Lydia, if this is one of your games—"

"It's not a game." A rare hint of desperation underscores her plea. "I just... I want to make things right. Freddie isn't a safe person to be with. I see that now. I've made some bad choices, and I need to deal with them."

I study her for a moment, searching her face. There's an openness to her posture that's unfamiliar, and the usual sharpness in her eyes is dulled by what seems to be genuine regret.

"Okay. I'll get in touch with my lawyer. He'll let me know what to do next."

"I'll tell mine to drop all claims on the divorce papers and we can go ahead with it directly."

"Good." My shoulders feel lighter knowing that Freddie won't be around Isabel anymore.

We stand in silence for a moment as we wait for Isabel to return. Moments later, she bounds down the stairs with her bag. I give her a hug, holding her tight and kissing her forehead.

"See you soon, my darling."

"Bye-bye, Daddy."

I watch the car pull away, Lydia at the wheel and Isabel waving from the passenger seat until they disappear around the bend. I'm still processing the bombshell Lydia dropped about Freddie and the hotels. A weight's been lifted off my shoulders, but I'm not getting the closure I was sure such a moment would bring. Maybe it'll take time—or maybe it's an unrelated issue causing the disquiet in my chest.

Rose.

I need to sort things out with her. She'll be happy to know this news about Freddie being out of the picture. I can start there.

Pulling out my phone, I tap out a message to her.

*Guess what? Lydia's dumped Freddie! She's come to her senses. And not only that, she's dropped the hotel claims. She said it was all Freddie's doing. It's such a relief. Hopefully we're shot of him for good.*

My thumb hovers over the 'send' button, and I can't help but smile. This impulse to reach out to Rose first, even before my family, tells me so much about how important she is to me. I hit send and lean against the doorframe.

I'm still grinning when the phone buzzes with her reply.

*Seriously? That's incredible news! So happy for you, John!*

I start to type back, then pause. A slow warmth spreads through me, not just from her words, but from the realization of their significance. She's the first person I wanted to share this with, the first person who came to mind in my moment of relief.

Message gone, I pocket my phone and head inside, feeling lighter than I have in weeks. But my mum and brother should hear the news too—directly from me rather than through the grapevine. I call Mum first, and she answers after a couple of rings.

"John, dear, is everything alright?"

"Better than alright, Mum," I say, unable to hide the cheer in my voice. "Lydia's dropped the legal stuff about the hotels. It's all over."

There's a sharp intake of breath on the other end. "Oh, thank goodness. That must be such a relief for you."

"It is. It really is." After I've chatted with Mum, I call Jamie and let him know. I'm so lightheaded, it makes me a little giddy. But there's unfinished business with Rose. And really, the only person who can finish it is me. I have to decide where I want things to go.

Freddie's gone. Lydia has withdrawn her claim.

Rose and I don't need revenge anymore. Really, was it ever about revenge? Maybe in the beginning. But most of it was about us. And it still is. All those times we were 'pretending' weren't pretend at all. I've never felt this real about anyone.

Christ, my divorce isn't even settled, and I swore to myself I wouldn't get into any more entanglements—but how can I ignore this? This feels more genuine than anything in my life. The timing is shit, but if I don't act, I could lose one of the most precious people in my life.

Rose Darwin.

"Fuck," I whisper to the empty room, a crooked smile curving my lips. I've fallen for her utterly and completely.

There's no going back now, and I don't intend to.

# 25

## *Rose*

I swipe the last speck of dust from the ugly sideboard in the hallway at Ardencairn. This place is stuck in a time warp—and not a good one. I get John's frustration with it, but I think he'd do well to modernize some of the furniture even if he can't replace the building. My heart twinges as I realize this might be the final time I see this place.

It's my last day.

Doing the job I'm paid to do is what I have to focus on, but it feels pointless. I could just throw this duster away and walk out. Why am I bothering?

Cleaning is hard work for lousy pay, and the only reason I've enjoyed this job so much is John. Just getting to be with him has kept me going. Wherever I'm sent next will never be as good. And I've heard nothing back about the jobs I applied for. Guess they don't want someone with nothing much on their CV—or Freddie and his parents have found a way to blacklist my name after all.

"Good afternoon."

I jump at the sound of John's low voice. Where did he spring from, and how long has he been standing there? My instinct is to go to him and curl into his embrace, but I can't do that. I need to put distance between us—start training myself to live without him. I haven't seen him all day, but I wasn't expecting to as he messaged me to say he was at a meeting with his lawyer. I didn't hear him coming back. If he'd parked at the front like guests, I would have heard his car, but he usually goes around the back and comes in that way.

"Hi."

He steps closer, hands buried deep in his trouser pockets. His eyes search mine, filled with something raw and unspoken.

"Have you had a good day?"

I give a little shrug.

"How are you feeling?" He cocks his head a little.

"How do you think?" My fingers fiddle with a rogue strand of hair that's slipped from my updo. "It's not like last days are ever that great. And this one... well..." If he doesn't know, I'm not going to tell him. Let's not complicate things anymore. I get that he's not a mind reader, but I've sent signals that are loud and clear.

"Look, let's not talk about endings, okay?" He reaches out, tucking the stray strand of hair behind my ear. His touch sends shivers down my spine, igniting hope where I thought none was left.

"But that's what it is," I breathe out, allowing myself to lean into his hand for just a second before pulling away. "I'm finished here."

"And is that... well, is it really what you want?"

"Don't you?"

His beautiful eyes link with mine. "Not really. If I had my way, I wouldn't let you leave. But you're a free woman. You're young, you have an exciting road ahead. I'm not sure you'd want me in your plans."

"But..." My throat tightens, words sticking behind a dam of emotions.

"I've fallen in love with you, Rose." His words send pleasurable tingles to every nerve end. "I never expected to feel this way again. Truth be told, I never expected to feel this way, period. Because what I feel for you is so strong. But I'm well aware I'm overstepping. I just don't want you to leave without me at least telling you and putting the cards on the table. Whatever your feelings and wishes are, I'll accept them. No questions."

"Love?" I repeat. John loves me?

"Completely and utterly." He steps even closer. "That's how I feel. I'm fully aware you might not return it."

"Of course I do." Warmth floods through me.

"You do?" His eyes widen like he's surprised to hear it.

"Yes." Tears well in my eyes. "You're exactly what I want."

A smile grows on his lips. "I can hardly believe it." His voice is a little hoarse. "Of course I hoped. Everything we went through together. It felt so real, but I didn't want to presume."

"Same. I thought you were done with relationships."

"I was. I never expected to find someone I cared for this much." He opens his arms, and I fall into them, into the place I belong and feel so safe and happy.

"But what about your family? What if they don't accept me?"

"Isabel adores you." He strokes my hair. "Jamie won't mind. He never interferes in relationships."

"But your mother?"

"Yeah, she'll be less than delighted at first." He huffs a little laugh. "But she wants me to be happy. And she's smart enough to see you make me happier than I've been in years. She'll come around."

"Really?" I peer up at him.

"Trust me." His hold on me increases and really, I don't trust anyone as much as him.

"We'll face whatever comes together."

"Okay." I lean into his touch. "Together."

His arms circle me, strong and sure, pulling me against the solid plane of his chest and he places a soft kiss on my forehead.

I look up and smile. I'll never tire of looking into his beautiful eyes. "You're mine now, Mr Knighton."

"I certainly am." His lips touch mine, soft and addictive. I join him, opening my mouth to him and letting our tongues touch. An electric current zips through me at the contact.

"More than okay." I tug him closer. All I want is to drown in the feel of him, in the reality that John wants me.

He yanks me flush against him, and I fist my hands in his shirt and hold on, my body melting into his solid frame.

Every touch is electric, his fingers igniting my nerve ends as they skim under the hem of my work tunic. My skin prickles with goosebumps, and I shiver, my nipples pebbling against the lace of my bra. I arch into him, craving more contact, needing to feel his hands on me properly.

Heat floods my core as John slides a thigh between my legs, grinding against me. I whimper and rock my hips, the delicious friction sending sparks of pleasure radiating out to my fingertips. It builds and builds until I'm enveloped in the inferno, surrounded by the scent of his cologne and the heat of his body against mine.

He leads me backwards until the backs of my knees hit the couch. With a gentle push, he urges me to sit. I sink into the plush cushions, my heart pounding in anticipation as he kneels between my parted thighs. His fingers find the waistband of my black work trousers. I lift my hips as he drags the trousers off and peels them down my legs with deliberate slowness, his knuckles grazing my skin and making me shiver.

Cool air washes over my heated flesh as he removes the trousers completely, leaving me in just my black lace panties. The damp patch at the apex of my thighs is unmistakable. John's eyes darken at the sight. He hooks a finger into the fabric and tugs it to the side, baring me to his hungry gaze.

"Love how wet you are already."

Then his mouth is on me, and I lose the ability to think, to breathe. His tongue delves between my folds, circling my clit with teasing flicks before suckling the sensitive nub. Two thick fingers press inside, curling to hit that spot that makes me see stars. He pumps them in and out, fucking me with his hand as he devours me.

It's almost too much. The filthy sounds of his lapping and sucking fill the room, mingling with my needy whimpers. My whole body is on fire, quivering as he stokes my arousal higher and higher. Electric pleasure licks through my veins and gathers in a molten pool low in my belly.

I yank impatiently at my tunic, suddenly desperate to be naked, to feel more of my skin against his. The offending garment gets tangled as I try to pull it over my head, and I make a sound of frustration. John chuckles against me, the vibrations shooting straight to my core. He releases me just long enough to help tug the tunic off, along with my bra.

A chill skims over my freed breasts, my nipples instantly tightening into aching peaks. I cup the soft mounds, massaging and pinching, sending zingers of sensation straight to where John's mouth has returned. His tongue delves inside me as his nose bumps my clit, and my back arches clean off the couch.

"Oh God, yes!" I grind against his face. "Just like that. Don't stop!"

He groans, doubling his efforts, licking and sucking and fucking me with complete abandon. I writhe beneath the onslaught. The tension inside me ratchets tighter and tighter, winding me like a spring about to snap.

With a keening cry, I shatter. Ecstasy crashes through me in relentless waves, and I convulse, my inner muscles clamping down on his fingers. He works me through it, drawing out everything I have until I collapse back onto the couch, boneless and gasping.

My surrender is complete, my body still shaking with aftershocks. I lay bare before him, my skin flushed. He sits back on his heels, just drinking me in, his gaze so heated it's almost a physical caress.

"You're so damn gorgeous," he murmurs. "And I love you."

My heart swells at the awe in his gravelly voice. "I love you too."

He moves to sit beside me, holding me, and I nuzzle into his neck. We sit for a few peaceful minutes, heartbeats completely synced. With a contented sigh, I drag my fingers across the bulge in his jeans. "I love you, John. So much."

"Which bit of me?" He raises an eyebrow.

"All of you." I straddle him, cupping his face in my hands.

He lifts his head to meet my gaze, and the sheer adoration in his sea-blue eyes takes my breath away. "I love you too. More than I ever thought possible."

He kisses me, deep and slow and achingly sweet, pouring so much emotion into the slant of his lips on mine. And I know with unshakable certainty that what we have is rare and precious. A once in a lifetime love.

As we lose ourselves in lazy kisses and gentle caresses, I grind against him. I've never felt so cherished. Like I'm where I'm meant to be.

In the arms of the man who owns me, body and soul. He's mine, and I'm his.

At the sound of a car door outside, John's head springs up.

"Shit. Surely not my mother again."

"Oh God." Talk about déjà vu. I jump off his lap and search for my clothes. John stumbles to the window to look out. It's already dark, which means it must be around five o'clock.

"Oh fuck. It is her."

"Should I go and hide?" I ask as I wrestle my tunic back on.

"No. Listen, why don't you stay tonight?"

"But I haven't got any more clothes. I need to go back to the apartment and get my stuff."

"I'll give you a lift later."

I check my phone. "If I go now, I'll make the bus. Let me sort stuff out tonight, and you can come for me tomorrow. It's just one night. Then my weekend's free, and I can be here."

"Okay." He kisses me again. "Just be careful. I don't like you being out in the dark on your own."

"I'll be fine. I do it all the time."

"I know. But still..."

The doorbell rings. Thank God he locked it this time.

"I'll nip out the back door."

"I love you." John gives me another kiss. "And I'll see you tomorrow." He steps back, raking a hand through his hair. "Text me when you get there."

"Will do." I give him a smile and a wave before heading to the back of the house. I hear him chatting at the front door as I pull on my coat and slip out into the night. The estate grounds are quiet and dark, the lights of Ardencairn casting long shadows over the path leading to the main road. I'd much rather stay with John, but I really need clothes and to tell Sienna what's going on. Also, I'm not ready for a confrontation with Vanessa. Hopefully John will tell her about us. After she knows, I'll meet her, and hopefully she'll accept me.

The damp earth squelches under my boots as I make my way across the sprawling grounds. A chill blooms at the base of my neck, not entirely from the cold air. The vast shadows of the ancient trees feel like they're closing in on me, and I hug my coat tighter around myself.

A rustle from the nearby bushes halts my steps. My heart thuds against my ribcage. Probably just a rabbit. But the sense of unease lingers, creeping up on me like ivy on old stone walls.

Then, out of nowhere, a hand clamps over my mouth, cutting off my startled cry. "Don't scream," a voice hisses in my ear, a voice I recognize all too well. Panic floods through me, icy and sharp. I thrash against the iron grip, but it's no use; he's too strong.

Freddie.

What the fuck is he doing?

"Just keep quiet." His breath is hot on my neck, stinking of fury and something darker. He forces my wrists in front of me and clamps handcuffs on me, then drags me toward a car parked in the shadows, away from the path, away from safety.

"Let me go!" I try to scream, but it comes out muffled and weak. My mind races with fear, every awful possibility flashing before my eyes.

He shoves me across the seat from the driver's side and climbs in after me, slamming the door before I can scramble out. The locks click into place, trapping me inside with him. Kneeling awkwardly on the seat, I fumble for my phone, but the cuffs make it impossible.

I've just managed to get it out of my coat pocket when Freddie snatches it from my grasp.

"I'll have that. Thank you." He rolls the window down and tosses the phone onto the driveway outside. He starts the engine, and, with a manic smirk, he reverses. I see my phone on the ground in the headlights, then with grossly accurate precision, he drives over it.

"Freddie, please..." I plead, my voice barely above a whisper.

"Please?" He mocks me, a twisted grin on his face. "Oh no. I'm going to make sure you regret ever crossing me. Your little fairy tale is over."

Tears prick my eyes, fear gripping me tight. How did things spiral so quickly out of control? "You won't get away with this." My voice is stronger than I feel.

"Already have, sweetheart." And with those chilling words, he exits the car, leaving me alone in the darkness, heart pounding, trapped.

I'm alone, encased in cold metal and glass, my heart hammering against my ribcage. I try to steady my breathing, to think clearly, but panic seizes me, a relentless vice.

Why has he left me here? What's he doing? There has to be a way out. My eyes scan the interior for something, anything that could help. The glove compartment? Empty. Under the seats?

"Help!" My voice is hoarse as I pound on the window with my bound hands. It's futile; the thick glass doesn't even wobble. I slump back into the seat, my chest tight with sobs I refuse to release.

"John…" His name spills from my lips, a whisper of hope that can't reach him. If only I could tell him where I am.

My gaze falls on the horn, and I lean forward, pressing down hard. The blare cuts through the night, a beacon begging for attention. I keep at it, the sound relentless, but it seems the vast grounds swallow the noise whole. No one comes. Not a soul.

"Please, someone…" But my plea dissolves into the blackness, unanswered. I'm utterly alone, and there's nothing I can do but sit, shaking and terrified, in the darkness.

# 26

## *John*

"Sit down, Mum. There's something I've got to talk to you about." I couldn't sound more formal, but I just want it over with. Who can tell how she'll react or how long she'll take to adjust to the idea? So, the sooner I give her the facts, the more time she'll have to digest them.

"Oh goodness, John. What is it? You're not ill, are you?" She takes a seat on the couch where I've just spent the last half hour debauching my love. Just as well she doesn't know that.

"No, no, nothing like that." I sit on the armchair opposite and sigh—not just at what I'm about to say, but at the state of this house. It's never been cleaner, but it's outdated. I've wasted too much time and energy in my battle with the planning department when I should have spent time on the interior. But that's something I can worry about later. "It's about Rose."

"Rose?" My mother's eyebrows arch, then knit together in confusion. "Who?"

"The woman who was cleaning in place of the regular cleaner."

"Oh... Yes. Her... What exactly about her?"

I swallow and look away. "She and I... We're in a relationship."

"Pardon?" She sounds shocked, as I knew she would be.

"Look, I know it might sound mad, but I've fallen for her. And she feels the same."

"She's very young." Mum breathes out through gritted teeth. "And she's your employee."

"Former employee." I point out. "And yes, I'm aware she's young, but that doesn't matter to me or to her."

"Love knows no age," Mum murmurs, almost to herself. Then, peering up at me, her gaze softens. "If you love her, I suppose that's what counts."

"Really?" I narrow my eyes a little, not sure this can be all. It seems almost too easy. "You're okay with it?"

"Of course, love." She gives me a warm smile. "If she makes you happy, that's all I need to know. After living through an absolute nightmare of a marriage, I only want my children to be happy and never to suffer as I did."

"Thanks, Mum." I go over to the couch, sit by her, and squeeze her tight. "That means the world to me. And I'm so sorry for what you went through. I wish I could have done something."

"You stayed close, and that's enough. You're my son, not my guardian." She pats my back. "I appreciate you just being here and not cutting ties with me, even when your father was still alive."

"I wouldn't do that."

"Exactly." She smiles with a twinkle of mischief in her eye. "Now, tell me more about Rose. Does she have any idea of the sort of stubborn man she's dealing with?"

I let out a dry laugh. "I think she has a fair idea."

Mum's reason for stopping off is her usual one—she's passing on the way back from a friend's. I wish she'd start forewarning me of visits, though at least this time the doors were locked.

I offer her dinner, but she declines, saying she wants to get home for the cat, and this was just a fleeting visit. If I'd known that, I'd have told Rose to wait. I would rather have given her a lift than had her walk through the dark grounds to the bus stop.

As Mum gets into her car, I check the time on my phone. Rose will be on the bus by now; otherwise, I'd have gone after her. I let out a sigh and pocket my phone. Patience has never been my strong point, but I really need to learn it. Waiting until tomorrow feels like an impossible task.

Mum's car crunches down the gravel drive, and I wave at the tail-lights. A wisp of unease tickles the back of my neck. I glance over at the gate, half-expecting to see a figure looming in the darkness. But it's just my mind playing tricks, and I brush off the feeling.

A car horn is blaring somewhere nearby, probably an alarm going off on one of the parked vehicles in the Country Club Car Park. It's not unusual for that to happen, though it sounds oddly erratic.

Shutting the door with a snap, I blow out a long breath and run a hand through my hair. It's done. Mum knows about Rose, and it was surprisingly painless. I whip out my phone and shoot Rose a quick message.

*Survived the mum talk. She's fine about us. Such a relief. Let me know when you're home. Love you, beautiful xx*

Hitting send, I jog up the stairs two at a time. The bleak upstairs corridor still has a faint smell of Rose's perfume. I flick on the light. As I head past Isabel's room, I notice Rose has tidied all the cuddlies away again and arranged them in a basket at the end of the neatly made bed. This room is the nicest one in the whole house.

My own room is as opulent as ever but feels like a dark and unwelcoming room now. I need Rose to work her magic in here, brighten it up, and make it ours.

I draw the curtains closed against the world. The fabric falls into place with a satisfying swish, sealing me inside my private sanctuary.

I shed my clothes and head toward the en suite.

Steam billows around me as hot water cascades from the showerhead, enveloping me in a cocoon of warmth. With each droplet that slides down my skin, I think of Rose. I want her in here with me where she belongs. After tomorrow, I won't have to worry about her being somewhere else. She'll be here.

I rest my palms against the cool tiles, letting the water blast me. In the fogged-up mirror of my mind, I sketch out our future together. Images of shared laughter, tender moments, and hot sex drift around.

A smile lingers on my face as I rinse the soap from my body, the water sluicing away all the doubt.

Once I'm fully clean, I towel off my hair and glance at my phone. Nothing from Rose. The silence from that sleek piece of technology is as loud as a siren in my ears. This is not like her. I rake a hand through my damp locks. She's usually quick to reply.

Maybe she's just caught up chatting with her friend. That sounds more than likely.

With a shrug, I pull on my lounge pants, the fabric clinging slightly to my still-damp skin. I'll give her a call after I've had dinner.

An intense ringing starts up downstairs. The smoke alarm. Seriously? Those things have a mind of their own sometimes. I toss the towel away and head out of the room to go and sort out the now deafening noise.

But then, something catches my attention—a smell that's out of place. My nose wrinkles. Smoke—thick and acrid.

"Fuck!"

My heart hammers against my ribcage as an ominous orange glow flickers from the stairs. Memories of the Gladstone flood back. The sight steals my breath away. I'm trapped. My escape route cut off.

"Fuck, fuck, fuck!" Panic surges through me. The fire is big; it's spreading quickly. I grab my phone, calling emergency services with shaking fingers.

"Fire service? Yeah, my house is on fire. The Lodge at Ardencairn Country Club. Please, hurry!" I bark into the receiver, my gaze fixed on the advancing inferno.

The voice on the other end is calm, but I'm not taking it in. I need to find a way out. Even as I try to figure it out, my thoughts fly every which way. How the hell did a fire start? And catch so quickly?

Something's wrong. Deep in my gut, I know it. This isn't just an accident. What if something has happened to Rose? My heart thrashes inside my chest.

I need to get out. I need to find Rose.

# 27

## *Rose*

The cold press of glass against my cheek anchors me in this nightmare. My bound hands slap uselessly at the car window, each impact sending a dull ache through my wrists, but there's no escape. No air. No mercy. Just the furious glow of fire, bright and violent, painting the night in sickening hues of orange and red as it consumes John's house.

A house I'd begun to imagine myself in. A life I'd just started to believe in.

The flames claw higher, licking at the sky like they're hungry for more, and a high, breathless panic coils in my chest. I've seen this before—years ago—but it never really left me. The helplessness. The unbearable knowledge that someone I love might be dying inside. My chest constricts, and the memory crashes in, vivid and sharp: my mum turning back toward the burning doorway. Her silhouette swallowed whole by smoke. The dog barking. My father's arms holding us back as we screamed. How she never came out.

History is repeating itself. Only this time, it's not an accident. It's Freddie's doing. He knows. That bastard knows.

A sob breaks loose from my throat as the crackle of fire grows louder. It's in my ears, under my skin, in my blood. I squeeze my eyes shut and turn away.

Freddie grabs a fistful of my hair and yanks my head around, forcing me to face the house.

"This is what happens to people who cross me." His voice is low and oily, like he's savouring every second.

I don't fight him. I can't. It's all gone—every ounce of strength, every thread of hope. What did I think he'd do? Make threats? Shout a bit? Not this. Never this.

My vision swims again, and not just from the smoke outside. Where is John? Oh God, please let him be out. Please let him be safe. Is he still in there? Maybe his mother is still with him. They might both already be dead.

Freddie leans close, his lips almost brushing my ear. He doesn't say the words outright, but he doesn't need to. It's all deliberate. It's theater. A twisted encore to my worst memory, crafted just for me.

"You should know," he breathes, "I'll always come out on top. You tried to outsmart me. Stupid girl. You never learn."

He sits back with a satisfied exhale, like a man admiring his own work. And I stare out at the inferno, a scream caught in my throat, my soul unravelling one flame at a time.

I swing around to face him, my heart hammering in my chest. His smirk is a slap across my face, and I can't help it—I scream. It's a raw sound, full of fear and fury.

"Let me out!" I tug at the handcuffs, the metal biting into my wrists, but they won't give.

"Come on, Rose, you're not making this any fun." Freddie chuckles, and the sound makes me want to kill him. He leans back, all casual-like, as if we're watching some TV drama and not John's life going up in smoke.

"Help me!" I'm shouting, praying someone will hear. But there's only Freddie, revelling in the control he has over me.

My breath comes out in sharp gasps—I have to get to John. Somehow.

"Please," I beg, because despite everything, part of me wants to believe Freddie isn't entirely soulless. But the glint in his eye tells me otherwise, and I realize that any mercy from him is about as likely as a snowstorm in July.

My skin is raw, and my heart is a blaze of panic. Freddie's sitting smug as a cat with the cream, and I can't stand it.

"You think you're so clever," I spit out, "but they'll catch you. They have to."

Freddie arches an eyebrow, his grin never wavering. "Who will?" His voice is sickly sweet.

"The police. You'll be put away for this."

He laughs. "You still don't get it, do you? I know people. I've got someone ready to vouch for me. A cast-iron alibi. No one will believe your hysterical nonsense, especially when John has famously tried to get this building knocked down and been repeatedly thwarted. People will think he started it himself, then got caught in a mess of his own making—which is closer to the truth than they'll know. The two of you brought this on yourselves."

Hot oil boils in my veins. I want to wipe that smirk off his face. Maybe I could smash him with my cuffed hands. It doesn't matter if

I get hurt in the process. Not now. Not if I can do enough damage to prove I was with him.

"It's always who you know, not what you know."

"Not this time. You won't get away with this." I lunge at him with my cuffed hands. It's a clumsy and futile attempt, but I need to do something, anything. I won't let him see how scared I am.

"Feisty." He dodges my swings easily. "But really, it's unbecoming. You should accept defeat with a little grace."

"Grace?" I laugh, bitter and sharp. "You wouldn't recognize grace if it hit you in the face." I attempt to smash the cuffs into his head again, this time putting full weight behind it. He moves out of the way, and his elbow rams the horn.

"I've had just about enough of you." He grimaces, holding my arms tightly so I can't move them.

A sudden rapping on the glass startles me. Freddie too looks around in panic. Blinking through tears, I see a face peering in through the window behind Freddie. It's Greg—the guy we helped get to the homeless shelter a couple of weeks ago.

"Help!" I scream. "Help me. Call the police."

Freddie seems in two minds about whether to drive away or to deal with Greg. Greg, however, has his phone out and stands back.

"Fire brigade too," I yell, "John's house—it's on fire!" I don't know if he can hear me, though he'll be able to see it for himself.

Freddie curses and shoves the door open. He's on Greg in an instant. Fuck. My heart pounds against my ribcage as I watch them grapple, Freddie trying to knock the phone from Greg's hand.

"Get off him!" I scream, finally managing to ram the door open. Freddie forgot to lock it in his haste. That means he's rattled. He's making mistakes.

Greg's phone skitters across the ground as Freddie tussles with him. Greg might be skinny, but he's tall and holding his own. He drags him away from the phone, and I grab it. It's still connected, and I yell into it.

"Police and fire service... to Ardencairn house. Quick, please. We're being attacked right now by Freddie Blackwood, and the house is burning." I'm probably making no sense, but I want to get everything out. I need them to know Freddie is here.

"Put that down!" Freddie yells at me as Greg still grapples to hold him back. "And you." He breaks Greg's grip. "Look what you've made me do." Freddie throws another punch, and I wince, feeling like it's my own face he's hit and not Greg.

"Stop it," I yell.

"I'm okay," Greg says. "Stay back."

If Greg's managing okay, then I'm going to see if I can find John. My legs pump furiously, propelling me toward the inferno that was once The Lodge. It looms ahead, a beast of fire and smoke roaring against the silent night sky. My heart pounds in time with my footsteps, the heat from the blaze intensifying as I get closer.

"John!" I cry out, hoping, pleading, that he's somewhere safe, not trapped inside it. I'm aware that I still have Greg's phone in my bound hands. I raise it to my ear and hear the voice of emergency services still coming through.

"Hello? Can you tell us if you're still there? Please stay on the line if you can. Help is on its way." The voice is talking, and I want to reply, but my mouth is dry. I cling to the tiny bit of hope that someone will get here in time—but what will they find when they get here?

If my mum could walk into a burning house for a dog, then I can damn well do it for the man I love. And nothing is going to stop me.

# 28

## *John*

The heat sears my heels as I stumble out the back door, gasping for air. The garden is a blur of night shadows, and the stench of smoke clings to every breath I take.

I'm out. I'm bloody out.

The fire service is on its way. Who knows what they can salvage? I clutch the basket of Isabel's cuddly toys, which I grabbed from her room on my way past. Priorities. I don't think my daughter would have got over losing these precious babies of hers.

Flames lick the sky, a roaring tangle of orange and red that casts a hellish glow on everything. My house. I may have hated that old building, but this isn't the end I would have chosen for it. How the fuck did it start? Faulty electrics? Whatever it was I'm damned if I know how it took so quickly and cut off my main escape route so efficiently. Thank God for the dodgy old backstairs. Normally they're off limits as they're unsafe, but they stood long enough to let me escape down them.

A scream slices through the night. I turn, heart lurching. Someone is sprinting around the corner.

"John!" Rose barrels into me out of nowhere, almost knocking the breath out of me.

"Rose! What the hell are you doing here?" I drop the basket of teddies next to a bush and catch her in my arms. "Why are you here? What are these cuffs for?"

"Oh, John," she gasps, tears rolling down her face. "Thank God you're out."

"Who did this to you?"

"Freddie," she sobs. "He's—he's completely lost it."

"Freddie?" My blood boils at the mention of his name, and I grind my teeth. "I'll fucking kill him." I examine the cuffs, searching for a way to release her. "Let's get you out of these."

"There's no time for that." Her words spill out in a frantic tumble. "He's fighting with Greg right now. We need to stop them. I don't want Greg to die—he helped me."

"Greg?" Christ almighty, I've no idea what's going on, but Rose is already jogging away, and I follow her.

"Freddie grabbed me, out of nowhere. There was no reasoning with him. He cuffed me, smashed my phone to bits, and forced me into his car."

"Christ…" My jaw tightens, and I put my arm around her shoulders as we hurry through the dark grounds. I kick myself that I wasn't there for her and she had to endure this on her own.

"He left me in the car while he set fire to the house."

"Damn him." Anger pulses through every vein in my body. "When I get my hands on him."

"Then he drove me here and made me watch." She chokes on the words. "If Greg hadn't shown up… I don't know what he would've done. We have to help him."

"Okay, we'll get to Greg." I speed up. "Just stay with me, Rose. I'm not letting you go."

Shouts from across the grounds make us break into a sprint. Two figures are locked in a violent tussle.

"Freddie thinks he's untouchable," Rose says as we run. "He bragged about connections. He's convinced he'll walk away from this."

"Like hell he will." My jaw clenches with determination. I won't let Freddie manipulate the system again. Not after everything he's done.

My blood boils at the sight of Freddie laying into Greg on the fringe of the golf course, far enough from the burning house that the flames don't reach us here, but close enough that I can still smell the smoke.

"Stay here." I hold Rose's shoulders. "Let me do this."

"Be careful." Her voice trembles. "I don't want to lose you."

"You won't." I give her a quick kiss on the cheek, then head straight for Freddie.

Greg catches my eye for a split second—just long enough for me to see the panic and pain there—and then I'm moving. No hesitation. No thought. Just instinct.

I charge forward and rip Freddie off him, my fingers digging into his shoulder as I yank him back with a snarl. "You've ruined lives long enough, Freddie. This ends tonight."

My fist slams into his jaw with a crack that travels up my arm, a burst of pain that feels like satisfaction, like justice—like revenge. For Rose. For Greg. For every goddamn time I had to stand still while my father hurt someone I loved.

He stumbles, and I follow, fuelled by years of fury I've never unleashed.

For the helpless kid I used to be.

For the man I've fought to become.

And for the woman who trusted me—with her pain, her truth, and her heart.

Greg rolls away, coughing, dragging himself to safety, and I plant myself between him and Freddie, ready for whatever comes next.

Freddie lunges, swinging wildly, but I've got the weight of something deeper behind me. My own darkness. The shit I never got to throw back at my father. Now I get to give it to someone who deserves it just as much.

"You want to destroy lives? You picked the wrong one this time."

We're a mess of fists and fury, crashing through the damp grass and churned mud, the smoke from the burning house curling in the night like ghosts of everything I could've lost.

I drive Freddie back step by step, my muscles burning, my blood roaring. "You're finished!" I shout, my voice hoarse. "You don't get to lay a finger on her again. On anyone."

This isn't just a fight. It's years of silence breaking open. A reckoning. And I'm not walking away until I make damn sure Freddie doesn't either.

# 29
## *Rose*

My heart thunders against my ribcage like it's as desperate to escape as I am from these cuffs. I'm rooted to the spot, my breaths ragged and shallow. I should go to Greg and check he's okay, but I don't want to get caught in the scuffle. John's hands are clenched around Freddie's throat as I edge around them, keeping my distance.

"John, don't!" I cry out, but my voice is lost in the void between us. My hands shake, and I have to remind myself to breathe. Inhale. Exhale. It's all I can manage right now. "Don't get hurt." In my head, I'm screaming at him not to do anything so serious to Freddie that he ends up in as much trouble. John could kill Freddie. And then what? Prison? I can't lose him. I won't.

John's fist connects with Freddie's jaw in a brutal arc, the sound of the impact shockingly loud. Freddie's head snaps back, and for a moment he teeters, his eyes unfocused, before crumpling to the ground like a discarded puppet.

"Greg?" John's voice is a low growl as he moves past Freddie's prone form toward where Greg lies panting.

"I'm okay." Greg's trying to push himself upright, but his movements are sluggish, his eyes glazed.

"Stay down, mate. Help's coming." John kneels beside him, checking he's okay. I break into a jog to get to them.

But before I reach them, Freddie staggers up, and lunges for me. "Rose!" His hand curls around my neck, not enough to choke, but enough to send paralyzing fear through me.

"Let her go!" John leaps to his feet.

"Or what, Knighton? You'll hit me again?" Freddie's sneer is ugly. "If you try, I'll snap this pretty little neck."

"Get off me," I choke out.

"Shut up." His grip tightens.

"I said, let her go." John's jaw is tight, his eyes flash red. "The police are on their way. It's not just your face that's going to be in a mess. Your reputation will be shot too."

"You've got nothing on me." But Freddie's words are less certain.

"I mean it. Get your hands off her now!" John says.

"Make me," Freddie spits back, his fingers still coiled around my neck. A shiver of fear runs down my spine, but anger is bubbling up too, hot and fierce.

I can't just stand here, a damsel in distress. That's not who I am. I'm Rose Darwin, and I don't wilt—I fight. With my heart thundering against my ribs, I muster all my strength and elbow Freddie hard in the stomach. He yelps, caught off guard, his grip loosening just enough for me to move.

"Nice try," he sneers, regaining some of his composure and grabbing hold of me.

"Let go of me, you prick." I twist my body and drive my knee into his groin with all the strength I can muster. Freddie doubles over, gasping for air, and I swing my cuffed hands up—hard—slapping him right across his smug face.

"Rose!" John's there in an instant, pulling me away from Freddie and shielding me with his own body. "Are you okay?"

"Yeah." Adrenaline surges through me so fast I feel dizzy with it. "I'm fine."

John's chest rises and falls with rapid breaths, and his eyes are dark storms of worry and rage. But when he looks down at me, there's that softness too, that gentle assurance that's only for me.

"Thank God." His hand finds one of mine still cuffed, and he squeezes tight even as we both watch Freddie stagger back, assessing the damage I've done.

A blur of motion catches my eye, and I glance over to see Greg pushing himself up from the ground. His face is a grimace of pain and determination as he stands on unsteady legs, brushing dirt from his clothes. He's a mess, but he's on his feet.

Freddie's eyes dart between me, John, and Greg, who's now squaring up like he's ready for another round. The arrogance melts off Freddie's face, leaving behind a flicker of doubt—a rare crack in his otherwise unshakeable facade.

"Come on then, you coward," John taunts, a muscle ticking in his jaw. "You going to take us all on?"

Tension thrums through John's hand, still clasped around mine. His palm is sweaty, but his grip is rock solid—like he would take on the world if it meant keeping me safe.

But before anyone can make another move, a distant wailing cuts through the standoff. Sirens. Growing louder, getting closer. We all freeze.

"Fuck the lot of you." Freddie backs away, realizing he's lost this round. He's not just out-manned; he's about to have an audience.

He bolts, sprinting across the grass toward his car.

"Shouldn't we stop him?" Greg yells.

"No." John puts his hand on Greg's shoulder. "Whatever he does, he can't get away. He'll get caught this time."

His car's engine roars to life, and within moments, Freddie's speeding off, tires screeching as he vanishes down the winding track that leads away from Ardencairn Country Club.

The sirens are deafening now, and blue lights pulse through the trees.

I press my hands to my thighs, trying to ground myself, but they won't stop shaking. My lungs stutter as I take a breath that's too shallow. The adrenaline still pumping through me makes my limbs tremble, and I'm not sure if it's fear, rage, or a noxious blend of both.

John lets out a long breath beside me, his shoulders sagging slightly, and that small motion makes me want to take him in my arms and hold him there forever.

"Are you okay, Greg?" I ask, forcing my voice to be steady as I turn to him.

"I think so." Greg looks at his hands, then rubs his neck like he's not sure he still has control over his own body.

The voices of police officers echo through the night, urgent and sharp. Torches flash in arcs, bobbing through the darkness like searchlights sweeping a battlefield.

"They'll want to take statements." John touches my back gently, his palm warm and solid.

I flinch, not because it hurts—but because it doesn't. Because for the first time tonight, the touch is safe. Comforting. Real.

The ground feels unsteady beneath my feet, as if the world hasn't quite settled. I reach for John's hand, needing something to anchor me, even with these damned cuffs. He doesn't hesitate—he just threads his fingers through mine, strong and certain.

The night is far from over, but John's alive. I'm alive. We're together. And no matter how much smoke still lingers in the air, or how loud the sirens scream, I know we've survived something we'll never forget.

# 30

## *John*

The roar of water jets drowns out the hiss and crackle of the fire as the firefighters get to work, their hoses slicing arcs through the smoke-filled air. I stand rooted to the spot, Rose's cuffed wrist still in my grip, the metal cold and foreign against my skin. The blaze is slowly being tamed by a swarm of yellow-helmeted heroes, but I can't seem to look away.

My heart's still hammering like it hasn't realized the danger is over. Every breath tastes of smoke and adrenaline, the kind that buzzes in your blood long after the threat's passed. The heat from the fire still clings to my skin, but it's her I'm holding onto—like if I let go, everything might come crashing down again.

"I can't believe this is happening," Rose murmurs, almost to herself. Her green eyes flicker with the reflected firelight, picking up the reds and golds like embers, turning something soft into something raw.

"Me neither." My voice comes out rougher than I expect. I squeeze her hand tighter, needing the contact as much for myself as for her. "But we're safe now. And I even managed to get Isabel's teddies out. I dumped them in a bush."

Her head turns sharply, and for a heartbeat, there's surprise—then a fragile smile that cracks through the ash and fear still clinging to her.

"You saved the cuddlies?"

"I sure did." I manage a small grin, but it comes with a wave of something I don't want to name—relief, guilt, maybe disbelief that we're even standing here.

She lets out a quiet laugh, soft and shaken, then leans into me like a wave finally giving up on the shore. I slide my arm around her shoulders, pulling her in close, pressing my lips to her hair. The scent of smoke clings to us both, but beneath it, there's her—warm, real, alive.

And for the first time tonight, I let myself breathe.

The police are questioning Greg a few feet away, their voices low but urgent. Two paramedics approach, their jackets catching flashes of red and blue in the dark. I stay close to Rose, keeping her within arm's reach like she might vanish if I blink too long.

"Is there any chance we can get these cuffs off?" I ask, my voice still hoarse from the shouting, smoke, and fear. "It's been a long enough night for her already."

The paramedic stands beside Rose, his tone kind but brisk. "I'll get one of the officers to bring the cutting gear." He gently takes her wrists and lifts a torch, the beam catching on the sharp metal digging into her skin.

I watch the light skim across her hands—red, raw, marked by a night she never should've been part of. My fists curl reflexively. I should've protected her better. Guilt coils low in my gut, stubborn and deep.

The paramedic lifts a walkie-talkie and speaks into it, talking to someone about cutting gear.

I instinctively straighten, my spine taut like it's bracing for the next blow, as I spot the officer in charge walking over.

He begins the formal questioning, his voice calm and steady, and we go over everything. I recount the events in order, keeping my tone level, but inside I'm pacing, still keyed up, still hearing echoes of fire and fists and Rose screaming my name.

All the while, my eyes drift back to her. She's here. She's safe. But I won't unclench until those fucking cuffs are off.

"Right," the officer finally says, flipping his notebook closed. "We may need to call you in at some point for further questions after Mr Blackwood is in custody."

A breath loosens from my chest, the first real one in what feels like hours. My shoulders sag a fraction. It's not over—not fully—but we're out of the fire now. Literally.

I shift closer to Rose, brushing my hand against her back, grounding myself in her warmth, the familiar rise and fall of her breath. I can still feel the imprint of fear in my bones—but it's fading now, washed away by the presence of the woman beside me and the quiet knowledge that, somehow, we made it through.

"Where's the lady with the cuffs?" A firefighter appears, looking around.

"Over here." I hold up my hand as he approaches.

The hulking figure strides over, cutting gear in hand. "Arms out, love," the firefighter says.

Rose holds her cuffed hands out. The firefighter positions the cutter, and there's a brief moment before the sharp clink of metal echoes through the air. The cuffs fall away, clattering to the ground. Rose stares at her wrists for a second, rubbing them gently, then she launches herself into my arms. Her body crashes against mine, and I automatically wrap her up tight, my hands splaying across her back.

"Thank you," I say to the firefighter, who nods.

Rose buries her head in my chest, her breath warm against my shirt, and I hold her close.

In this hug, there's something raw and real. Relief, gratitude, and love... So much love.

Two days later, I stand in the doorway of The Lodge, my hands shoved deep into my pockets, surveying the wreckage. Charred beams loom overhead, and the smell of burnt wood lingers like an unwelcome guest.

"God," I mutter under my breath, "where do you even start with something like this?"

"Well, you start at the beginning, don't you?" Rose squeezes my hand and smiles.

I'm so lucky to have her here with me.

"Right." I let out a short laugh. "The beginning. And where would that be in this mess?"

"With us." She wraps her arms around my waist. "The where doesn't matter. It's the who that does."

"That's a very good point, but I still feel like I should at least attempt to clean some of this up." It's a warped sense of fate that I might be able to build the house I always dreamt of here now. But it comes at a price. It was common knowledge that I wanted to knock down the old house, so I'm not above suspicion. And Freddie Blackwood will play on that fact like the scumbag he is.

"Just as well I'm maid for you." Rose makes jazz hands and laughs.

"You certainly are." I let out a laugh. "Bet your former employer never realized just how appropriate that pun would be in our case."

After surveying the damage, we make our way to the main hotel at Ardencairn, where we're staying for now. The suite I've taken is a stark contrast to the soot-stained walls of the Lodge. Everything is pristine and welcoming. This is exactly how I'd like any future home with Rose to look.

"Hey." I spot Jamie and his partner coming down the grand staircase. They're all smiles and open arms.

"John, Rose." Jamie claps me on the shoulder while his partner, Owen, pulls Rose into a hug. "How bad was the damage?" Jamie asks.

"Bad," I reply. "But no more than expected."

"Well, at least you have this place," Owen says.

"Indeed." I nod. "And I've never been happier to be a hotel owner and have plenty of places to stay at my disposal."

The suite is big enough for all of us—not just Rose and me, but Isabel too. That thought alone makes something tight in my chest unfurl, like a cautious bloom in early spring. We're safe. Together. Starting again.

Later on, Isabel barrels in like a small cyclone, her schoolbag bouncing wildly off the doorframe as she charges through it. Just seeing her—whole, untouched by the chaos that nearly swallowed us—makes my throat tighten. She spots me, and her face lights up, brilliant and pure.

"Daddy!"

She launches herself at me with such momentum that I stagger back a step, catching her weight against me. I grunt with the effort—my ribs still sore from the fight—but I still wrap my arms around her, grounding myself in her familiar warmth. God, we nearly lost this.

"Is Rose...?"

"I'm here too," Rose answers softly, stepping out from the bedroom like something out of a dream. She's changed into soft clothes, hair loose around her shoulders, and her smile—warm and a little tired—hits me right in the heart.

Isabel wriggles out of my arms and launches into Rose's, her excitement bubbling over. "Does that mean you live with us now?"

"Yes," I say without hesitation. My voice is quiet, but solid. Certain.

Rose glances at me with a mix of surprise and tenderness but says nothing. Her eyes say enough.

"Yay! I always wanted you two to be together." Isabel pulls back, practically vibrating with joy. "Are you gonna get married? Will you have lots of babies?"

I blink, caught completely off guard. For a heartbeat, I'm frozen. But then Rose lets out a laugh, light and real, and I shake off the panic.

"Whoa, slow down, tiger," I say, ruffling Isabel's hair. "Let's just take it one step at a time, shall we?"

Rose beams at us. "Your dad managed to save all your cuddlies from the fire. I've set them up in your room."

"You got all of them?"

"Yeah. Thankfully, they were all nicely put away in a basket, so they were easy to pick up."

"Rose did that."

"I know." I give Isabel's hair another playful tousle. "And you need to learn to do it too."

She grins, then races off to inspect her reunited plush crew. I let out a long breath.

Rose moves to my side, her hand finding mine. I curl my fingers around hers, the contact grounding me again. Her skin is warm, her grip firm.

For the first time in a long while, my thoughts aren't haunted by what I've lost—but by what I'm lucky enough to have.

I'm not naïve. Life can turn on a dime. But right now, with Rose beside me and Isabel laughing in the next room, I finally let myself believe in something more than survival.

Maybe this is what healing feels like. Quiet. Solid. Full of hope and love.

# 31
## Rose

I fold my last sweater—the soft gray one with the hole in the elbow that I like wearing around the apartment—and place it in my suitcase. It's strange how my entire life fits into two bags and a cardboard box. Then again, when you've had to start over from scratch, you learn which possessions actually matter. The rest is just stuff that weighs you down, collects dust, reminds you of things best forgotten.

The bedroom door creaks open behind me. I turn to see Sienna balancing two steaming mugs of tea, her ginger curls tucked messily behind her ears. Her oversized glasses have slipped down her nose again, but she's too preoccupied with not spilling the drinks to push them back up.

"Thought you might need this." She nudges the door wider with her hip. "Packing is thirsty work."

I take the mug gratefully. "You're a lifesaver."

"So..." Sienna perches on the edge of my now-stripped bed, her eyes scanning the nearly empty room. "This is really happening, then?"

I sink down beside her, cradling the warm mug between my palms. "Yup."

"You excited?" Her voice is gentle, genuinely curious rather than judgmental. That's the thing about Sienna—she never makes you feel like you're being interrogated, even when she's asking about the big stuff.

I laugh, a nervous hiccup of sound. "It feels right, but also… I don't know. Big."

Sienna nods, understanding written across her face. Her expression is always so open, so honest. "After what Freddie did to you, I'm not surprised you want some security." Sienna's voice hardens slightly. "But are you sure you're not rushing into it?"

"I'm not sure about that, but I am sure about John. I know he's right for me."

"Thank goodness for that."

I take another sip of tea. "I'm going to miss this," I admit quietly. "Miss you."

"Don't get soppy on me now," Sienna warns, but her voice wobbles slightly. "Besides, I'm already planning all the fancy dinner parties you'll have to invite me to at The Lodge once it's rebuilt."

I giggle and check my phone. "Eleven-thirty. John will be here any minute."

I wrap my arms around her just as my phone buzzes with a text. I check it, my heart doing that familiar little leap when I see John's name on the screen.

"He's here."

Sienna nods, reaching for the suitcase. "Right then. Let's get you on your way. And good luck with the interview."

We say our goodbyes, and she helps me down the stairs with my luggage. Outside, the November air hits me with its particular Edinburgh chill—not the biting cold of deep winter, but the damp, insidious kind that seeps through layers and settles in your bones.

I scan the street and spot John's car, gleaming black and imposing, parked directly in front of the building.

I give Sienna one last hug as John gets out. He shakes Sienna's hand before lifting my cases into the boot.

"Ready?" he says.

"As I'll ever be."

After he closes the boot, he steps closer, one hand coming up to tuck a tendril of hair behind my ear. "Hello," he says quietly, as if we're alone rather than standing on a busy Edinburgh street.

"Hello yourself," I reply, smiling.

He leans down and I rise to meet him, our lips connecting in a kiss that's both familiar and thrilling. His hand cups my cheek, thumb brushing gently across my skin, and I feel that now-familiar warmth spreading through me—comfort and desire intertwined.

When we part, he studies my face with that intense focus that used to unnerve me. "You okay?"

I nod, though I can feel tears threatening again. "Just... it's all a bit much, isn't it? Saying goodbye to Sienna, us moving in together. The interview. Everything happening at once."

He guides me to the passenger side, opening the door. "Second thoughts?" I catch a flash of vulnerability in his eyes.

"Not about us." I slide into the seat. "Never about us."

He walks around and gets in on the driver's side, starting the engine before turning to face me again. "So what, then? The interview? Because if you're not ready—"

"No, I want to go," I interrupt. "I need to go. It's a good opportunity."

He nods, pulling away from the kerb. "It is. And you're more than qualified."

I stare out at the familiar streets, trying to organize my jumbled thoughts. "It's not just the interview. It's... everything with Freddie. I can't help thinking it was all my fault, somehow."

John's hands tighten on the steering wheel, his knuckles whitening momentarily. "I need you to dismiss that thought right now," he says, his voice low and intense. "Freddie Blackwood is clearly psychotic. None of what happened was your fault."

My fingers twist together in my lap. "But if I hadn't tried to get revenge on him,"

"Then he would have found another way to punish you for daring to stand up to him," John cuts in firmly. "Men like Freddie don't need reasons, Rose. They need control. When you threatened that control, he lashed out. Remember the Gladstone? Now your actions have helped put him away."

"It's just hard not to replay it all, you know? Wonder if there was a moment I could have changed things."

"I know." John's expression softens as he glances at me. "But now he's been caught and arrested. Those charges are serious. He'll be out of our lives for a long time—forever, in fact. I've got a good lawyer who'll make sure Freddie is kept away or tagged and on a restraining order for the rest of his life."

The certainty in his voice is comforting, but it also stirs something uncomfortable in my chest. "I don't want you to think that's why I'm with you," I say suddenly. "Because you can protect me from him. Or because you have the means to hire expensive lawyers."

He frowns slightly. "That's not what I think at all."

"I know, but..." I struggle to articulate the tangled mess of feelings inside me. "After everything with Freddie, I promised myself I'd never put my faith in a man to 'look after me' again. I don't want to be that person."

"Rose," he says. "You are the most fiercely independent person I've ever met. Sometimes frustratingly so." His mouth quirks up in that half-smile I've grown to love. "If anything, you're the one looking after me."

The light changes, and he returns his attention to the road, but reaches over to take my hand in his, his thumb tracing circles on my skin.

"That's your little joke." I smile despite myself.

"It's not a joke." He shakes his head. "Before you bullied your way into my life—"

"Bullied?" I protest, laughing.

"Forcefully entered, then," he amends. "Before that, I was... existing. Not living. You changed that."

I look down at our intertwined hands, his so much larger than mine, yet holding on with such gentleness. "I feel so safe with you," I murmur. "But I still want to be independent. Need to be. Which is why this interview is important."

He nods. "I know. And I respect that. I wouldn't want you any other way."

We drive in comfortable silence for a few minutes.

"You know," John says eventually, "I never thought I'd have someone living with me again. After Lydia left, I swore it would just be me and Isabel."

I glance at him, noting the tension that still appears around his eyes at the mention of his ex-wife. "And now?"

"Now I can't imagine it without you."

Something warm unfurls in my chest, chasing away the last of my anxiety. This is what makes us work, I think. Not grand gestures or dramatic pronouncements, but this—quiet certainty, mutual respect, the safety to be exactly who we are.

I settle back into the seat, watching as we approach the office building where my interview awaits. The nervousness is still there, fluttering beneath my ribs, but it's manageable now—just another challenge to face, not the overwhelming dread I felt earlier.

"You're going to be brilliant," John says, as if reading my mind. "And if not, there are plenty of other opportunities."

I nod, drawing strength from his confidence in me. "You're right. It's just one interview."

"Exactly." He squeezes my hand once more before releasing it to make a turn. "And whatever happens, we'll figure it out. Together."

Together. The word still feels new and precious, a gift I'm almost afraid to accept fully in case it's snatched away. But as I look at John's profile—the strong line of his jaw, the scars he no longer tries to hide from me, the slight tension around his mouth that betrays his own nervousness on my behalf—I know that this is different from what came before.

This isn't desperation or dependence. It's choice. It's trust. It's the beginning of something I never thought I'd have.

The building looms ahead, all glass and gleaming steel. It's the kind of place that screams "corporate" and "professional" and "we probably won't hire someone whose last job was cleaning houses." My palms are already sweating, and I surreptitiously wipe them on my skirt as John pulls into a parking space. This is it. My chance to prove—to myself more than anyone—that I'm more than my past mistakes and setbacks.

"Impressive building," John comments.

"Edinburgh's premier marketing agency," I recite from the job listing. "Industry leader in lifestyle brand development." The words feel foreign in my mouth, corporate jargon I'm not entirely sure I understand, despite spending hours researching the company.

John shifts in his seat to face me. "Ready?"

"Yes. I need to do this. For me."

"I know." His thumb brushes across my knuckles in that way that never fails to send a little shiver down my spine. "But there's no pressure. If you don't get this, something else will come up."

I squeeze his hand, grateful for his understanding. "The pressure's all coming from in here," I tap my temple with my free hand, "where a little voice keeps reminding me that just a few weeks ago I was scrubbing toilets and living on beans on toast."

"Nothing wrong with honest work," he says. "And you were brilliant at it. My house was never so clean."

I laugh despite my nerves. "Are you saying you only fell for me because of my superior dusting skills?"

"That, and the way you took care of Isabel and her toys." His eyes crinkle at the corners.

I lean across and press a quick kiss to his lips, drawing strength from his steadiness. "I should go in. Don't want to be late."

He nods, serious again. "You'll be brilliant. Just be yourself."

I gather my bag, checking my reflection in the visor mirror—blonde hair neatly pulled back, minimal makeup, the smart teal dress Sienna insisted brings out my green eyes. Professional. Capable. Not at all like someone who had their life torn apart and stitched back together in the space of a few weeks.

The lobby of Archer & Bell Marketing is exactly as intimidating as the exterior suggests—all polished marble and minimalist furniture, with a reception desk that appears to be carved from a single slab of some expensive-looking wood. The receptionist, a sleek young woman with an impossibly neat bob, looks up as I approach.

"Rose Darwin," I say. "I have an interview."

She checks something on her computer, then offers a professionally warm smile. "Please take a seat. Someone will be with you shortly."

I perch on the edge of one of the angular, uncomfortable-looking chairs, trying not to fidget.

"Rose Darwin?"

I look up to see a woman in her thirties standing at the entrance to the corridor, iPad in hand, expression pleasant but unreadable.

"Yes, that's me." I stand, smoothing my dress and picking up my bag.

"Excellent. I'm Meredith, Head of Creative. Please follow me."

The interview room is less intimidating than I expected—a medium-sized conference room with a round table rather than the imposing boardroom setup I'd feared. There are two other people waiting: a middle-aged man with kind eyes behind wire-rimmed glasses, and a younger woman with an undercut and impressive silver earrings.

"This is David, our CEO, and Sasha, who heads up our lifestyle division," Meredith introduces them as I take my seat. "We're delighted you could join us today."

The first few minutes pass in a blur of pleasantries and standard questions about my background. I stumble slightly when explaining my departure from the gallery, offering a carefully edited version that emphasizes "seeking new challenges" rather than "was fired after my ex decided to physically abuse me and I left him."

But then David asks about my experience with client relations, and I find myself on firmer ground, describing how I'd built relationships with artists and collectors at the gallery, understanding their needs and matching them to the right pieces.

"I believe good marketing comes from the same place," I say, surprising myself with my confidence. "Understanding what people truly connect with, what speaks to them on an emotional level, rather than just what they think they want."

Sasha nods, looking genuinely interested for the first time. "Can you give us an example of how you've applied that philosophy?"

I think for a moment, then describe a particular sale I'd facilitated—an uncertain collector, a challenging piece, the careful way I'd helped them see beyond their initial impression to the artwork's deeper value. As I speak, I feel something shifting in the room, the atmosphere warming slightly.

Then Meredith glances at her notes and asks, "I notice there's a gap in your employment history between the gallery and your current position. Can you tell us about that period?"

My mouth goes dry. This is the moment I've been dreading. I could lie, invent some story about travelling or caring for a relative, but something in me refuses to start this potential new chapter with dishonesty.

"After leaving the gallery, I went through a difficult personal situation," I say carefully. "I took whatever work I could find while I regrouped, which led me to a cleaning position with an agency called Maid for You."

I see the flicker of surprise cross their faces, perhaps even a hint of dismissal in Meredith's eyes, and something inside me hardens with determination.

"It wasn't the career path I'd planned," I continue, my voice growing stronger, "but it taught me invaluable lessons about adaptability, attention to detail, and the importance of creating environments that make people feel comfortable and valued—all skills that I believe would benefit me in this role."

David's eyebrows lift slightly, and I see a glimmer of what might be respect in his expression. "An interesting perspective," he says. "And how did you move from that position to your interest in marketing?"

For the next few minutes, I weave the narrative of my recent weeks.

By the time we reach the final questions about my future goals and what I'd bring to the team, I've hit my stride, speaking with a passion and clarity that surprises even me. These people don't know about Freddie, about the mess my life became. They're seeing me as I am now—capable, resilient, eager to rebuild.

"Well, Rose," David says as the interview draws to a close, "this has been illuminating. We have a few more candidates to see, but we'll be in touch within the week."

I thank them, gathering my things with hands that are miraculously steady. Meredith escorts me back to the lobby, her professional mask firmly in place, giving no hint as to my chances.

"Best of luck," she says, and then I'm back in the marble expanse, walking on legs that suddenly feel wobbly with the release of tension.

Outside, the late autumn air is crisp against my flushed cheeks. I spot John's car, and something in me eases at the sight. I walk toward it, mentally reviewing the interview, picking apart my answers, trying to gauge whether I've done enough.

Did I talk too much about the gallery? Not enough about my specific marketing knowledge? Was my explanation for my employment gap convincing, or did they see straight through to the mess underneath?

John steps out of the car as I approach, his expression carefully neutral, but I can read the question in his eyes.

"Well?" he asks simply.

I shrug, suddenly exhausted as the adrenaline ebbs. "I don't know. I did my best, but..." I gesture vaguely, unable to articulate the swirl of hope and doubt inside me.

"Your best is more than enough." He opens the passenger door for me.

As I sink into the seat, I'm not sure I believe him, but I appreciate the sentiment, nonetheless. I did what I came to do—showed up and took a step toward reclaiming my life. Whether it leads to this particular job or not, there's victory in that.

I kick off my interview heels with a groan of relief. The sleek leather interior wraps around me like a cocoon, and for a moment, I just sit there, letting the tension drain from my shoulders. John slides into the driver's seat. He's wearing his navy suit and pristine white shirt—the one that makes him look like a model, even with the scars—and his hair is slightly rumpled at the back, as if he's been running his hand through it while waiting.

"I'm sure you were brilliant," he says, his faith in me so unwavering it makes my chest ache. "Did they say when you'd hear back?"

"Within the week." My stomach churns with uncertainty. "So now I just wait and try not to obsessively check my phone every five minutes."

John smiles. "I think this calls for a celebration."

"A celebration for possibly not completely bombing an interview?" I raise an eyebrow. "Your standards are concerningly low."

"For taking the step. For putting yourself out there." His gaze is suddenly intense. "I know how hard that was for you, after everything."

Something warm spreads out in my chest, chasing away the lingering anxiety of the interview. This is what still surprises me about John—not just the understanding, but how he never makes me feel weak for needing it.

"So," he continues, finally starting the engine, "I thought we could go to the Taybury for lunch. My treat."

"The Taybury?" I repeat with a smile spreading across my face. "Sounds delightful."

"I seem to recall you enjoyed the dessert there."

"'Enjoyed' is an understatement. Maybe we could skip to that again today." I lean back in my seat, watching his profile. "I'm thinking we should properly christen our first day of cohabitation. In private. With considerably fewer clothes."

"That," he says, "is the best suggestion I've heard all day."

His hand finds mine across the console, his fingers warm and sure as they intertwine with my own. "Penny for them?" he asks quietly.

"Just thinking about everything. How different things were the last time we went to the Taybury. How far we've come."

He nods, understanding without needing elaboration. "It's been quite a journey."

An understatement if ever there was one.

We stop at a traffic light, and John turns to look at me properly, his expression softening in that way that still makes my heart skip. "You know," he says, "I've never been more grateful for the agency sending me you as a cleaner."

I nod, letting my free hand drift to his thigh. "Me too. I was *Maid for You* in every possible way."

"You certainly were."

# 32

## *John*

We step into the sleek reception of the Taybury. I stride to the desk, keeping Rose close to me, give the receptionist my name and show her my ID. "I need a room for business, please."

Business. If only she knew the kind of business I'm here for this afternoon.

"Yes, Mr Knighton." The receptionist doesn't blink—just nods politely and starts tapping away at her keyboard. Efficient, professional, and trained not to flinch when couples show up looking like they plan to christen the furniture, especially when one of them owns the place.

Rose hovers just behind my shoulder, and I catch her gaze in the glass reflection behind the desk. She's looking at me like I'm something worth admiring, and that smacks me bang in the heart. That anyone—let alone her—could look at me like that still blows my mind.

"Just let me authorize a key for you," the receptionist says. I nod, hands loose at my sides, but my heart a steady thump of anticipation. Not just for what's about to happen, but for everything else—for us.

"And will you be requiring dinner reservations this evening?" Her gaze flicks to Rose and back to me.

"Yes, thank you. At seven."

That gives us three hours. More than enough time to make Rose forget all about the nerves that came with applying for her dream job. She didn't just apply—she *went for it*, and that makes me prouder than I can say. No matter what happens next, she chased something for herself. She stepped into the fire and didn't flinch.

The receptionist hands me the key card, tucked in a neat little paper sleeve. "Room 412, fourth floor. The lifts are just to your right. Is there anything else I can help you with today?"

I shake my head and slide the card into my pocket before turning to take Rose's hand. Her fingers curl around mine like they belong there.

At the lift, I press the call button and steal a sideways glance at her.

The lift doors open with a soft chime. We step in, and the moment the doors slide shut, the outside world fades.

I turn to her, cupping her face. Her green eyes are bright with mischief, her lips parted slightly, expectant.

"You are amazing," I say, and I mean it, utterly and completely.

She smiles. "And you are very sexy."

My lips twitch—just a little. The smile that only she can draw out of me. "Thank you," I murmur, letting my voice dip low, "but for all your brilliance, you're still wearing too many clothes."

The lift stops with a soft jolt, and the doors glide open on a familiar corridor—cream and gold, pristine and polished. The carpet hushes the sound of our steps as we walk side by side.

I count off the doors without meaning to. 406. 408. 410.

"Here we are." I stop in front of 412 and pull out the key card.

The green light flashes, a soft electronic chirp, and the lock clicks open. I push the door inward and step back, motioning for her to go first. She brushes past me, close enough that her coat grazes my arm, and every hair on my body stands to attention. The scent of her, light and floral with a hint of something darker—something *her*—wraps around me as she crosses the threshold.

God, she's stunning. And she's here. With *me*.

The room is decorated just as I like—neutral luxury, elegant lines, and at the centre, a king-sized bed with sharp white linens that dare us to mess them up. On the desk, the champagne waits in its bucket of ice, already beading with condensation.

"When did you arrange that?" She motions to the bottle.

I shrug, one corner of my mouth lifting. "Perks of being the boss. I hoped we'd have something to celebrate."

I don't say it outright, but I *knew* we would. Rose isn't the sort to let life pass her by. She went for the job of her dreams, and I'm still riding the rush of admiration that came with watching her do it. It doesn't matter if she doesn't get it. It matters that she tried.

"We do," she says softly. "Us."

That word sends a thrill through me so potent I have to take a breath before moving. *Us*. Something whole. Something worth protecting.

"Yes, exactly."

I close the door behind me and cross the room toward her, slow and deliberate. Her eyes never leave mine. I reach up and brush a strand of hair from her cheek, fingers trembling slightly despite the steadiness I project. She leans into my touch, and I swear I feel something inside me crack open. No fear, no doubt. Just *her*.

"I'll never tire of you." The words come out low and raw, dragged from a place I rarely expose. But she brings it out of me every time—the soft centre behind all my walls. The part that now believes I can have this, *keep* this.

A smile spreads across my face, unguarded, probably stupid-looking, but I don't care. It's hers.

She rises onto her toes, and I bend to meet her, our lips brushing in a kiss that starts soft—tentative, reverent—but quickly ignites something deeper.

My heart kicks into gear, pounding like it's trying to match the pace of my racing thoughts. I slide one arm around her waist and pull her flush against me. My other hand tangles in her hair, tugging just enough to tip her head, to claim her mouth more fully.

She tastes so sweet and warm, like everything I've needed for years and never had the words for. Her fingers slide up my chest, over the beat of my heart, and land on my shoulders, anchoring herself to me.

Then she kisses me like she's starving, and I return it like I never want to come up for air.

When my teeth graze her lower lip, she gasps into my mouth, and I swallow the sound greedily, deepening the kiss, needing more. Always more. Her hands slide up, burying in the hair at the nape of my neck, and the feel of her touch there—gentle but possessive—sends heat coursing through me.

This isn't just lust. It's a promise. A reclamation.

For once, I don't feel broken or scarred or second best. I feel wanted. Chosen. Loved.

And I plan to show her in every possible way, that she's not just my lover. She's my future.

I walk her backwards, slow and steady, until her back meets the wall. Then I step in, closing the space between us, letting her feel exactly what she does to me. The heat in her eyes sharpens when she feels the hard press of my arousal through my trousers. She likes knowing she affects me. *Hell*, I like it too. Every second with her ignites something feral in me, but it's never just about the physical. Not with her.

"God, Rose," I murmur, pushing her top away and moving my lips to her neck, trailing kisses along her soft, warm skin. "I need you so badly. That night in the fire..." My voice roughens, chest tightening. "It made everything painfully clear. I love you. I don't know if I can ever put it into words just how much."

She tugs my face back to hers, eyes blazing. "Show me," she breathes.

I kiss her hard, with no apology. This isn't about gentle declarations—it's about raw need, about love that wants to tear through walls. My hands grip her hips as I press her into the wall, wanting her closer, always closer. Her fingers fumble at my buttons, eager and desperate. Her hands tremble, matching the tremors inside me.

I find the hem of her top, locking eyes with her as I lift it slowly, savouring each brush of my knuckles against her warm skin. When it clears her head, I toss it aside, returning my hands to her body. I've missed the feel of her—even though I touched her this morning. Even though I'll touch her tomorrow. It's never enough. Never will be.

My fingers trace the edge of her bra, delicate cream lace with embroidery that makes her look like art. My personal collection.

"Is this okay?" My voice comes out husky, caught somewhere between reverence and hunger.

She nods, breathless. "Always."

I smile as I push the straps down, watching her body respond to every touch. She doesn't shy away—she stands proud, offering herself like she *knows* she owns me. And she does. Every inch of me.

"You're beautiful," I say, letting my fingers ghost along her collarbone. She shivers beneath the touch, and I follow it with a firmer hand to her breast. "And all mine."

Her eyes darken at those words, and I step around behind her. "Turn around."

She does, obedient and teasing at the same time, her back straight, her breathing deep. I press my chest to her spine, my hands exploring the shape of her hips, the lines of her ribs. She tilts her head as my lips find the place where her neck meets her shoulder—the spot that always draws a shiver from her.

Her body answers me like it was made to.

"Cold?" I whisper against her skin.

"No," she breathes. "Definitely not cold."

I let my hands roam higher, memorizing every inch of her again, like I haven't already done it before. When I cup her breasts through the lace, her breath catches, her nipples hardening beneath my touch.

I step back only to start undressing, shrugging off my jacket and tossing it over a chair. Her eyes follow me in the mirror, hungry, watching every movement like she's savouring it. I rip open my shirt without ceremony and let it hang off my shoulders.

She faces me again, and her hand lifts, tracing the slope from my collarbone down across my chest, and my breath stutters in my throat. Her touch is soft but confident, claiming me just as surely as I claim her.

"I'm so hungry for you," she says.

I catch her hand, pressing a kiss to her palm, lips lingering there. "And you can have me. But not before I've had you."

That brings a smile to her face, the kind that makes me lose my mind. I shrug out of the shirt and step forward again, drinking in the sight of her.

Slipping down the straps of her lacy bra, I push the fabric off her breasts. My gaze travels over her exposed skin. She stands straighter, letting me look my fill.

"Beautiful." I trace a finger along her collarbone. A flush blooms across her skin, following the path of my touch.

My hand slides to her waist, through the thin fabric of her skirt, and I turn her to face the wall again. My chest presses against her back, and I breathe onto the nape of her neck as I find her zipper, drawing it down slowly. Her skirt loosens, and I slip my hand inside, palming her hips before pushing the garment down. It pools around her ankles, and she steps out of it, now dressed only in her panties and heels, her hair tumbling loose.

"Your shoes," I murmur.

She turns back to face me and kicks them off, losing some height, but not a shred of presence. She still owns the room. She owns *me*.

I cup her face, thumbs brushing her cheekbones. The moment softens between us for a second—heat simmering rather than burning.

Then she kisses me.

And I'm gone.

Arms around her, mouth devouring hers, chest to chest, skin on skin—everything explodes into flame again.

We kiss like we're breathing each other in, like nothing else exists outside the heat between us. My hands roam her back, exploring familiar curves with renewed hunger, then dip lower to cup that perfect ass. I give it a slow squeeze and feel her gasp into my mouth. That sound undoes me. She raises her arm around my neck, and I lift her just enough to feel the shift in power—and her trust in me.

Then I go further.

One arm sweeps under her knees, the other cradles her back, and I lift her clean off the floor. She laughs—startled, delighted—and the sound is everything. I carry her the few steps to the bed and lower her down gently, even though I'm seconds from losing all restraint.

The sheets are cool, but I don't give the chill time to settle. I follow her down, covering her body with mine, anchoring us together again as our mouths find each other's. I deepen the kiss, one hand braced beside her head, the other already exploring her breasts, her nipples pebbling at the touch. My knee nudges between her thighs, and she opens for me, beautiful and willing.

Her lips are slick and hot under mine, her breath hitching as I kiss a slow trail along her jaw, down the column of her throat. Her pulse races under my mouth. I take my time, branding her with every kiss, every stroke of my tongue. She arches into me when I reach her breast and take her nipple into my mouth, rolling it with my tongue, letting my teeth graze the peak just enough to draw a breathless sound from her.

I'm addicted to every one of those noises.

My free hand cups her other breast, thumb circling until the nipple is hard as a diamond. She's so responsive, so alive under my hands—under *me*. Her fingers tangle in my hair, pulling slightly, and I hum against her skin in approval. I switch to her other breast, giving it the same slow, thorough attention, until she squirms beneath me.

I know what she wants. I feel it too—my cock throbs with an ache only she can relieve. But not yet.

I'm not in a rush. I want her on the edge before I even touch her where she needs me most.

I start my descent, lips and tongue trailing down the line of her sternum, tasting every inch of her. Her skin's warm and smooth beneath my mouth. I kiss along her ribs, into the dip of her navel, and let my tongue linger there. Her stomach tightens under the attention. My hands hold her hips firmly, thumbs stroking slowly along the soft skin just above her panties.

I glance up and catch her watching me—eyes wide, chest rising fast. She looks wrecked already, and I haven't even *begun*.

"These need to go," I say, my voice low and rough as I hook my fingers into the lace.

She lifts her hips in silent invitation.

I draw her panties down at an excruciating pace, loving the way her breath shortens, the way her thighs tremble just a little. I drag the fabric past her hips, her legs, down to her ankles—my knuckles brushing against bare skin the whole way—before tossing them aside. My eyes drink her in.

Fuck, she's stunning.

All soft curves and flushed skin, rosy in the lamplight, stretched out and waiting for me.

"You're gorgeous." My hands slide up her calves, owning her like she's the most precious thing I've ever touched. And she is. "Absolutely incredible."

She doesn't hide. She never does. She *knows* what she does to me—and she owns it.

I lower myself to her slowly, deliberately, because this isn't just about pleasure—it's about worship. I press a kiss just below her knee, then a little higher. The tiniest movements. The faintest brushes. And still, her legs tremble beneath my hands. Her skin tastes like sweet honey, and I plan to devour every part of her.

She tenses as I inch my way up her inner thigh, kiss by kiss, so damn close but not yet there. I switch sides and start again, dragging this out because I *can*, because watching her come apart under my mouth is one of life's rarest privileges.

She makes a frustrated little noise, a sweet, impatient whimper that makes my mouth curl into a smug grin. I blow gently against her slick skin just to hear her gasp.

"Patience," I murmur, glancing up at her through my lashes. She's flushed and wide-eyed, gripping the sheets like she's hanging on for dear life. "Good things come to those who wait."

Her voice is shaky. "Is that a promise?"

I grin. Not soft. Not teasing. Pure predator.

"Absolutely."

I wedge her thighs farther apart, exposing every part of her to my gaze. God, she's beautiful. Open. Wet. Desperate for me. She doesn't try to hide. I lower my head, letting my breath tease her slick centre. Her hips jerk, and her hands twist into the sheets again.

I kiss close to where she needs me, building the tension, winding it tighter. I hear her whisper my name. "John. Please... Oh, please."

Fuck, she sounds wrecked.

I look up again. She's staring down at me, completely undone, and something raw and fierce settles in my chest. This woman is mine. No one else will ever see her like this. No one else will ever *taste* her like this.

"Since you asked so nicely." My voice is low and rough. Then I add, with a wicked curl of my lips, "My good girl."

And then I give her what she wants—what *we* both want.

I press a kiss directly onto her clit, gentle at first. A reward. A promise fulfilled. She gasps, hips jolting, but I grip her thighs and hold her firm. No escape now.

I part her folds with my tongue, slow and thorough, tasting her properly. She's sweet and slick, and the noise I make—half groan, half growl—is completely involuntary. I can't get enough.

"You really are the tastiest dessert I've ever had," I murmur against her, lips brushing her most sensitive bundle of nerves as I speak. She shudders, the vibrations pulling another moan from her throat.

I set to work.

Every stroke of my tongue is intentional. I know exactly how to touch her now. What makes her hips twitch. What makes her fingers clutch the sheets like she's clinging to sanity. I circle her clit, not too soft, not too hard—just the way I *know* she needs.

She arches beneath me, breathless, gasping my name. Nothing else exists. Just her. Just this. Just us.

I work with the focus I usually reserve for golf course designs and balance sheets—only this is a hundred times better.

She threads her fingers through my hair, not tugging, not guiding. Just *holding*. It's the kind of touch that says trust, and fuck, that lights something deep in my chest.

I hum against her in appreciation, and she shudders—yeah, she *felt* that. I smile against her, then seal my mouth around her clit and suck gently. Her hips buck, wild and uncoordinated, but I keep her steady, one hand sliding up to her belly to press her down just enough. Not holding her back—just anchoring her while I work.

Her taste, her scent, the way she gasps my name like it's the only word she knows—it's all heat and need and raw. And I'm hungry for it. All of it.

I flatten my tongue and drag it slowly up her, relishing the way her thighs twitch. She's close already—I feel the tension winding in her, the way her body braces for what's coming. I shift to teasing strokes, circling her clit with the precision that makes her breath catch and her hands tighten in my hair.

Glancing up, I catch her looking down at me—and Christ, the look on her face. Wide eyes, lips parted, like she's barely hanging on. She sees me. *Sees* me—between her thighs, eating her out like it's the only thing I've ever wanted. And right now, it is.

Our eyes lock, and when she moans, a pulse of heat fires straight through me. I groan against her, low and involuntary, because yeah, I *feel* it—how much she's giving me, how close she is. My hand leaves her thigh, and my fingers glide through her slick heat before pressing gently inside.

She gasps, hips lifting, and I feel her clench around my fingers. My cock is rock hard and on the verge of blowing. This is so fucking hot. But I need to keep control. I've got to last the distance.

I press deeper, slow and sure, curling until I find that spot that makes her tense all over. She cries out, legs straining against me, and I murmur into her, "That's it. Let me feel how much you like this."

Her breath stutters, body moving against my hand now, chasing every stroke. I pick up the pace just a little—thrusting in a rhythm I know will push her higher—while my tongue keeps teasing her clit in slow, deliberate patterns. Sometimes dead on, sometimes just grazing the edges. Keeping her guessing. Keeping her climbing.

She's gasping now, her beautiful breasts heaving. I *love* the way she lets go—completely unfiltered. She tightens again around my fingers, that telltale build-up.

"Please," she breathes, voice breaking, and I don't even know what she's asking for—but I'll give her everything.

"I've got you," I growl against her skin, my voice ragged with need. "Let go for me, Rose. I want to feel you come on my tongue."

She's chasing it, grinding down like she needs more, *needs me*. And fuck, I *give* it to her. I don't pull back. I press in. Devour. My world narrows to her taste, her sounds, the way her thighs tremble against my jaw.

She's close. I can *feel* it—her body wound tight as wire, the sounds spilling from her lips unlike anything I've heard before. Raw, wrecked little sobs, my name falling from her mouth. Her fingers tighten in my hair—hard enough to sting—but I don't stop. Hell no. If anything, I double down.

I focus everything I have on her clit, lips and tongue working in perfect sync with the steady rhythm of my fingers inside her. Every stroke is deliberate, every flick designed to send her higher. She's shaking now, breathing in broken gasps, and when she tries to speak, the words fall apart.

"I'm—" she starts, but it's lost to a moan—and I know. I *know*.

I don't stop. I keep her right there, teetering, then I push.

She comes apart on my mouth with a cry that hits me right in the chest—loud, unguarded, beautiful. Her body bows, tight with release, thighs trembling around my shoulders as I ride the wave with her, only just stopping myself from coming in my underwear. She clenches around my fingers in rhythmic pulses, and I keep going, keep *giving*, coaxing every last tremor from her until she's breathless and spent.

Only when I feel the peak start to ebb do I ease up—tongue softening, fingers slowing but staying inside, grounding her as the aftershocks ripple through. She collapses onto the bed, arm thrown over her face, her breasts rising and falling like she's just run a marathon.

"That's my Rose. Such a good girl."

I press a kiss to the inside of her thigh—gentle, reverent. Then another, higher this time. I work my way up her body, slow and unhurried, tracing a path over her soft skin. Her taste still lingers on my lips, and I'm drunk on it.

I slip my fingers from her gently, and even though I know she's wrung out, I feel the small shift in her body—like she misses the connection already. I know I do.

"Beautiful. So. Fucking. Beautiful. When. You. Come." I punctuate the sentence with soft kisses to her hips, her stomach, her breasts, and finally, her lips.

She's catching her breath, still a little wrecked. And I'd do it all over again just to see that look on her face one more time.

I'll never stop doing it if it makes her this happy. She's mine, all mine, and I couldn't love her any more than I do at this moment.

# 33
## *Rose*

John kisses me on the lips, but I can hardly breathe, never mind return it. He braces himself above me on strong arms, and I see him watching me with an expression of such naked longing it makes my chest ache.

"That was so good," I manage.

His smile is slow and satisfied. "Only the best for my beautiful girl."

The shine of my arousal is on his lips and chin, and a fresh wave of desire rolls through me. I reach up to return his kiss, tasting myself on his tongue as it slides against mine.

It's languid at first, a gentle reconnection after the intensity of the orgasm he's just given me. But it doesn't stay gentle for long. John's body presses against mine, and I feel the hard length of his cock still confined in his trousers.

I slide my hands down his back, feeling the play of muscles beneath warm skin. My fingers find his belt, fumbling slightly with the buckle.

"Time for me to thank you properly for... that."

"No thanks necessary. The pleasure was all mine, as always."

"Not all yours." My fingers move to his zipper. "Definitely not all yours."

John shifts, helping me as I push at his trousers. They slide down his hips, revealing his classic black boxer briefs stretched tight over his thick cock. I trace my fingers along the waistband, watching his abdominal muscles tense at my touch.

"I can't wait for this," I whisper.

He stands from the bed, and in one fluid movement, his eyes never leaving mine, he fully removes his trousers and steps out of them. He stands before me without shame, magnificent in his near nakedness, his desire evident in the substantial bulge straining against his boxer briefs.

I sit up slowly. My legs still feel slightly tremulous from my orgasm, but a new energy hums through me—the desire to make him feel even a fraction of what he just gave me.

"Come here," I say.

The corner of his mouth lifts in that almost-smile that makes my stomach flip. He steps closer until he's standing at the edge of the bed, between my parted knees. From this position, I have to tilt my head back to meet his gaze.

I reach out, tracing the hard line of his erection through the fabric. He inhales sharply, muscles tensing at even this light contact. I explore him with tentative touches, loving his shape, his size. A small damp spot has formed where the tip presses against the cotton, and I run my thumb over it, drawing a soft groan from above.

I hook my fingers into his waistband and slowly draw the fabric down. His cock springs free, hard and flushed, the prominent vein running along the underside that I know so well.

I glance up to find him watching me intently, his breathing slightly faster than before.

"Beautiful," I murmur, deliberately echoing his earlier compliment to me.

A flicker of amusement crosses his face, quickly replaced by something darker as I wrap my hand around his shaft. The skin is impossibly soft over steel hardness, hot against my palm. I stroke him exactly the way I know he likes it.

"Rose," he groans when I swipe my thumb over the sensitive head, gathering the moisture there to ease my movements.

"I love the taste of you," I tell him, looking up through my lashes.

His hand cups my cheek, his thumb brushing my lower lip. "You're so incredible." The intensity in his eyes nearly undoes me. I lean forward, maintaining eye contact as I place a soft kiss on the tip, then I part my lips, taking just the head into my mouth, swirling my tongue around the sensitive ridge.

John's hand moves to my hair, and he weaves his fingers into it. I take him deeper, hollowing my cheeks as I establish a rhythm—slow at first, teasing.

His taste is clean, slightly salty, distinctly male. I work him with a combination of hand and mouth, using my fingers to cover what my lips can't reach. Each time I take him a little deeper, his breathing grows more ragged, his fingers tightening slightly in my hair.

"God, Rose," he murmurs, voice strained. "You're so fucking good at this...."

The praise sends a flush of pleasure through me. I never enjoyed doing this with Freddie, but with John, it's powerful, intimate, and an act of worship rather than service. I want to break his control, to make him feel as undone as he made me.

I pull back to catch my breath, using my hand to maintain the stimulation. "You're the hottest guy I've ever been with and the only one I ever want to be with." I take him in my mouth again, deeper this time, relaxing my throat to accommodate more of his length. One hand cups his balls gently, feeling their weight, while the other grips his thigh for balance.

John's hips make small, aborted movements, as if he's fighting the urge to thrust. I appreciate his restraint, but part of me wants to see him lose it.

I take a deep breath through my nose and take him deeper still until I feel him nudge the back of my throat. My eyes water slightly at the intrusion, but the choked sound he makes is worth any discomfort. His hold on my hair deepens, anchoring me without hurting.

"Rose," he warns, voice ragged. "If you keep that up…"

I pull back just enough to speak, my lips brushing against him as I form the words. "That's the idea."

A soft laugh escapes him quickly turning into a groan. I establish a rhythm, taking him deep on each downstroke. My jaw aches slightly, but the sounds he's making—barely restrained grunts and gasps—spur me on.

His free hand caresses my face, thumb tracing the spot where my lips stretch around him. The tenderness of the gesture contrasts with the raw carnality of the act, and something about that combination makes me squeeze my thighs together, arousal building again despite my recent release.

I feel him harden further, a subtle change that signals he's getting close. His breathing has taken on a ragged quality, and the muscles in his thighs are tense beneath my hand.

"Rose," he says again, more urgently this time. "I'm gonna lose it."

I hum acknowledgment, the vibration making him curse softly. I don't pull away, instead redoubling my efforts, wanting to taste his pleasure, to feel him come undone because of me.

His fingers grasp more firmly in my hair, a silent claim that sends a tingle down my spine. "Rose, I'm going to—"

I answer by taking him as far as I can. It tips him over the edge—his body goes rigid, a guttural groan escaping him as he pulses against my tongue.

I hold steady, swallowing what he gives me, easing the pressure but not pulling away until I feel the last tremor run through him. Only then do I release him gently, sitting back to look up at his face.

John looks totally spent—cheeks flushed, hair mussed where I must have gripped it at some point, eyes dark and slightly unfocused. I've never seen him so unguarded, so completely vulnerable, and something fierce and possessive unfurls in my chest at the knowledge that I did this to him, that I'm the one who broke through his careful control.

He sinks onto the bed beside me, pulling me into a kiss that's tender despite its passion. I wonder briefly if he's bothered by tasting himself on my lips, but he shows no sign of hesitation, his tongue sliding against mine with lazy purpose.

When he finally pulls back, his hand cups my cheek, thumb wiping at the moisture at the corner of my mouth. "That was..." he begins, then shakes his head slightly, as if words are inadequate.

I smile, pleased at his speechlessness. "Good?"

"Beyond good," he says, voice still rough. "You're extraordinary."

The compliment warms me more than it should. I lean into his touch. "I wanted to make you feel the way you made me feel."

He pulls me into another kiss, this one lazy and exploring. His hand slides down my back, over the curve of my hip, coming to rest on my thigh. We lie together, kissing and holding each other for what might be minutes or hours. I'm not counting, and this is so blissful.

John rolls on top of me, pushing my hair behind my ears as he kisses me. I feel him hardening again against my stomach.

"Already?" I murmur against his lips.

He chuckles, the sound rumbling through his chest. "What can I say? You inspire me."

His fingers trace patterns on my inner thigh, moving higher with each stroke, and my breath catches in anticipation. Despite my spectacular climax earlier, my body responds to his touch as if starved.

"I think," he says, voice dropping to that commanding tone that makes my stomach flip, "we're just getting started."

He gently guides me onto my back, his body following mine down to the mattress. The weight of him pressing me into the sheets feels like an anchor, keeping me from floating away on the tide of sensation. His eyes, dark with renewed desire, hold mine as he positions himself between my legs, his knees nudging my thighs further apart.

"I know I say it a lot, but you really are beautiful," he murmurs, one hand tracing from my collarbone between my breasts, over my stomach, to rest at the juncture of my thighs. "So responsive."

His fingers dip between my folds, finding me still slick and sensitive from before. I gasp as he circles my clit with feather-light touches, just enough to rekindle the embers of desire without overwhelming my sensitive nerves.

"Oh, fuck," I breathe, hips rising to meet his hand.

He leans down, lips brushing my ear. "Be a good girl for me, Rose," he whispers, the command sending an unexpected thrill through me. "Let me take care of you."

Something about his tone makes me melt into the mattress, surrendering to whatever he has planned.

"Yes," I whisper back.

He rewards me with a kiss—deep and thorough—before pulling back to kneel between my spread thighs. The position offers me a perfect view of him in all his naked glory. His body is a study in contrasts—powerful muscles and elegant lines, smooth skin and rough scars, strength and vulnerability intertwined.

His cock stands proud between his legs, already fully hard again. I watch as he takes himself in hand, giving a few slow strokes that make my mouth water in remembered appreciation of his taste, his weight on my tongue.

One large hand slides beneath my lower back, tilting my hips slightly. The other guides his cock to my entrance, rubbing the head through my folds to gather moisture. The teasing contact makes me gasp, sensitized nerves firing at even this gentle touch.

"Ready?" he asks, eyes holding mine.

I nod, beyond words now, wanting nothing more than to feel him inside me. He presses forward slowly, the tip of his cock breaching me with gentle insistence. I feel the stretch, the delicious burn as my body accommodates his size.

"God," he groans, pausing when he's just inside. "You always feel incredible."

I wrap my legs around his waist, urging him deeper, and he complies, sinking into me with agonizing slowness. The sensation is overwhelming—fullness bordering on discomfort, then tipping into pleasure as my body adjusts. When he's fully inside, he stills, giving me time to acclimate, his forehead pressed against mine.

"Okay?" he asks.

"More than okay." I roll my hips against him.

The movement draws a hiss from him, his hands tightening on my hips. "Whoa, steady. Let's take this slow."

I smile. "I'm not sure I can."

He chuckles, the sound vibrating through both our bodies, then he shifts his weight onto his forearms, bracketing my head. The movement changes the angle of his penetration, drawing a gasp from me as he hits spots that send sparks shooting up my spine.

"Better?" he asks, knowing full well it is.

In answer, I tighten my inner muscles around him, gratified when his eyes flutter briefly closed. Two can play this game.

His first thrust is measured, controlled—pulling back slowly before pushing in with deliberate force. I arch beneath him, hands finding purchase on his broad shoulders. He establishes a rhythm—steady, deep strokes that make the bed creak in protest and drive little gasps from my throat with each forward movement.

"You take me so well," he murmurs, gaze fixed on where our bodies join. "So perfect."

The praise washes over me like warm honey, sweet and enveloping. He's always so openly appreciative of my body and responses. It makes me want to give more, to show him everything. He's all I've ever wanted—even before I knew I wanted it.

I meet his thrusts with eager movements of my own, our bodies finding a natural synchronicity. The drag of his cock inside me creates friction that builds upon my earlier pleasure, promising another peak if we maintain this delicious rhythm.

John shifts again, angling his hips to hit that spot inside me that makes stars explode behind my eyelids. I cry out at the contact, fingers digging into his back hard enough to leave marks. He grunts in satisfaction, repeating the movement with precision.

"There?" he asks, though my reaction has made the answer obvious.

"Yes," I gasp, "right there. Don't stop."

He maintains the angle, increasing his pace slightly, each thrust firm and purposeful. I feel the coiling pressure building in my lower belly. My breaths come faster, short pants that match the rhythm of his movements.

"Oh, God." The tension inside me is a live wire, ready to spark. "I love how you fill me. I want to come... I need to."

"Okay. Anything for my good girl." He slows his pace abruptly. The words send a fresh wave of arousal through me, my inner walls clenching around him in response. He makes a strangled sound, clearly affected despite his control.

His hand slides between our bodies, thumb finding my clit. The dual stimulation—his cock filling me so completely, his thumb circling that sensitive bundle of nerves—pushes me rapidly back toward the precipice.

"Please," I gasp, closing my eyes.

His own breathing is ragged now. "Look at me, Rose. Look at me, beautiful."

I force my eyes open, meeting his gaze. The connection feels as intimate as our physical joining—perhaps more so. There's vulnerability in his expression that catches me off guard, a naked need that goes beyond physical desire.

"I want to feel you come around me," he says, his voice rough. "I want to come with you."

A fresh surge of heat courses through my veins. His thrusts grow more forceful.

"Please, John," I whimper. "I need to—"

"Yes," he interrupts, thumb pressing more firmly against my clit. "Now, Rose. Come for me now."

The orgasm crashes over me with stunning intensity, radiating outward from where we're joined. My back arches, a broken cry tearing from my throat as my inner walls clamp down around him in rhythmic pulses.

John groans, his own control shattering at the feel of my release. His hips stutter, losing their steady rhythm as he drives into me with abandoned force. I feel the exact moment he follows me over the edge—his body going rigid, a guttural sound torn from deep in his chest, the hot pulse of his release inside me.

"I love you so much," I cry.

For a suspended moment, we're frozen in shared ecstasy, bodies locked together at the apex of pleasure.

"And I love you," he rasps. "You're my world."

Slowly, the tension drains from his frame. He collapses partially on top of me, careful to keep most of his weight on his forearms, his face buried in the crook of my neck.

The only sound is our ragged breathing filling the quiet room. I feel boneless, satiated in a way I've only ever experienced with him. My fingers trace lazy patterns on his sweat-dampened back, following the ridges of his spine.

After several moments, John raises his head, looking down at me with an expression of absolute adoration. He presses a gentle kiss to my lips, then carefully withdraws from my body. I wince slightly at the loss, suddenly aware of tender muscles and a pleasant soreness.

He moves me gently so that my back presses against his chest. His arm drapes over my waist, hand splayed protectively across my stomach. I feel surrounded by him, and it feels like coming home.

"You're not just *maid* for me, Rose. We're *made* for each other."

It takes a second for the pun to register, then I groan, laughing softly. "How much mileage can we get out of that one?"

"It'll be with us forever."

"Forever." I echo the word as if it's a vow, smiling as I curl into him, his warmth wrapping around me like a shelter. The word settles deep in my chest. Forever isn't a scary thing now. It's exciting and beautiful.

Because it means *us*, not just a fleeting moment or fantasy. It's real. It's solid. It's mine.

For the first time in as long as I can remember, I feel whole. No missing pieces, no shadows lurking in the corners. Just love. Safety. A future I *want*. And as John's arms tighten around me and his lips brush my hair, I know with absolute certainty—I'm exactly where I'm meant to be.

# 34

## *John*

The Caribbean sun beats down on my skin. I'm stretched out on a wooden lounger, my body lazy with heat and rum, watching Rose tilt her face to the sky. Her hair streams down her back in waves of blonde, catching the light like spun gold. Paradise feels earned after everything. I take another sip of my cocktail and let the tension of the past month melt from my bones.

The private villa sits just fifty yards from the Barbados shoreline, its deck suspended between the turquoise sea and the shelter of palm trees. White sand stretches in a gentle curve to our left and right. We haven't seen another soul since we got here.

"I think I could stay here forever." Rose lifts her oversized sunglasses and sits on the other lounger. "Seriously. Why do we live in Scotland again?"

"Because you'd miss the rain," I reply, unable to suppress a smile. "Your constitution would wither away under constant sunshine."

She snorts and lies back on the lounger, the movement causing her bikini top to shift slightly. I feel the familiar tug of desire low in my belly, watching the fabric tauten against the swell of her breasts.

"My constitution seems to be adapting just fine." She raises her cocktail glass in a mock toast. "To adaptation."

I clink my glass against hers, the ice cubes tinkling. "To adaptation."

A pre-Christmas holiday is maybe a little insane. December was always going to be a complex month—what with the division of Isabel's time, the expectations of the festive season, plus everything else that's happened this year. But then Rose got the marketing job she was desperate for, and suddenly there was another reason to celebrate, one that's purely ours. So here we are, a week of tropical indulgence before heading back for the Christmas rush. Rose asked, after all, if we could go to Barbados after Paris, and I wouldn't like to disappoint her.

"Any word from Isabel?" Rose asks, always attuned to where my thoughts might drift.

I check my phone, though I know there's nothing new. "Just the photo from yesterday."

Lydia's taking Isabel for ten days of "mother-daughter bonding" since her relationship with Freddie fell apart. Hopefully, whoever she chooses next will be someone a lot nicer.

"She looked happy." Rose reaches for my hand across the gap between our loungers. "And you know she's counting down the days until she gives you that mystery present, she picked out."

I squeeze her hand, grateful for her understanding of the complexities that come with co-parenting. "I know. It's good for her to have this time with Lydia. Especially now that things have settled."

"Settled" seems an inadequate word for the explosive implosion of Lydia's relationship with Freddie, and the implications of his actions on all of us. This is part of the healing process.

Lydia, to her credit, cut ties immediately and publicly. Perhaps motivated by self-preservation, but it still eased some of the tension between Lydia and me. Nothing creates common ground quite like mutual contempt for the same person, as Rose and I know too well.

Rose sits up, swinging her legs over the side of her lounger to face me directly. "This week is about celebration. Let's not think about you-know-who while we're here—" she gestures at the pristine beach "—in actual paradise."

I smile, setting my drink down on the small table between us. "You're right." I reach out to brush a wisp of hair from her face. These small intimacies still feel like privileges, moments of wonder.

Rose leans into my touch, turning her face to press a kiss against my palm. "I know I've said it before but thank you for this. For all of it. I never imagined I'd be celebrating a career breakthrough in the Caribbean with..." She pauses, her eyes softening. "With someone who actually believes in me."

"Anyone who doesn't believe in you is a fool," I tell her, meaning every word. "I'm just lucky I was smart enough to recognize what I'd found."

She smiles. "Aw, that's so sweet."

"Must be the rum," I reply dryly, but we both know I'm joking. The truth is that Rose has drawn life from me that I'd buried after the fire at the Gladstone.

She raises one knee on her lounger with a contented sigh. "Here's to Caribbean sunshine, and whatever comes next."

I lift my own glass in response, watching the light filter through the amber liquid. The deck creaks slightly beneath us as a breeze picks up from the ocean, carrying the scent of salt and distant rain. Up the coast, clouds are gathering, promising an afternoon shower that will vanish as quickly as it arrives, leaving everything refreshed in its wake.

"To whatever comes next," I agree.

I lean back, watching the sea sparkling like someone has upended a vault of crushed diamonds over it. "You know what I was thinking about this morning?" I swirl the ice in my glass. "Everything we have to look forward to when we get back." I've spent so many years looking backward or focused on surviving the present. But now, the future spreads before us like this beach, bright and full of possibility.

Rose turns her head, sunglasses still pushed atop her head like a crown, squinting against the light. "I like that." She props herself up on one elbow, giving me her full attention. "Tell me about all these good things I have to look forward to with you."

I take a breath, enjoying the anticipation in her eyes. "Well, there's the Gladstone Hotel reopening in February."

"That's so exciting." Her smile widens.

"Then there's the house." The new plans came through just before we left, and the architect is confident they'll be approved.

Freddie did us a favor in a roundabout way by burning it down. His involvement has been proven beyond doubt, and now I get to build the house I always wanted to with Rose's artistic input to keep me right.

"Show me again." Rose stretches across to my lounger. I pull out my phone, finding the digital renderings my architect sent over.

She settles beside me, her bare shoulder pressing against mine as we scroll through the images. The redesigned Lodge is so modern and appealing compared to the ugly old thing it's replacing.

"I still think the kitchen should open directly onto that back terrace." Rose points to the screen. "Morning coffee watching the sun rise over the golf course? That's worth sacrificing a bit of wall space."

"Noted." I make a mental note to discuss it with the architect. The builders said we can break ground as soon as the frosts are over. Mid-March, hopefully. We could be in by Christmas next year.

"And we don't have to worry about you-know-who in our lives."

Rose gives a little snort. "Yes, we're free of him."

I bring her hand to my lips, pressing a kiss against her knuckles. "We are."

Her expression softens. "The best thing he ever did was to bring us together."

We sit in comfortable silence for a moment, smiling at each other, as the waves lap against the shore. A light breeze stirs the palm fronds overhead, casting dappled shadows across the deck.

"So that's it?" Rose says. "A hotel opening, a house being rebuilt, and the continued absence of my dreadful ex? That's your list of good things?"

I turn to face her, taking in the playful challenge in her eyes. "Those are just the practical items. The measurable ones."

"And the immeasurable ones?"

I run my thumb along the inside of her wrist, feeling her pulse quicken beneath my touch. "Those are a bit harder to put into words."

Her lips part slightly, her gaze dropping to my mouth. "I've always found you quite capable with words when properly motivated."

"Is that so?" I let my voice drop lower, watching the effect ripple across her skin in a wash of goosebumps despite the heat.

"Mmm," she confirms, shifting closer on the lounger. "But sometimes I prefer action to words."

The air between us grows heavy with intention, the conversation forgotten as something more primal takes its place. Somewhere in the distance, thunder rumbles—the afternoon storm approaching across the water.

Rose puts her cocktail down on the deck with deliberate care, her eyes never leaving mine. There's a shift in her expression—subtle but unmistakable—as she stands, adjusting the ties of her bikini bottom with idle fingers. My body responds before my mind fully registers her intent, heat pooling low in my abdomen as she crosses the short distance between our loungers. The wooden deck creaks softly beneath her bare feet, marking each step toward me like a countdown to ignition.

I shift on the lounger, making space, but instead of sitting beside me, she plants one knee on either side of my thighs and settles onto my lap with deliberate slowness.

"Hello," she murmurs, her face now inches from mine, her legs warm against my outer thighs.

"Hello," I manage, my hands finding their way to her hips as if magnetized. The thin fabric of her bikini bottoms does little to disguise the heat of her skin.

The sudden proximity of her fills all my senses at once—the coconut scent of her sun cream, the weight of her against my rapidly hardening cock. I'm wearing only swim shorts, and they provide no concealment of my body's immediate, visceral response to her.

"Mmm," she hums appreciatively, shifting her weight slightly to press more firmly against my erection. "Someone's paying attention."

"Hard not to," I reply, my voice rougher than I intended.

She smiles—that particular smile that's equal parts innocence and sin—and reaches behind her neck to untie her bikini top. The simple movement transforms her posture, arching her back and lifting her breasts. My fingers tighten involuntarily on her hips as she unties the second string around her back and lets the small triangles of fabric fall away.

Her breasts are so perfect—full but not overly large, with pale pink nipples that harden under my gaze. The contrast of her tan lines accentuates their shape, drawing the eye to what's normally hidden.

"God, Rose," I breathe, unable to form more coherent thoughts as blood rushes southward.

She laughs softly, clearly enjoying the power she wields in this moment. "Like what you see?"

"Always," I answer truthfully. Whether she's dressed in elegant dresses, one of my old t-shirts, or nothing at all—Rose never fails to amaze me.

"Show me." She takes my hands from her hips and guides them upward.

I cup her breasts, feeling their weight, their softness. My thumbs brush across her nipples, drawing a sharp intake of breath from her. The sound sends a bolt straight to my groin, my cock now fully hard and straining against the confines of my shorts.

Rose releases my hands, but they remain where she placed them, continuing their exploration of her sun-warmed skin. Her own hands trail down her stomach in a lazy, sensual path that makes my mouth go dry with anticipation. She drops her fingers into her bikini bottoms, gently touching herself.

"I love watching you watch me." Her voice drops to a register that sends shivers across my skin despite the heat. "Your eyes get so dark."

I swallow hard, transfixed, as her fingers slide higher again, circling her nipples, pinching them lightly between thumb and forefinger. Her eyes flutter closed for a moment as she pleasures herself, a soft sigh escaping her parted lips.

The combination of visual and physical stimulation is almost overwhelming—her weight on my lap, the sight of her touching herself, the knowledge that we're completely alone with nothing but sea and sky as witnesses. My hands drop to her thighs, fingers digging into the soft flesh there as I fight the urge to rush.

"You're driving me mad," I tell her, my voice strangled.

She opens her eyes, pupils dilated with desire. "That's rather the point."

We've been together long enough now to know each other's bodies, to understand the specific rhythms and touches that drive the other to the edge. But there's still a sense of discovery, of newness, that keeps our encounters from becoming routine.

My previous relationships—including my marriage—never contained this particular alchemy of physical desire and emotional connection.

Rose shifts again, a deliberate rolling of her hips that drags a groan from deep in my chest. The thin layers of fabric between us do little to dampen the sensation as she rocks against my erection, creating friction that sends sparks of pleasure shooting up my spine.

"Do you know," she says conversationally, as if we're discussing the weather rather than grinding against each other in the open air, "what I've been thinking about all morning?"

"Tell me." My hands slide up to grip her waist, not sure if I want to still her movements or encourage them.

"This." She gestures to our position, to the lounger, to the deck. "You, me, nothing but sunshine and privacy." Her fingers trace the scars on my cheek—remnants of the first of the two fires that nearly took my life this year—with familiar tenderness. "No interruptions, no schedules, no clothes."

I capture one of her wandering hands, bringing it to my lips to kiss her palm. "Seems like a reasonable agenda."

"I thought so." She reclaims her hand to trace my collarbone, then my shoulders, mapping my body with unhurried focus. "Especially the no clothes part."

The lounger beneath us creaks slightly as she shifts her weight, leaning forward to brush her lips against mine in a kiss that's barely there—a tease, a promise. I chase her mouth as she pulls back, earning a playful smile.

"Not yet," she murmurs, though I can feel the racing of her pulse where my hands encircle her wrists, belying her composed exterior.

I release her to slide my hands up her bare back, pulling her closer so that her breasts press against my chest. The contact of skin against skin sends a jolt through both of us.

Her laugh dissolves into a gasp as I capture her mouth, kissing her with all the hunger that's been building. She tastes of rum and lime and salt, her lips soft and yielding beneath mine. One of my hands tangles in her hair, cradling the back of her head as the kiss deepens, turning urgent.

When we break apart, breathless, the gleam in her eyes has intensified. "That was nice." She teases kisses along my jaw to my ear. "But I'm still wearing too many clothes."

"Easily remedied." I run my fingers along the ties at her hips that are keeping her bikini bottoms in place.

"Not yet." She captures my hands, guiding them back to her breasts. "First, I want to feel your hands everywhere."

I'm happy to oblige, cupping the soft weight of her breasts, thumbs circling her nipples until they're hard as diamonds. She arches into the contact, her head falling back slightly, hair cascading down her back in a golden curtain. The sight of her lost in pleasure—eyes half-closed, lips parted, skin flushed—is enough to make my cock throb painfully against the constraints of my shorts.

"Beautiful," I murmur.

"These need to go." She tugs at the fabric of my shorts.

I lift my hips slightly, allowing her to draw the shorts down. The process requires some awkward manoeuvring given our position on the lounger, but we manage it. With some wriggling and a shared laugh when I nearly tip us both onto the deck, my shorts end up discarded somewhere near our forgotten cocktail glasses.

The relief of being freed from the confining fabric is immediate, my cock springing up between us, hard and ready. Rose's gaze drops to take in the sight, her tongue darting out to wet her lower lip in a gesture that sends another rush of blood southward.

"Much better." She wraps her fingers around my length. Her touch is confident, knowing exactly how much pressure to apply as she strokes upward, then down, her thumb circling the sensitive head.

Her hand continues its maddening exploration, her eyes never leaving mine. "I love watching you come undone."

"And I like to be inside you when that happens." I reach for the ties at her hips that secure her bikini bottoms.

She releases me to help, untying one side while I work on the other. The small piece of fabric falls away, leaving her naked astride me. She's all golden skin and curves, her blonde hair slightly wild from the sea air, her eyes bright with desire. Even now, part of me marvels at the reality of her, at the fact that this vibrant, beautiful woman has chosen me, scars and all.

Her smile widens as she shifts again, positioning herself directly above my cock. One hand reaches between us, guiding me to her entrance. "There's nothing I love more than you inside me."

She holds my gaze as she slowly begins to lower herself onto my cock. We both freeze for a heartbeat, suspended in the exquisite tension of the connection. Then she continues her descent, taking me inch by inch, her body hot and tight around me.

"Fuck," I breathe, the word torn from me as she settles fully, my cock completely bedded inside her. My hands grip her thighs, feeling the slight tremor in her muscles as she adjusts to the fullness.

"That's the general idea," she agrees, her voice strained but amused. She braces her hands on my shoulders, her nails digging in slightly as she rocks her hips.

The sensation is overwhelming—the wet heat of her wrapped around me, the visual feast of her naked body joined with mine, the knowledge that we're completely alone here with nothing but ocean and sky as witnesses. My head falls back against the lounger, a groan escaping my throat.

Rose stays motionless for several heartbeats, both of us savouring the moment of complete connection. Then she begins to move, rising slightly before sinking back down, establishing a slow, deliberate rhythm. Each movement sends waves of pleasure radiating outward from where we're joined, building like the tide climbing the shore.

"You feel so good." Her hands slide from my shoulders to my chest, her fingers splayed wide, as if trying to touch as much of me as possible. "So perfect inside me."

Words fail me entirely as she increases her pace, her body rising and falling with growing urgency. I can only watch, transfixed, as she takes her pleasure—her head tipped back, exposing the elegant line of her throat, her breasts bouncing gently with each movement. The sight of her lost in sensation is almost as intoxicating as the physical pleasure itself.

I slide one hand between us, and my thumb circles her clit as she rides me, drawing a sharp cry from her lips. Her inner muscles clench around my cock in response, sending a jolt of almost unbearable pleasure up my spine.

Her breath comes in short, sharp gasps, her movements growing more erratic as she chases her release. I'm fighting my own battle for control, determined to hold back until she finds her pleasure.

"Don't stop," she pleads. "Please, John, don't stop."

As if I could. As if there's anywhere else in the world I'd rather be than right here, watching her come apart in my arms. My free hand tangles in her hair, pulling her down for another kiss as my thumb maintains its relentless pressure on her clit. She's trembling, teetering on the edge.

"Let go," I murmur against her lips. "Like a good girl."

She breaks the kiss with a gasp, her forehead pressed against mine as her body tightens around me. For a moment, she's perfectly still, suspended in that exquisite space between anticipation and release. Then she shatters, a cry torn from her throat as pleasure crashes through her in visible waves.

The sight of her climax—her face transformed with ecstasy, her body pulsing around my cock—nearly pushes me over the edge as well.

"Fuck. I love you." I can't last long like this, not with the visual feast of her, not with the memory of her orgasm still fresh, not with her looking at me like I'm the only man in the world. My hands grip her hips hard.

"Fuck." I feel the familiar tightening, the gathering storm. "I'm going to—"

"Yes." She leans in to speak directly into my ear. "Come for me, John. I want to feel you. I'm still going. I can come again too..." Her breathing falters. "I can feel it... Oh God."

She thrusts her hand to her clit and rubs like crazy. I drive even deeper inside her, and she gasps, then clenches around me. Her eyes roll back, and she convulses with a scream. I stiffen as my climax rockets through me, spilling my hot seed deep inside her.

"Holy fuck." I can barely draw breath. Pleasure so acute it borders on pain washes through me in endless waves. She shudders against me again, an aftershock of ecstasy rippling through her, making her cry out again. The intensity of our combined orgasms leaves me panting.

I move my arms around her as she goes floppy and lands on my chest. I hold her close as the storm passes. We remain connected, her limp in my embrace.

We stay like that for a long moment, neither of us willing to break the connection. Her weight on me is perfect, grounding, real. When she finally shifts slightly, I feel the loss of her immediately, a cooling emptiness where her heat had been. But she doesn't move far, just readjusts to a more comfortable position, still straddling my lap, her arms looped loosely around my neck.

We lie together, our bodies bared to the elements. The warmth seeps into my skin, a physical echo of the contentment flowing through me. "When Maid for You sent you to my door, this outcome wasn't exactly the outcome I imagined."

"Me neither."

"I never thought I'd find anyone like you."

She runs a fingertip over my chest. "I feel the same." Then she sits up. "Race you to the water?"

"Seriously? You want to move?"

"Yeah, come on, we can wash off in there."

I take a moment to drink in the sight of her. The woman who started as my cleaner and somehow became essential to my happiness. "You're on."

As we race toward the waves, her hand clasped tightly in mine, something shifts inside me—something weightless, like the last of the darkness finally lifting. The future looks like the horizon stretched out before us—endless, luminous, full of promise. A life we'll build together, one fearless, messy, beautiful moment at a time.

Whatever comes, we'll face it side by side. That's the vow I make without words, just in the way I hold her hand, in the way she squeezes back.

The water greets us like a baptism, cool and clean against overheated skin, and when she laughs, I laugh too. The sound catches in my chest, and it's wonderful. With her arms looped around my neck and the waves cradling us, I hold her close, my heart wide open.

In this perfect, weightless moment, I know what peace feels like. I know what love *is*.

It's Rose. It's *us*. And it's forever.

## The End

# Also by Lexi Blair

# About Lexi

**Lexi Blair** writes steamy, modern romances set in Scotland, where smart women and irresistible sexy guys spark, clash, and burn their way to happily ever afters. Expect passion, power, and plenty of spice.

When she's not writing, Lexi can usually be found people-watching or plotting new ways to bring readers all the swoons, spice, and happy ever afters.

SIGN UP TO LEXI'S NEWSLETTER FOR EXCLUSIVE UPDATES AND TO ACCESS SOME INCREDIBLE **NSFW** ART BY ARTIST RAQUEL NEKRO TO ACCOMPANY THE SERIES!